Farewell, My Denmark

Farewell, My Denmark

Tina Peterson Scott

Foutz
Fables&More

Mesa, Arizona, USA
foutzfablesandmore@gmail.com

Cover Design by Eden Literary
http://www.edenliterary.com

ISBN-13: 978-0-9891581-5-2

Thank you to Valerie, Joyce, Joan, Anna, and Terry, and the many wonderful women in ANWA who have supported and encouraged my writing for years. A special thank you to Jennifer Griffith for helping me edit this novel to perfection, to my kids for their love and support, and to my dear husband who encourages my writing and who thinks I'm brilliant.

"And all they who have given their lives for my name shall be crowned." Doctrine & Covenants 101:15

Chapter 1

April 22, 1863

I stood on the back step and swallowed back my nerves. Nothing in my seventeen years had prepared me for the conversation I would have tonight. I peered in the direction of the barn but didn't see any light. Isaac hadn't arrived.

Fog covered the earth like an ocean of shadowy white. Not even a vague outline of our three-winged home was visible. It set me on edge. I pulled my shawl tight around my shoulders steeling myself against the cold, damp air. Then, praying Isaac wouldn't be long, I hurried across the courtyard.

I lifted the wooden plank that secured the barn each night. The heavy door groaned as I pulled it open making goose bumps prickle up my neck. The ghostly fluttering of the startled swallows did not frighten me, yet as soon as I stepped into our barn, I heard the skittering of tiny feet, and forced back a scream.

Although I knew field mice loved to call our barn home, I shuddered at the sound of their scurrying. I hated mice. My heart drummed in my chest, and I was no longer certain of the wisdom in asking that Isaac meet me here.

Once my eyes adjusted to the blackness, I stepped forward and lit the lantern, relieved by the warm glow it cast about the barn. Had Isaac read my book of scripture? I couldn't bear the thought of what it would mean if he hadn't, and walked to the stall where we penned our cow for the night, rubbing between her ears.

"It is good," I told her. "You'll see. He will have read the scriptures, ja?"

My family was beginning their journey to America in the morn. We had prayed about it a year ago. I'd had such a strong affirmation to my prayer about immigrating. I touched my hands to my chest, remembering. It had felt so right.

And then Isaac had proposed. Somehow it felt wrong loving him the way I did. But, regardless of my desire to live in Zion, I would stay in Denmark as his wife, if he honored me by reading the scriptures.

When the large double-door creaked open once more, I drew in a breath to prepare for the evening's task; receiving the long overdue answer to my one small test of his love, and the only way I could feel right about staying. Four months ago I had asked Isaac to read our Book of Mormon and pray about it before judging my new religion.

I straightened my apron, and rushed to greet him as he stepped into the barn. "Isaac!"

"Catherine, my love." His eyes shone in the lamplight. "Good evening." He took off his cap, revealing his light brown hair, and strode forward. Pulling me into his embrace he twirled me before letting me down. "I brought your book although I don't understand your hurry. I plan on wearing down the road to your aunt's house, and could give it to you tomorrow or the next day just as easily." He grinned, and patted his pocket, pulling out the worn Book of Mormon.

I beamed at this declaration, having worried when I'd see him next. "What did you think?" My pulse quickened in anticipation. "Did you like it?" I bit my lip back, hopeful.

"Nej." He grimaced. "It's not for me and I did not read it."

Isaac peeled his thumb through the pages as though it was a catalogue. "You say a man wrote this?"

His attitude unnerved me and my shoulders drooped. "Didn't the missionaries tell you? I sent them to your home ages ago."

A brief look of annoyance crossed his face, surprising me, but then it smoothed into a look of sadness. "Father sent them away."

"Oh." I gulped. This is why he hadn't mentioned them to me. "Well, a prophet translated it from an ancient record." Why did I find it so hard to talk about my religion with the man I loved?

"That's right." His eyes rolled heavenward. "Gold plates."

I nodded. "Ja, ja. It's all right that you haven't read it, we can read it together." I smiled hopefully. "We can start tonight." I hadn't meant to sound this eager. I raised my chin and looked him in the eye.

He put his hand to his cheek, frowning. "I've heard stories, Catherine—stories about Joseph Smith wanting to be the American president—and how his followers aren't Christian." He shook his head. "I still can't believe that your family joined with him."

The weight of his words crushed me. Still I faltered. Hoping to disguise my frustration, I raised my hands to smooth my braids, but my hands shook, so I pretended to smooth the crisp white apron covering my dress.

"Joseph Smith was martyred long before we even heard of the Church of Jesus Christ of Latter-day Saints," I said in our defense. "And you know that we are Christian. How could you say such a thing?" I pulled my lips into a pucker.

Was this lack of interest in my religion truly evidence that he didn't love me? That is what I had decided on as a sign to settle my unsettled heart.

If he read the Book of Mormon, then he loved me. If he even showed interest, I would stay in Denmark to be his wife regardless of whether or not he ever converted. If he didn't read it, didn't show interest, I should consider it a breach of his love and immigrate to America with my parents, trusting myself to the Lord's care.

"Father wanted me to burn it, but I saved it from the rubbish pile." He handed the book to me, holding it between his thumb and finger.

I slipped the book into the pocket of my apron, blinking back my disappointment. I had been so sure of his love—so sure he would read it. For me.

Once free of my scriptures, Isaac paced the barn. I wondered if he had never felt the promptings of the Holy Spirit. Had he not even thought to pray on this most important matter?

Isaac turned and came to me in all tenderness, taking my hands in his and kissing them. My heart skipped a beat, thinking that maybe he teased me and had actually read the scriptures.

"Catherine. Love." His lips pursed briefly before he continued. "Let's not do this again, now. You are merely upset because your family is leaving in the morn. We have our whole lives ahead of us. If it is important I read your book, I'll do it another day."

How I ached to believe his words, but they rang hollow and I knew I could not trust them. With my hopes dashed to pieces, I smiled feebly in response.

Isaac pulled me to the handmade wooden bench. As we sat together he began brushing his fingers up and down my hand—something he did when he wanted to appease me.

Usually thrilled by his attentions, tonight I only felt the emptiness of my broken heart, and stared down at my wooden shoes. I loved him desperately, and did not want this to be our last night together. Nor did I desire it to be a night of sorrow. But I felt the Holy Spirit urging me forward, whispering that I needed to stand firm in my decision to leave Denmark with my parents, and I knew that I must.

I looked into his periwinkle eyes. Should I tell him—confess my plan to leave? Or should I take the coward's way and write him a note?

He touched my cheek and kissed me. I savored the musky smell of him while returning his kiss, my heart a tangled mess. "We love each other, ja?" He touched his forehead to mine. "Don't be angry with me. I'll read it if that's what makes you happy. I will."

He had said these words to me before, yet I felt my resolve melting away. I needed to confess my new plans before I changed my mind and decided to stay.

"I'm leaving for America in the morning with Mama and Papa." I rushed through the hated words. They tasted bitter like spoiled milk as they passed over my tongue.

He frowned, and gazed into my eyes. I saw the shock and pain there. I had hurt him. Seeing his pain caused more of my own. I wanted to take it back—I wouldn't leave him—I'd stay by his side forever. He loved me, I knew it. And I loved him.

"We were to be married—and now you leave me?" He stood and moved to the other side of the barn where he folded his arms and met my gaze with a scowl.

He had proven himself in every way to be a kind and generous man. I wanted to beg his forgiveness for the pain I'd caused him, beg him to marry me, to take me in his arms and love me forever. But my mouth didn't open.

I found myself once again by his side and placed my hand on his arm, wanting to offer him reassurance. He jerked away but made no further movement except to glare stonily toward the horse stall.

"Isaac, look at me please." My voice quavered. "You know of my feelings."

"You said that you love me, ja?" He glared at me. "But this is not love." He stomped across the barn again, this time pitching harnesses, grooming brushes and even a hay hook in his anger. Then, he turned to face me, fire raging in his eyes. "Father warned me this would happen. You're brainwashed, the whole lot of you!"

He'd never before raised his voice at me. I quaked at the energy of his tantrum and remained speechless while wondering what I could say to calm his sudden temper. Remembering the kindness of his spirit, I gained a modicum of courage and went to his side once again. Isaac was hurt and it was my fault. He had trusted me to marry him, and I needed somehow to make it better.

"Please, Isaac, stop." I clung to his arm. "I cannot bear this."

He thrust me away.

Caught completely off guard, I stumbled before regaining my balance. Our cow bellowed at the disturbance. This was not the Isaac I had loved.

"Your family has planned all this year to leave and you wait until the eve of your departure to tell me that you're following with them?" His face reddened as he spoke and it was as though a stranger stood before me. "And what about your aunt? Who will care for her now?" He shook his head, his face snarled in disgust. "This new religion has changed you—it's changed your whole family!"

I uttered a silent prayer that he could see the truth of the gospel—that he would understand that the true love of Christ only made people better—and that my leaving was a direct result of his lack of support toward me and my new religion.

"If you had listened to the missionaries, you would know that the gospel can make us closer." I folded my arms against my stomach, wishing for my Isaac to return and talk this out rationally. "It's not too late. We can start tonight. We can read the scriptures together."

If he apologized and then showed an interest in learning the gospel, I could eventually forgive his act of impulsive behavior. I reached out to him.

"Don't!" He jerked away from my touch as though I had burned him. The movement knocked over the empty milk can. "I'll have nothing to do with liars!"

Liars? "Mormons aren't liars, Isaac." My voice rose in frustration. I took a deep, calming breath and continued. "I do love you, this is not a lie, but I could never marry a man who doesn't think I know my own mind."

A blaze sprang into his eyes and he raised his hand. Isaac actually thought to do me harm! Refusing to run, I braced myself for his blow. This was the man I had hoped to marry only moments earlier.

The barn door flew open and Isaac lowered his hand. His chin rose in defiance. Papa stood in the doorway amongst the billowy fog. His face shone in the lamplight—his gun at his side. I rushed into Papa's arms, never more grateful to see him than at that very moment.

"It's time for you to leave, son," Papa said calmly.

With no more than a moment's pause, Isaac strode toward the door and stopped. He glared at me while speaking. "Gladly. You're fools, the lot of you!"

I gasped and pressed my fingers to my heart.

"I hope you Mormons get what you deserve—a burial at sea!" Isaac never spared me another glance before storming into the darkness and out of my life.

Taking my handkerchief from my apron pocket I tried silencing my sobs. Papa held my trembling frame until the sound of Isaac's galloping horse was a distant memory.

"Oh, Papa!" I moaned. "What have I done?" Overcome with grief, I collapsed in his arms.

"There, there, Princess, the Lord will provide," Papa soothed. I leaned on his support as we walked into the house, and then I ran to my room.

From the comfort of my bed, I sobbed the night away. By morn's first light, there were no more tears to cry—or so I thought.

Chapter 2

I entered our bedroom to remind Berta that time for our departure ran short. My heart ached for Isaac, though I took solace in knowing I'd be with my sister. She was always such a comfort to me, and in turn, I would help steer her mind away from Jens. She had been to see him yesterday, like a dreamer chasing her fairytale. I understood those feelings too well.

Her packed bag lay untouched in the corner, and Berta paced around the room, her wooden shoes plodding against the wooden floor in quiet harmony. I noticed a lump of muslin on the bed. Her petticoat. The one she should be wearing. What was going on with my sister to set her so ill at ease?

I went to her hoping to quell her fears. "The Lord will guide our journey." I held her hand in mine. "He will lead us to kind and honorable men."

Berta gave me a sideways glance. "I'm too nervous to wear the petticoat." She leaned and pulled it from our bed. "Will you wear it for me?"

"What is wrong?" Cautiously I reached for the petticoat weighted with a portion of the family's funds, afraid of what this meant. "You know you can tell me anything." I slipped on the undergarment.

Wary of thieves along the way, we'd painstakingly sewn

small pockets all around it to hold Papa's coins. We would build our new life with this money.

Berta said nothing as I dressed, but continued pacing the floor. Something was terribly wrong.

Hoping to alleviate her fears by pretending all was well, I smiled. "Come, Papa is waiting for your things." I finished tying my apron, and picked up her bag. "We'll have great fun along the way, like we did at the beach near Kerteminde last summer."

Rather than return my smile or do any of the things I hoped, she straightened with a determined expression and went outside. I followed, of course. Last night's fog still clung to the earth like a bad omen and I heard more than saw Mama settling our little sisters, Mary and Ana, into the wagon already overfull with the few tools Papa could bring with us. Mama must have sensed something amiss for she joined Papa.

"Where are your things, Berta? I've left room for them here at the back." Papa patted the wagon. "It is time we left."

Berta remained silent until Papa quit packing to watch her. Nervous, I reached for her hand, but she fidgeted away and stepped forward.

"Papa, Mama, I will stay with Aunt Thora in place of Catherine." Berta stood resolute before our parents.

I gasped and stepped back. Her words chilled me like a bucket of ice water. Indeed Mama must have felt the same for the color drained from her face and she clutched Papa's arm for support.

"Nej," Papa said. "I cannot allow this."

"But, Papa, you were allowing Catherine to stay."

"You have to come." I went to her. "We will be together as a family. It will be good, ja?"

"Nej." She stepped closer to Mama and Papa.

Would she stay behind and lose her faith of the restored

Gospel of Jesus Christ? I chewed my bottom lip.

"Papa, someone needs to help Aunt Thora. It should be me. I will stay." Berta clasped her hands together.

Horrified, I watched the expression on Mama's face turn from dismay to one of pained consideration.

Thora, Mama's only living sibling lived a day's journey to our south. Mama didn't get to see her often, but she did her best to exchange monthly letters, some filled with cherished family recipes. Mama's previous correspondence that I'd be coming to help had been accepted humbly by my aunt.

"Perhaps ..." Mama began and then stopped, still in thought.

"Nej, Mama Nej!" I shouted. "Don't you understand? She is only doing this because of Jens."

Berta glared at me, but I didn't care. Mama and Papa needed to know.

"Is it true?" Mama turned to Berta, her eyebrows pinched together with concern.

She hesitated and the pink color of a blush appeared on her face.

"I told you, ja?" I said, my voice more subdued and respectful. "Papa, please don't let her go." How could my sister stay—and for him? Berta needed to get away from Jens just like I needed to get away from Isaac. I could see this truth clear as a sunny sky this morn. Now, with the faithful Saints leaving Denmark, Berta would be alone in her faith.

"It is partly true." Berta glanced down. "Jens will ask me to marry him if I stay. He told me as much yesterday."

Papa crossed his arms and frowned. Mama pursed her lips.

"The Jorgensens are against the Mormons," Papa scolded. "I cannot leave you here to marry such a boy."

"Papa, he's not like his parents, or Isaac. I will give him a Book of Mormon, and I am sure he will read it."

Berta sounded hopeful and naïve like I had been only

yesterday. I could not let her be parted from our family on false hopes. A fierce desire to protect her from the same sorrow I had experienced surged in me.

"He is not interested in our church or he would have told you so." I stepped near and touched her elbow. "Please don't separate our family on a whim."

"You are bitter because of Isaac and cannot see Jens for his good qualities."

I gasped and stepped away. I was not bitter.

"Berta, dear, we cannot leave you here in the hands of a wolf," Mama chided. "See what almost happened to Catherine and learn from her mistake."

Mama's words hurt me but I knew they were true. For Berta's sake they needed to be said.

"Would you feel differently if he was a member of our church?"

"Of course it would be different," Mama said.

"Mama, Papa." Berta took their hands in hers. "I shall not marry a wolf, and I promise you this day that I shall not marry anyone who believes differently than I." She paused for a moment gazing wide-eyed at Mama and biting her lip. "Aunt Thora lives far away, but Jens loves me, I know he does. He will join the church and then come to marry me."

"Berta, please! Don't do this. Come with us to Zion," I pleaded. "We're your family. We're the ones who love you." Saying goodbye to Isaac was difficult, but to Berta? I didn't know if I could survive this.

"Mama, I love you. I really do," Berta said gently. "But my heart is here in Denmark. Jens will be a good husband."

I touched my hand to her shoulder. "He will never be the kind of husband you deserve." Jens never thought of anything or anyone but himself. Couldn't Berta see it? "He only wants what will make his life easier, and remember he is bound by his parents' rules if he desires to inherit."

Berta didn't respond to my pleas or my tears, but continued talking only to our parents.

"Mama, Papa, do not make me stay here! I will never be happy without Jens and I cannot leave Denmark without him," she pleaded. "If you force me to leave, you will ruin my only chance for happiness." She wiped tears from her face. "And you know Aunt Thora needs my help."

Talk of Aunt Thora was always a tender subject. I knew I had lost the battle when Mama and Papa didn't say anything right away. They seemed to be talking with their eyes. I wanted them to fight for her, to make her come, for I could not bear to leave my Denmark without Berta.

Knowing that Mama would be more comfortable immigrating if someone stayed to care for her aging sister did not comfort me in losing mine.

"Thora needs our help," Mama whispered to Papa. "She refuses any financial assistance from us, but she has agreed to let one of our daughters stay with her and help."

Papa walked to the front of our wagon, helped Mary and Ana down, and then returned. "Let us say a prayer. The Lord will know what is right." He knelt and removed his cap.

Saying a prayer was a good thing. I knelt with Papa on the ground. The Lord had prompted me to immigrate and I knew he'd do the same for Berta. With everyone in a circle, we each joined hands.

After Papa finished the prayer, he kept his eyes closed for the longest time and I watched for his declaration that Berta should accompany us.

"Berta will stay and help care for Aunt Thora." Papa stood, helped Mama up, and brushed the knees of his breeches with his cap before returning it to his head.

I remained on the ground unable to move, but watched the

disturbing scene play out before me like a nightmare as I knelt on the damp earth.

Tears streamed down Mama's face and she embraced Berta who melted into her arms, sobbing. Then Mama pulled away, and with tears still shining in her eyes, she pressed something small into Berta's hand.

Berta opened her fingers and choked back her sobs. "Mama, I can't take your locket."

"I want you to have it." Mama folded Berta's fingers back around the treasure. "It will help you remember who you are. We will be on the other side of the ocean, but I am still your Mama and I will pray for you every day. Take my Book of Mormon also." Mama pulled the book out of her travel bag and handed it to Berta. "It is the only thing as dear to me as my family. Keep your faith in mind when dealing with Jens."

"I will, Mama, I will," Berta choked in reply.

Six-year-old Mary jumped up and rushed to Berta, clinging to her. "Nej. Don't stay! You must come, please!"

All the tears confused and upset little Ana. She toddled to Berta and reached her arms up. "Come with us, please!"

Mama pried the girls loose and ushered them back into the wagon. Slowly, I rose and stepped closer, afraid that this wasn't a dream, afraid to say goodbye, and most certainly afraid of never seeing my beloved sister and confidant again.

As I took another step near, I studied her, trying to memorize each feature of her face—her perfect blue eyes—her perfect nose. Her blonde hair, braided and tucked under her bonnet, refused to be bound by rules and always wanted to fly free in the breeze—as did she. Berta's gaze locked with mine and we rushed into one another's arms.

"I love you so much," she bawled. "How will I ever live without you?"

I wiped the tendrils of hair from her face. "You are the best sister anyone could hope for. I will miss you dearly." I cupped her face with my hands, wiping a tear from her cheek and then pulled the embroidered handkerchief from my pocket, handing it to her.

Berta looked at me with wide eyes. "Grandmother Erichsen's," she said reverently. "She helped you make this."

"When I was ten," I reminded her. "It is now yours. Keep it to remember me." It was difficult parting with my special handkerchief but I saw in her eyes that she would love it as much as I did.

Berta put it into her pocket and then pulled out hers, handing it to me.

"This is the first thing you embroidered yourself," I said, amazed that she'd part with it.

"It was a trick for me to sew around the corners," Berta said.

"You had to take it out five times." I remembered. "But look at the other corners." I lifted the cloth. "They each lay perfectly."

"It is now yours."

I nodded, blinking at my tears. We embraced once more. "I love you," I said, and then shaking with sobs, took my place in our wagon.

Only Papa stood near.

"What will we do without you?" Papa murmured.

"I don't know what I'll do without you, Papa," cried Berta. "I will stay in Denmark, yet I will think of you every day and I'll love you always."

Papa took her hands in his. "I arranged for a carriage, thinking Catherine would need it, but it won't arrive until mid morn. You will be all right until then, ja?"

Berta nodded and chewed her bottom lip.

"This is travel fare to Thora's, and enough for a wedding should you desire it." He placed a small bag of coins into her open palms.

"Nej, Papa. It is too much."

"I only wish it could be more," Papa said. "We must go now else we miss the ferry." He turned to join us, but Berta thrust herself upon him and wept. It was the only time I had seen Papa break down, for he cried with all the tenderness of a loving parent losing his child.

He never bothered wiping away his tears upon joining us in the wagon. Silently, Papa led the horses toward the Storebaelt without looking back. But, knowing that I might never see my sister again in this life, I couldn't keep from craning my neck to watch as she waved.

Doing the Lord's will was not supposed to feel like this. I should feel joyful and full of conviction. I'd never felt worse.

Tears fell unchecked as I waved my farewell, morose and unsure of anything. Would my sister be safe? Would we?

Chapter 3

A variety of bushes and soon-to-flower brambles lined the shore on either side of the wide dock. Fog continued to hang over the water, though only wisps of the moist whiteness clung to the earth. Still, I detected the outline of our ferry as it approached.

The large vessel rode low on the water's surface and had a railing around the low-lying craft. Two enormous black smokestacks protruded from the center near the wheelhouse. One of the ferry's deck hands stood at the head, calling directions to the man at the wheel.

I wondered if the ferry could hold us as well as all of our belongings. I'd never seen such a group of people, most of them strangers. Someone trying to gain the front pushed against me, nearly sending me to the ground. "Pardon me," he said.

I nodded and turned my attention back to the dock.

The man behind the wheel raised his hand. Thinking he'd seen me, I started to wave back. The deep blast from the ferry startled me, and let me know my error. He was merely blowing the horn. The ferry slammed against the dock and the deckhand threw a large rope to shore. Another man caught it and tied it with impressive speed to a wooden post.

"Catherine!" Ester Knudsen, one of my childhood friends wove her way forward. "You are joining us then?" She gave me a quick hug.

"Ja, ja." I turned, not wanting to say more. A lump formed in my throat, and I didn't want to show my emotions in front of everyone.

Ester would not be dissuaded so easily however, and took my elbow as she guided me to a large rock. "What has happened?"

"Please don't make me confess it." My voice quavered, and I hated my weakness.

"Dear friend, share your burden with me." She placed her hand on my shoulder. "It will help you feel better."

"Isaac did not approve of Mormons." I could not speak the cruel words he'd spoken. I could not confess that the man I loved wished me dead.

"Poor thing." Ester embraced me. "Is there something I can do?"

She meant well, I know she did, but I shook my head. No amount of coddling or sympathy could help. "I just need time."

Ester left me then, and I felt the kindness of her action. My emotions were too raw to discuss them on this day.

Wounded by the memories that Ester had evoked, I walked away from the others to stand at the water's edge. I couldn't help but wonder if the dark liquid felt as good as when we'd played in the sea near Kerteminde, so I slipped out of my wooden shoes and removed my woolen stockings. I stuck one toe in the water and immediately pulled it back out. The frigid water was colder than a winter storm.

A large, orange-hued glutinous object hovered just underneath the water like a translucent ghost. I wondered what it might feel like to float through life with no worries other than what to eat that day. I reached my hand into the water, stretching to touch it.

"Catherine!"

I jerked my hand back and guiltily raised my eyes up at Mama. "I was only curious to feel it."

"And a fine thing if it would have stung you. Such a silly notion; trying to touch a stinging jellyfish." She shook her head with a frown. "Your curiosity will get the better of you one day." Her extended hand held my shoes and stockings. I took them and put them on.

"Hmph." I rolled my eyes. Learning about new things was good, not bad. But I remained silent as Mama led the way back to Papa and the girls.

Soon I realized that there weren't as many strangers as I'd thought, since it seemed every familiar face turned toward me in surprise. My face warmed, and I turned away, but the buzz of speculation hummed in the air like a swarm of bees.

Each person I knew tapped my shoulder, expressed concern at my being there and curiosity as to Berta's whereabouts. At first, I gave a polite explanation, Berta wanted to stay in my place, and therefore I could follow with my family. But, as others gathered around like I was some strange bird, questioning our location and motives, I developed a sore headache—my eye twitched from the stress of it. I fervently wished Berta were there to offer support, and clutched her handkerchief as a thin replacement.

When the excitement over my immigration finally passed, we waited for our turn to board the ferry and cross the Storebaelt. I stood at the water's edge worrying about my future and stared through moist eyes toward the unknown horizon. Why should I leave when I wanted nothing more than to stay in Denmark with Berta? Couldn't we be Mormon here just as easily?

Mama wrapped her arm around my shoulders.

"Mama," I began.

She silenced me with a finger to my lips. I looked into her grief-stricken face and knew I couldn't utter the words I wanted to say—longed to say. Mama needed me. I embraced her hoping to offer her the same comfort and strength she offered me. Papa put his arms around us too, and once again the weight of his sorrow at having our family divided pressed down on me.

He looked down at us with emotion in his eyes. "The Lord will provide," he whispered huskily.

Then Papa guided us back to our place in line and one-by-one we boarded the ferry. Mary rushed into my welcoming arms. She helped hold my emotions together and I clutched onto her. I would be strong for my little sister. I sighed a deep breath and stepped onto the vessel that would take me away from my home and Berta.

Waves lapped against the ferry, rocking it, and it took a moment to gain my footing. Mary wiggled, wanting released to explore, but I kept her fast to my heart.

"Stay with me until the others are settled and the ferry has departed toward Sjaelland," I said.

With two short blasts, the ferry lurched forward into the sea. I stumbled and nearly dropped my little sister. Once I regained my balance, she turned, studying my face for a moment as though it was her first time seeing me.

"Will you be getting married soon, Catie? If not, Berta will be married first."

I clenched my jaw against an irritable response.

Mary looked solemnly around the ferry and then pointed to a boy not far from us. "Peter is nice, ja? Maybe you could marry him."

My lips turned up sarcastically. Peter was a fine boy—for a twelve-year-old. "Nej." I patted her head. Only a six-year-old could think a twelve-year-old was marrying age.

"Well, hurry it up, ja," Mary advised. "You're almost as old as Mama."

"Oh! Seventeen is not old. You take that back." I set her down, folded my arms, and glared at the little imp.

Sometimes she could be so impossible.

"Your friends, Joanna and Marta are both already married," Mary continued. "Maybe you can find someone in the big city, København." She smiled and her eyes lit with hope.

København, indeed. I glanced about the ferry, wondering how many had heard Mary's outburst. As I did so, I saw several better choices than Peter. My face grew hot and I turned away. After last night's ordeal, I wasn't ready to consider anyone, regardless of their age.

Mary kept me busy then, chasing her from one end of the ferry to the other. She peeked over the ferry's edge, and laughed when sea spray blew into her face. As we moved farther into the Storebaelt toward the isle of Sjaelland and away from our island of Fyn, my heart tugged.

We were leaving my family's home—a three-winged structure made of the traditional half-timber with a thatched roof, built by my great-great-grandfather and continually occupied by his descendents—until today.

We were leaving my grandparents' graves. They were buried in the little church cemetery near town, and cared for by Mama and me—until now.

We left it all: our furniture, handmade by Papa, Grandmother's china, the great carved chest given to a dear friend had originally held fabrics and linens embroidered by Mama for her wedding dowry, most of Papa's tools, handed down from father to son, had also stayed. None of these precious things could come, but more than that, we left our ancestors, our heritage, our Danish culture. Everything that made up our lives in Denmark had been sold for the sake of our testimonies and our desire to gather with the saints in Zion.

There was one extravagance that Papa had allowed, my great-grandfather's gold watch. It was expensive and beautiful, and it still kept perfect time. He kept it as a legacy of our family's love.

Great-grandmother Erichsen had traveled all the way to Switzerland to purchase it for her husband as a twenty-fifth anniversary gift saying she couldn't wait until they were wed fifty years to give a gift that reflected her deep devotion.

"Catie, why are you crying?" Mary tugged on my apron.

"I'm not crying." My voice cracked, giving me away. I forced myself to recover, smiled for her benefit, and gave Mary a squeeze. "It's the salt air."

I hoped she believed my lie but knowing that she might require a distraction, I turned her attentions to our island.

"Look, Mary, and watch our Fyn get smaller as we near Sjaelland." I needed to be strong for my little sisters. We had prayed on more than one occasion as a family about immigrating and knew it to be right.

Mama turned her knowing eyes to me. "You made the right decision."

I nodded but said nothing.

As our island grew smaller in the distance, the emotion in me swelled until I thought I might burst. I already missed Berta. A painful lump formed in my throat and I turned away. Sjaelland lay ahead, a dark line on the horizon. The foundational columns for the new bridge rose from the sea.

"See the pillars." I lifted Mary back into my arms and pointed them out.

Papa held Ana in his arms and they also looked. "One day they will form a great bridge from island to island."

But we would never see it finished.

Gloominess threatened to consume me. I struggled for a distraction from the pain of leaving our home and untied my bonnet. Releasing my hair from its braids, I let it fly with the wind. It swirled in the air around my face.

Mary laughed as a few strands tickled her nose. "Take mine off."

I complied with her request, and upon doing so, Ana wanted her hair unbraided as well.

We had spent considerable time this morning preparing Mary and Ana for our journey, and I glanced up, afraid of Mama's disapproval. Ana's bonnet had already been tucked neatly into Mama's apron pocket. The little girls and I watched as Mama unloosed the last plait of her own hair and shook her head. Her golden brown tresses flew in every direction.

Papa unexpectedly grabbed Mama and nuzzled her hair. I laughed as she blushed and swatted him away. I took note of the faces surrounding us, young and old, frowning in disapproval. But, not wanting the refreshing feeling to go away, I put Mary down and twirled around on my toes.

"Hello, new life, hello. Hello to Sjaelland!" I waved my bonnet as though the island could see. I had never been further from home than Kerteminde, and was truly excited to see the big city of København.

I heard Ester's voice behind me. "That's Catherine Erichsen, poor thing. She planned on staying here to marry Isaac Thompsen, but he left her. It is why she has come."

I turned to see to whom she spoke, wishing to silence her gossip with a glare. Instead, I accidentally glanced into the green eyes of a fiery-haired young man near my age. He watched me with laughing eyes and an amused smile. My heart skipped a beat. I plopped my bonnet atop my head and slunk down hoping to become invisible.

With Mama's hair already rolled neatly under her bonnet, she fussed with Ana's.

"I suppose," Mama said, "that we should provide a better example for your sisters."

Showing a little excitement could not be wrong, and with the silliness forgotten, my heart and mind had more time to wander to unsafe places. Before long, I once again felt the tearing of my soul and wished I had cried out, "Good-bye Fyn, good-bye Berta, good-bye love, forever."

We were not a people prone to giving large displays of emotion however, so I kept my thoughts to myself. With Mary once again in my arms, we remained silent for the remainder of the ferry trip.

Once we touched the shores of Sjaelland and began disembarking, I needed one more glance at the green-eyed young man, and stayed near the ferry. Partially hidden, I dared to look on the faces of the others as they came ashore, wondering if we'd meet. Most were families, but there were several who seemed to be traveling alone.

Two young men caught my attention; probably friends traveling together. Their features were not at all similar. The shorter one had an air of authority and seemed more confident.

He had a straight nose, nice cheekbones and the flyaway blond hair that I loved. Though I put little stock in looks, the young man's blond hair and blue eyes reminded me of Grandfather Erichsen.

The other, I had waited to see, was tall and awkward with freckles to match his bright red hair. His vibrant green eyes, quick to light up in joy were what held my interest. Yet, I ducked and hurried away as he glanced in my direction.

Mary and Ana, excited for a little space, ran to the lawn giggling and squealing their delight. "Come here you little imps." Papa chased after them, laughing.

Mama and I watched with amusement. He soon had them under his arms, lugging them toward us like great sacks of flour.

The train depot was a tall building made of red brick. Food peddlers lined the walkway. Gulls flitted back and forth, squawking, chirping, and on the ready for neglected crumbs and pieces of meat. Heavenly aromas of smoked fish, spicy pork sausage and marinated herring permeated the air. Only on very special occasions did we have store-bought meat. My mouth watered with longing.

"This smells good, ja?" Papa said as he drew near. "But nothing tastes as good as Mama's cooking."

We left home without a morning meal and my stomach growled in protest. Since the train was not here, Mama spread out a blanket and opened up a bag of food while Papa played with the girls.

Other families stretched out blankets or spread their meager meals on the lawn. I watched with a twinge of envy when a few of the single passengers purchased smørrebrød sandwiches, or smoked herring, or sausage links, and settled down to savor them.

Soon we were all spread out and eating a noon meal on the grass. I noticed the redheaded young man helping a small child on the blanket next to his. It was very sweet, and I wondered if they knew each other.

Mama served us the remainder of last season's apples, a few slices of havarti cheese, and some of her homemade rye bread. Even though it wasn't purchased from the vendors, I thought that perhaps the king himself couldn't eat a more elegant meal.

I leaned back, enjoying an apple and watching a couple of stilts wading in the shallow water, picking their noon meal from the wet sand. The black and white birds looked as though they were dressed for a fancy party. A ringed plover raced along the beach and out of sight.

"Papa, will we see King Christian, or perhaps a member of the royal family?" I shooed away a gull that tried to steal a piece of cheese. He screeched his protest.

"I think," Papa said, pausing to scratch his chin, "that where we are going, the royal family seldom goes."

"Never?"

"Why should they travel by rail when they have expensive carriages and servants waiting to drive them anywhere they wish, and a private yacht at their disposal?"

"I've heard that Hans Christian Andersen walks the streets of København telling stories." It had long been a dream of mine to meet someone famous, and it would be a special treat to meet our family's favorite author.

"Even if he were there, we could not stop to listen. Our ship will be waiting." Papa lifted his eyebrow, regarding my disappointment and continued. "All is well and good; we have his book of children's stories." He smiled and wiggled his eyebrows. "Don't be disappointed, but it's my understanding that he is currently out of the country."

This, in fact, did not disappoint, but allowed my mind to speculate about the possibilities of meeting our famous Danish author across the sea. We might bump into him while he was on a corner in the city of New York rehearsing the story of the Ugly Duckling to a crowd.

We would listen with rapt attention until he finished, after which Papa would nudge me forward. Embarrassed, I would curtsey.

He would tip his hat and then take my fingers in his gloved hand, offer a polite kiss, and then say something like,

"To meet such a Danish flower on this side of the ocean brings my heart great joy."

I, of course, would blush again at such flattery and tell him, "Thank you." Perhaps before we parted ways, he might even offer me one of his decorative paper cuttings.

I sighed.

"Papa, Catie is dreaming while she's awake again."

My eyes opened, and Mary was only inches from my face. Her eyebrows pinched together in concern, her lips a thin line. I frowned back at her and crossed my arms in false denial of her accusation.

Papa laughed. "The imagination is a wonderful thing, is it not?" His eyes twinkled. "Take your sisters and let them use up a little more of their energy before that train comes."

Nodding, I took their hands and we walked toward the far edge of the shore. Mary let go of my hand and chased a pair of gulls pecking in the grass. Ana followed her. With a shriek of alarm, the stilts fled. The gulls lifted into the air and landed a little farther down the beach. Mary and Ana pursued them, squealing their delight.

As we made our way back to Mama and Papa, the ground began vibrating. My heart raced, and as the train drew near I was overcome with two simultaneous emotions: one, the strong desire to "accidentally" miss the train to go live with Berta and Aunt Thora, and two, fear—both the fear of following through on my impulse, and the fear of not.

If I stayed on my present course, what would my new life be like? My insides shivered. I blinked through my tears and glanced from the ferry to the approaching train and from my parents to my little sisters.

Chapter 4

The long machine before us seemed endless. Large boxes with strange metal wheels balanced on two narrow tracks. This would carry us to København. I frowned. Was it safe? We inched closer to the acrid-smelling beast, awaiting our turn to enter.

"Are you nervous?" Mama's eyebrows lifted and her lips curved into a smile.

"Nej." My heart thrummed in anticipation. I had never ridden a train before, nor had I ever seen one. "Are you nervous, Mama?"

"It will be something, ja?" Her eyes were wide as she took Mary and Ana's hands. She heaved a breath, and led the way behind Papa.

Before we took our seat, Ester came on board with a blond gentleman. "Oh, Lars," she said. "You are so funny!"

Her parents followed behind with looks of annoyance on their faces.

When I sat, the train's humming vibrations filled me with trepidation, and I watched as every bench filled. With Mary beside me, I peeked out of the window. Smoke from the smokestack billowed into the sky like angry storm clouds and then dissipated into the air. The train filled with the sounds of chatter. Everyone seemed excited, happy. Not me. I clutched Berta's handkerchief to my stomach.

A loud, somber whistle blew and the escaping steam hissed.

The train lurched forward and then began to move. Startled, I grabbed hold of the bench. Ana slid forward unable to stop herself.

"It is well and good. Not to worry." Mama grabbed hold of Ana just before she plummeted to the floor.

Mary made a whimpering sound and went to Papa, clutching his arm. Moving to the side, I peeked my head through the open window and watched the wheels churn as they anxiously, dizzily, guided our way. The train so huge, the railings so slender—surely it wouldn't take much to knock us off track. My heart leapt into my throat, I caught my breath and pulled back inside.

"Did you see?" I placed my hand to my chest. "Mama, Papa, look out the window. See how fast the wheels are moving." My heart raced, and then a loud hiccough escaped my lips. My face heated with embarrassment.

I put my hand to my lips and glanced around. The excitement among the other immigrants echoed off the walls. No one heard, and I took a deep breath to ensure that there were no other hiccoughs.

Mama and Papa looked at me, both shaking their head. "Nej. It is best not to stick your head out of the window," advised Papa

"I want to see." Mary climbed off of Papa's lap and onto mine.

"Me, too." Ana wriggled from Mama's grasp and strained to see.

"Nej. You could get hurt or fall out." Mama motioned for the girls to sit beside her. They complied with a frown.

"It is not dangerous," I said, and leaned out the window again. The wheels clacked in rhythm. The salty sea air blew past with such fierceness that my cheeks flopped back and forth. I started to laugh, but felt a sharp pain.

"Ouch!" I closed my eye and plopped into my seat. "There's something in my eye. It feels like glass." I placed my hand over my eye, and, with my eyelid still closed, rolled my eye around trying to dislodge whatever it was.

"Mama, it hurts!" Tears watered my hand.

"Let me see." Mama sat next to me with her handkerchief. "Move your hand," she coaxed. "Open your eye."

I tried, but the pain was like nothing I'd felt before—sharp, cutting.

Mama dabbed the moisture with her handkerchief. "Look up," she said. When I did, she dabbed the cloth to my eye, and it instantly felt better.

"What was it?" I blinked and squinted.

"Possibly an ember." Mama held the handkerchief to display a nearly unnoticeable speck of black.

"That couldn't have been it. It's too small."

"Your eye feels better now, ja?"

"Ja." I nodded, and sat back.

Papa winked at me. "See the rolling hills of our land?" He asked the little girls. They glanced out the window and nodded. "The Vikings have a legend that explains why. Did you know that most of Denmark used to be underwater?"

"How did the cows stay alive?" asked Mary.

Papa rubbed his chin. "Perhaps they had rafts."

Mary tilted her head, her eyebrows squeezed together in puzzlement, but Ana smiled, satisfied.

I loved hearing of our legends but I didn't put much stock in this one unless they meant to say that Denmark had been underwater during the times of Noah.

I did know that some of the hills were actual burial grounds where the Vikings had buried a beloved chieftain—ship and all.

Having never been on the main island of Sjaelland, I turned my attention to the landscape, watching with satisfaction for a time. It was still my Denmark. The hills rolled and ebbed, facing one direction or another. Though not as large as on Fyn, they still looked like the dry land's version of a soft rippling of the sea on a sunny day. I breathed the sweet Danish air, fragrant with rich soil, grass and abundant greenery, and let it out in a sigh, taking brief contentment in watching as one farm ended and another began.

"Is that our farm, Papa?" Mary, once again beside Papa, stood on the bench and gazed with rapt interest at the changing scenery.

"Nej, daughter. We are on Sjaelland now. Our home is far away on the island of Fyn."

Houses dotted the horizon. Some were half-timber houses with thatched roofs, like ours. Others were simple wooden structures. Thick rows of the oak and ash trees that were also prevalent on Fyn separated each property. The earth was prepared in long furrowed rows that went first one way and then another depending on the tilt of the land. The sight reminded me of Mama's patchwork quilt.

After a time, the rhythmic clacking of the train against the rail lulled many of the immigrants to sleep. We were crammed into the general seating of the passenger cars, packed together like sardines. I twisted and turned, trying to get comfortable enough to rest.

Ester was three rows up from us. Her head rested on the young man's shoulder. Her parents dozed on the bench facing them. Sleeping in an upright position was not one of my talents. Turning my head, I closed my eyes and tried sleeping once more.

Something tickled against my neck. I slapped at and then scratched the sudden itch. I could sleep. I would sleep. Mary, the little imp, thought I was old. I took a deep breath, also remembering Ester's embarrassing declaration on the ferry, and Berta's standing alone in our yard. My eyes fluttered open and I glimpsed the verdant farmland again before forcing my eyelids shut.

A fly must have gotten into the train, for something tickled my nose. I wiggled it but when my nose still itched, I scratched the tip. The tickling sensation moved to my arm. I brushed at it and peeked to see nothing there. Mama opened an eye. She regarded me and then continued resting.

No amount of squirming or wiggling made me comfortable. I took my shoes off and rested my feet on the bench opposite me, careful not to disturb Papa. I leaned forward, and resting my elbows on my legs, placed my face in my hands. The moment my eyes closed however, Isaac appeared—an unwanted apparition—taunting my soul with his lies.

Ester stretched her arms and said something to the young man. I strained to hear their conversation.

"We saved money all year... still didn't have enough for the whole family... sent us ahead."

"How sad," exclaimed Ester.

When had she become such a flirt? I closed my eyes. When I did, Isaac was there once more, his face twisted in rage. That would not do. My eyes flew open, though it was of no use.

The train's continual mocking, no one loves you—no one loves you, drummed in my ears until I thought I would scream.

If only I could stay in Denmark just long enough to ensure Berta's happiness. Our being separated wouldn't hurt as badly if I knew she loved an honorable man.

Had I made a big mess of things? Perhaps I shouldn't blame Isaac for being angry with me. Perhaps his behavior and his getting upset only proved the depth of his love. Perhaps the Lord didn't have another man for me and I should have been more patient with Isaac. I shook my head.

Mama and Papa had occasional disagreements and Papa

never raised his voice. Nor did he throw things in anger or think to strike Mama—or any of us. This knowledge brought me only one conclusion. Isaac never truly loved me.

I sighed as I remembered the dimple in his chin, his purple-blue eyes lit up in mischief, and the way his soft hair fluttered in the breeze when he didn't wear his cap.

I thought there were no more tears left in me. Nevertheless, they fell down my face. Isaac probably never shed one tear over me, yet there I sat, a waterfall of emotion. It made me angry with myself.

I hope you Mormons—are buried at sea—I hope you Mormons—are buried at sea, the train mocked. At last, I made a resolution. I would give myself until we arrived in København to mourn the loss of him. After that, I vowed not to shed another tear for a man who didn't love and respect me.

I put my handkerchief, or rather Berta's handkerchief, in my apron pocket. I'd turned it into a waterlogged mess. Seeming to always read my mind, Mama handed me hers and patted my hand. How could she know? Yet I saw that she willed me better with all of her motherly love.

Mama and Papa had a love as true and pure as any I'd witnessed. Their lives fit together in perfect harmony. But would there be true love for me? I vowed to never settle for anything less than the total adoration that my parents shared—and prayed for the wisdom to find it.

"Mama, how did you know Papa was a good man before you married?" I dried my tears once again and waited for Mama to retell the story of how they met.

"Only the Lord can know the heart of another. It's up to us to ask and then patiently listen." She placed Ana on the bench beside her, laid Ana's head on her lap and stroked wisps of blonde behind her ear. "Papa came to the mill often." Mama smiled with her memories. "I watched from a window how he treated others and didn't know until after I became Mrs. Erichsen that he came only to see me."

Ana climbed back into Mama's arms, and stuck her thumb in her mouth. Mama kissed her forehead. "I knew how I felt about your papa, but I made the idea of marrying him a matter of daily prayer."

"But ..." I protested and then remained silent. I had prayed about Isaac.

I turned back to the window, frowning, and tried finding comfort in Mama's words. Perhaps, if the Lord willed it, I would be blessed to find a good man in Zion.

Maybe the Lord had someone truly wonderful in mind for me. The idea gave my heart hope. I brushed away another tear and then pressed my forehead to the glass, trying envisioning who He might send—a kind person who behaved with integrity even when upset—someone who meant what they said, and wouldn't break my heart as Isaac had. And, unlike Isaac, he should be a man in good standing with the Lord.

Mary awoke, rubbed her eyes, slid off of Papa's lap and came to sit with me.

"Catie, why didn't Berta come with us?" Tears pooled in her eyes. "Doesn't she love us anymore?"

"You must never think that." I took Mama's handkerchief from my apron pocket and dabbed at Mary's tears. "Berta loves us all very much."

"Why didn't she come with us then? I miss her."

"She had another dream to follow, but that doesn't lessen her love for you." It broke my heart to see how Berta's absence affected Mary—how I knew it affected us all.

"I know she wants to marry Jens, but I don't know how she can," Mary said.

"What do you mean?" I glanced over at Mama, hoping she didn't hear.

Mary leaned over, and brushing the bonnet free from my ear, whispered, "Aunt Thora lives in Svendborg. Jens will be too far away."

I shook my head. Mary was but a child with childish thoughts. I did worry, though, if Berta would see Jens before traveling to Aunt Thora's. How else would he know she stayed in Denmark?

"What are you girls whispering about?"

I turned to see Mama frowning at us. "Nothing." I shook my head and bit my lip hoping she wouldn't ask more.

"Berta and Jens can't get married," announced Mary.

My hands flew to cover Mary's mouth. Mama didn't need to worry more about Berta than she already was.

I looked anxiously over. "Our God will keep her safe. Mama, you know He will." As the words spilled from my mouth, I prayed that they were true.

"The Lord will provide us all with comfort," Mama said, her voice forcibly strong. "We shall always pray for Berta's safety and happiness now that she is not with us."

Had Berta thought to pray? My heart skipped with anxiety. Oh, please, I prayed, guide Berta to the man she should marry, even if that man is Jens. At least Berta had a good home to stay in until she married. And, perhaps while she was with Aunt Thora she would find someone else.

The benches were hard and uncomfortable. Rubbing my hind-side, I tried not to grimace. The crowded train had begun smelling of sweating bodies. I leaned over and re-opened the window, inhaling the fresh air.

We might have traveled in the nicer train-car had Papa not helped finance several of our friends' immigrations as well as our own. We, or rather Papa, had been fortunate in selling our farm's lease, and he delighted in being generous.

Unfortunately, even in the nearly twenty years since the

martyrdom of Joseph Smith, it seemed that persecution abounded toward those who discovered the true and living God. I didn't know why one religion would rail against another, but I'd heard other immigrants' tales. They'd been forced from their land after joining with the Mormons. Some nearly died as a result. I couldn't imagine being bullied and purposefully starved over religious differences.

In the Denmark I knew, everyone was as kind and generous as Papa. He radiated goodness in his soul. I observed Papa sleeping on the bench. His ears were rather large, and he had an old scar along his jaw that I seldom noticed. However, he was as handsome as any man I knew.

"Mama, are we there yet?" Ana, now awake, stood and stared out the window.

"No, dear." Mama brushed wisps of blonde away from Ana's face, and then kissing her pinkie finger, placed it lovingly on little Ana's cheek. "A tiny fairy told me to give you this."

Ana looked on either side of Mama and Papa, and then jumped off the bench and searched under it. "Where did the fairy go, Mama? Tell me 'cause I want to get a kiss for you too."

"Dear one, to me your kisses are much better than those of a mere fairy. If you'll share a kiss with me, I'll be the richest Mama in the world."

Ana climbed onto the bench, held Mama's face between her hands and kissed her cheek.

Mary plopped into Mama's lap then and hugged her tight around the neck, also giving her a kiss on the cheek. "I love you too." Mary giggled.

"How much do you love me?" Mama smiled, and I saw the twinkle in her eyes.

"I love you more than all the fish in the ocean, and more than all the fairies in Denmark. How much do you love me?"

Mama laughed and gave Mary a big hug. "Oh, I love you all

that, plus all the hugs in the world."

Mary's eyes widened. "Really?"

"Of course." Mama lifted Mary to the seat by the window. "Now let's enjoy some of this beautiful Danish scenery. You need to pay attention because when we get to America, I want you to remember this land. You are a Dane, true and proud."

"Ja, ja." Mary studied the farmland before her with all the concentration a serious six-year-old could give.

I remembered when Mama used to play these loving games with me. I longed to be six again, if only for a day, so that I could snuggle unburdened into Mama's arms.

I knew better than to test the Lord. After all, He'd prompted my immigration, but I longed for one more day. One day wasn't too much to ask. One day to forget the pain and to heal my wounded heart. One more day with Berta and to live and breathe in Denmark.

But I couldn't fool myself into believing that I'd pull myself together so quickly. An hour—a day—a month—a year, it was useless to think I would ever be whole again. The waves in the sea could crush a rock into sand, but no one had ever taken that sand and formed it back into rock.

Chapter 5

As we neared København, I looked for the familiar U-shaped farm homes with thatched roofs common on Fyn, and saw instead, rows of smaller, half-timbered houses bunched together. I pressed my face to the window, entranced. Berta and I had dreamed of coming here together one day to meet Hans Christian Andersen. Here I was without her.

Only a narrow sidewalk distanced them from the cobblestone streets. The homes were painted a variety of gay colors and connected as though one long house—with roofs made of tile. Most had planter boxes under the windows with this year's flowers already growing in them.

"Will they have cobblestone streets in America?" I loved the sound of horses' hooves on cobblestone streets. It was comforting and familiar.

"We'll have to wait and see," replied Mama.

Other passengers stood at the windows along each side of the train car, staring into the streets and trying to see the city. I remained seated, still worried the train might topple off the track.

"Papa, look! What is that?" Mary pointed out the window, her voice raised in excitement.

"Well, I'll be!" Papa exclaimed. "Bicycles."

Having heard of them, but having never seen one, I turned in the direction Mary pointed. Several men sat atop two-wheeled metal contraptions, pumping their legs up and down while bouncing over the cobblestone streets.

"I'll bet it's not too long before they start riding those bicycles everywhere," Mama said. "We're in a new age now, with trains and steamboats, and men riding bicycles in the middle of the street. Who knows what they'll think of next."

Papa nodded in agreement.

What would it be like to ride a bicycle? I tried to imagine myself on one but couldn't. They seemed rather tricky. If I were to try, I would probably fall to the ground and break my neck. How could anyone be that foolhardy? If Berta were here, would she try to ride one? I looked closer and was puzzled to see they seemed to be enjoying themselves. "Hmph!" I crossed my arms and turned away refusing to even consider it.

"Can I have a bicycle when we get to America?" Mary asked.

"We'll see, Princess." Papa patted her shoulder and gave her a hug. "First though, we'll need to be getting ourselves a handcart to carry all of our belongings. We'd look pretty silly traveling to Zion with all of us perched on one of those."

Ana giggled. So did I.

"I want to ride a horse to Zion," said Mary.

I had a hard time taking my gaze from the city and continued staring out the window. København was amazing with its tall buildings and city streets.

There were crowds of people. Many of the women wore dresses made of rich colors and plenty of lace. As the men walked, their tall black hats bobbed up and down.

Some buildings were made with tan brick—others with red. Some had fancy designs and people carved along the top, almost like a royal residence—others had rows of windows close together. Were they the homes of rich folk, or were they businesses? They must be businesses for who could live in such places?

One building was long. It had a green metal roof with nine elaborate dormers protruding from it. I gasped with delight. In the center was a tower with four large dragons perched atop it with their tails intertwined in a swirl toward heaven.

"That's the stock exchange building," Papa said, appearing amused at my reaction. "It was commissioned and built by the command of King Christian the Fourth."

No sooner had I overcome the marvel of that sight when

another extravagant building caught my attention. Its doors gave the appearance that it was a church, yet it looked nothing like the churches I had seen. The brick forming its walls were dark brown and it had a pointed tower gilded in gold with stairs on the outside that spiraled to the sky. It was an odd place to put stairs. I shouldn't want to climb its heights in the cold of winter.

"The tower of the Church of Our Savior," Papa said, pointing, "can be seen for miles."

The older, more traditional buildings made of cement and wood contrasted with newer buildings made from small red brick, many sporting neatly cut lawns that accented the city like green emeralds.

"Look, Papa! What's that?" I pointed to a man walking across a lawn with some sort of machine, the likes of which I had never seen.

"I've heard of them before, but I've never seen one. It's called a lawnmower—for cutting grass."

Mary and Ana started giggling. "You're so silly, Papa."

"No, Angels, I'm telling the truth. It's a new invention."

"But Papa, why don't they just let their cows and horses eat it like we do?"

"Well," Papa rubbed his chin. "The lawns are small and we are in the city. Do you think it's possible they don't own a horse or cow?"

We considered that possibility but it seemed like something too far-fetched even for one of Hans Christian Andersen's fairytales.

"They probably buy their milk at the market," I said thinking aloud. "If so, they wouldn't need a cow; and if they owned a bicycle they wouldn't need a horse either." I pressed my lips through my teeth and wondered if I'd guessed right. These people, though still in Denmark, lived in a world foreign to mine.

"When I grow up, I'm going to have a big house with a lawnmower for cutting grass, and a large fountain for the birds to swim in." Mary pointed to a large fountain with a statue of a woman at the top. "Look! Mama, Papa, she's naked!"

I watched the reactions to Mary's declaration with amusement. Mama grabbed my baby sisters and sat them in their seats so they could no longer see out of the window. "Hush!" she scolded.

Ester sat still, but her eyes turned to the window, her lips quirked into a smug expression. The redheaded young man and his friend, engaged in conversation, didn't seem to hear Mary. Several other heads bobbed up to see the fountain, including Brother Lindquist. His wife struck him on the shoulder with her umbrella and he immediately sat. I glanced at Papa to see his reaction. He turned his back to the window.

I followed his example.

"Mama," Mary protested. "I want to see København."

"Some things are best not to be seen," Mama said.

"I won't look at the statue again, I promise."

"Maren, dear, I'm sure the statue is out of sight now. Let the girls see the city."

This is why we loved Papa—he always looked out for us and softened Mama's stern ways. After giving him a frown, Mama relented and allowed the girls to resume their places at the window.

Having hoped one day to travel to København with Berta, I searched everywhere, for a glimpse of the royal castle, the king, or Hans Christian Andersen, but only saw hundreds of strangers in an unfamiliar city. While I was deep in thought, the train lurched to a stop.

The conductor pressed a lever and the doors opened. "Don't forget your belongings," he said as he ushered everyone off.

As we stepped off of the train, I accidentally bumped into a man. He glared at me, brushed at his arm, and walked away. This was a world I knew nothing of. We were thrust among the bustling throng of strangers and city-dwellers. My parents held fast to my sisters. I kept my eyes on them as we stumbled forward.

Strangers pressed against me. I heard a frantic cry from someone in the crowd, "My pocketbook! It is missing!" And

I remembered hearing woeful tales of others who had been robbed or tricked out of their things in the big city.

Papa would not allow us to lose our money to thieves' trickery. We had sent constant prayers heavenward from the moment Papa announced we were immigrating. One morning the answer had come to Mama like a ray of sunshine. "We will sew the coins into our petticoats."

Papa had agreed to the plan, but with one provision.

"Our little girls shouldn't be burdened by having to carry even a small amount."

The feel of my skirts weighing me down was a peaceful reminder that we need not worry.

Mary and Ana were too young to keep a secret, so we had always discussed the matter as though talking about a fairytale. "Tonight, after everyone goes to sleep, the little elves will come to visit." Mama winked at Berta and me. "They'll get to sewing right away and fill each little pocket with a secret."

Though they tried on several occasions to see the fabled elves, Mama made sure Berta kept the young girls extra busy playing, gathering eggs and helping around the house. By evening time, they always fell sound asleep.

No one could possibly be aware that every coin we owned was stitched tightly into our underskirts and in the lining of Papa's trousers.

I took Mary and Ana's hands and we made the trek from the train station to the wharf. All was well and good. I felt secure that should anyone try to pick our pockets or steal our bags, they wouldn't come away any richer.

As we neared the wharf, I looked around, marveling at the sight. Saints were everywhere—a sea of caps and bonnets—hundreds of people anxious to follow the Lord's will and travel to America. The air was charged with excitement. Mama and Papa kept hold of Mary and Ana so they wouldn't wander away.

"Look at this crowd." I overheard someone say. "There must be hundreds of us." Someone replied, "It will take hours to get us all on board." I had to agree. It would probably be nightfall before we took up anchor.

The crowd quieted, and I looked around. What was happening? A man in front stood tall and began speaking. It was Elder Barnett! My heart swelled in love for this man who had brought our family the gospel message.

"Brothers and Sisters, let us gather together." He motioned everyone forward. "We wouldn't want anyone to get lost from our group."

We pushed in closer, eager to hear his words.

"It is a glorious day here in Denmark where so many of the Saints of God have met for the purpose of sailing the ocean together in order to live peacefully in the land of Zion.

"It won't be long now." He paused and looked reassuringly toward the crowd. "Our journey will not be an easy one, but the good Lord willing we shall travel with the west wind and make it quickly and safely to our new home ..."

At the mention of our new home, my insides twisted in knots. I wasn't yet ready to leave my old home. I wanted more of Denmark, more of København. We'd just gotten here.

Would America have green-topped buildings sporting dragons? Would it have luscious rolling hills green with grass, and buildings so old they were covered with moss? Would America have castles and kings and fairytales?

America had none of those things. In my confusion I prayed that we could stay longer in Denmark, but even as the words formed in my mind, I knew it couldn't be.

Searching the crowd again, I assured myself that, indeed, it would be hours before we boarded. I couldn't leave København, not without pressing every detail into my mind and heart, to remember this place forever, for Berta.

Mama and Papa held on to the girls, and since I stood behind them, it wasn't difficult for me to slip unnoticed from the crowd.

Chapter 6

Rows of warehouses lined the dock. I nodded to passersby as I walked, ready to embrace København. I caught sight of a pair of lions made either of cement or grey stone, I couldn't tell which. They were carved into the base of a bridge. It looked as though the bridge rested upon their heads. A past king had probably commissioned its construction. The regal lions undoubtedly represented Denmark—proud and unafraid.

Moments later, I craned my neck skyward to see the bell tower of a cathedral made of enormous grey stones. The whole building reached into the sky—as did the wooden doors.

They looked heavy and I wondered how anyone could open them to enter. I walked closer and outlined one of the rough-hewn stone blocks with my finger. It was huge and magnificent.

If only Berta had come. Missing my sister made me pause for a moment, but since she wasn't with me, I needed to enjoy the city for the both of us. With Berta in mind, I had only one goal, to see the home of our favorite author. My pace quickened and I passed shop after shop. The buildings in this area were tall, though it seemed the shops occupied only the ground floor. They sold things here—jewelry and fine clothing—things I could never afford.

I stopped near a merchant. "Pardon me?" He straightened a stack of clothing outside his store. "Do you know where Hans Christian Andersen's home is?"

"Nyhavn." He glared at me, impatient and pointing. "Three

blocks south and one to the west."

If I hurried, I could get there with plenty of time to spare. I started on the run, avoiding shoppers as best I could. However, with my skirts weighted down as they were, I slowed to a more comfortable walking pace.

Customers filled the restaurants that lined the sidewalk. Umbrella-shaded tables outside buzzed with energy from patrons' eager chat. Near each door, signs touted the day's special. My stomach growled at the delicious aroma of frying fish. I peered up to the windows on the first, second and third floors. Could people actually be living above their stores?

One shop had trays of smørrebrød for sale in the window. I stopped to look. My mouth watered at the open-faced sandwiches made of sardines, shrimp, ham or tongue, each with different toppings. When I saw two rows of the sandwiches with smoked salmon, caviar, and a sprig of dill on top, I had to force myself away.

I walked the three blocks south and one west, and stood at the corner of an intersection. The sign across the street read, Nyhavn. My heart skipped a beat. On one side of Nyhavn, the earth dropped off almost instantly into the sea with boats crowding the edge. On the other side of the street, a row of tall buildings went on farther than a stone's throw—each one pressed tight against the other—and each painted differently. They looked like a string of multi-colored jewels. Mr. Andersen must live in one of them. I stepped off of the sidewalk.

"Get outta the way!" yelled one traveler and then another. Startled back to my senses, I rushed between two carriages and crossed the street. Then I heard the loud, resonant blast of a ship's horn.

"Oh," I exclaimed. "Mama and Papa will be so angry!" I took one last glimpse of the buildings, wistful, and wishing I could have found his exact home. Then I turned on my heel, chiding myself for wandering so far away. My parents were probably stricken with grief over my absence. Panic seized my breast and I ran toward our harbor hoping I was not too late to join them.

Unable to get there fast enough while wearing my wooden clogs, I pulled them off knowing I'd have to repair my stockings later, and grabbed them and my skirts up to hasten my arrival.

The horn blasted again. I'd gone too far. I would never make it in time. My lungs burned and my legs threatened to give way, but I ran all the harder. It seemed like an eternity. Had I really passed all these shops or was I lost? I kept running. This had to be the way.

I spotted the Saints ahead. The group was visibly smaller, but at least the ship hadn't left the dock. Moisture fell from my eye. I wiped it off with the back of my hand and nearly tripped, but I didn't stop running until I came upon the edge of the crowd.

Here I stopped and bent to catch my breath—it came in large pants and gulps. Sweat dropped from my forehead. My vision blurred, darkening temporarily, and my knees ached.

"Are you Catherine Erichsen?" The redheaded young man I'd noticed on the ferry greeted me.

"Have I missed the ship?" My heart still hadn't slowed to its normal rhythm, yet I straightened and pushed my way forward. He tried to keep up but was soon swallowed in the crowd. Every few feet I made forward, someone else greeted me and asked, "Are you Catherine Erichsen?"

I was in serious trouble. Although our steamship loomed ahead, and I knew I hadn't missed the voyage, it didn't bring me comfort to know that I'd worried my parents so.

"Are you Catherine Erichsen?" A handsome man tipped his hat and took my elbow.

"What?" I gave the stranger an angry frown, but undaunted,

he continued escorting me toward the front. "Who are you?" I demanded.

"I'm sorry. I didn't introduce myself." He turned a charming smile toward me. "My name is John Rasmussen. I'm from Jylland, and I'm here to help hasten your way to your parents' side."

Although Brother John Rasmussen had an authoritative manner and a few grey hairs at his temples, he appeared otherwise youthful. Still unconvinced that this stranger could get me forward faster than I could get myself, I tried to worm free. "Unhand me."

He immediately let go of my arm, but continued to push forward and allow me room to pass through.

"I'm assuming that you are indeed the missing Catherine Erichsen." His wry smile both angered and captivated me. "If not, I've taken charge of the wrong woman."

"I am she," I answered, regretful of my current situation. "I suppose Mama and Papa are sick with worry. Have they begun allowing passengers to board?"

"Indeed, miss. Our good captain has been boarding passengers for some thirty minutes now. However, your parents have refused to board without you."

A lump formed in my throat at the thought of them worrying over me. I slipped the clogs back onto my feet, and hoping to get through, I heaved a push at a gentleman in front of me.

"Beg pardon?" The young man with flyaway blond hair and eyes the color of a Danish sky in autumn turned with a frown.

I blushed, knowing of my rudeness. Yet, when Brother Rasmussen once again opened the way, I fled without apologizing.

This Brother Rasmussen from Jylland was quite adept at opening the way for the both of us, for he would not leave my side until he saw me safely to my family. Yet, I dared not give appearances of being overly dependent on his care lest he consider me a child, so I jutted my chin forward and feigned disinterest.

When I tried gaining the front on my own, the surrounding masses, unmindful of my efforts, formed a human barrier between me and my family. Since I was of a slight build and height, I feared that most did not refuse to move aside, but were merely unaware of my presence. Reluctantly, I let Brother Rasmussen once again take the lead.

I saw the captain first. He stood on the dock calling passengers' names, checking them, and allowing them to board. Mama and Papa stood near the captain with such an expression of worry and grief that I became paralyzed for a brief moment. Could they ever forgive me for causing them such worry?

Brother Rasmussen walked toward the captain, and my feet propelled me forward. My parents' faces washed over with relief when they saw me. I rushed into their waiting arms. Mary and Ana tugged at my skirt.

"Where have you been?" Mama hugged me tight as she sobbed. "We thought you'd run away."

Papa encircled us in his arms. "We prayed for your safe return." His voice was gruff with emotion.

"I'm so sorry," I said, humbled by their distress. "I didn't mean to worry you—I was foolish and wandered away." I would never worry my parents like this again. "Brother Rasmussen helped me push through the crowd." I smiled at him in gratitude.

"Come with us. Catie, we'd be so lonely without you or Berta," Mary said.

"We'd all be lonely without you." Mama smiled and hugged me once more, her embrace like a burst of sunshine on this otherwise dreary day.

The captain stood next to a wooden railing leading to the

steamship Aurora—a magnificent manifestation of painted steel with an enormous smokestack billowing grayish clouds into the already cloudy sky.

Rowboats perched along the ship's side, and our beloved red and white Dannebrog waved to everyone from high in the air. Many passengers already milled about on deck while awaiting our departure.

"Mr. John Rasmussen. A single man with no family," the captain called.

"That's our cue." Brother Rasmussen motioned for us. "Board with me."

We had lost our place in line, and didn't want to wait until all the others boarded. We thanked him and followed behind.

"I'm John Rasmussen, and this is the Erichsen family." Just as he indicated us, the sky opened up with a spring rain. Papa picked up Mary and Ana, and as one, the girls lunged toward me. I laughed. They squeezed me around the neck and kissed my cheek. After we set them on the ground, Mama secured their wool coats around them and straightened their bonnets so their heads stayed dry.

The dampness of my clothing and the chill in the air, set my teeth chattering. Brother Rasmussen lay his coat over my shoulders. I looked up, feeling suddenly shy at his gesture, but he gave no indication that it was anything more than an automatic reaction.

The captain glared at me. "Who is this young lass? Are you trying to sneak an extra passenger aboard?"

"No, sir," said Brother Rasmussen. "If I were trying to sneak someone on board, I wouldn't walk up and announce it. Check under Erichsen, you'll find her name along with her parents'."

Papa drew me near and placed his hands on my shoulders. "This is our daughter, Catherine. We didn't come forward earlier because we were separated in the crowd." He frowned at me.

Embarrassed, I chewed the remnants of a fingernail knowing I was the cause of these problems. The captain appeared unmoved by Papa's declaration. Brother Rasmussen stood beside the captain and flipped his passenger log to nearly the first page.

"Right here." He pointed to our names. "Hans and Maren Erichsen, and it lists their children, Catherine—"

"That's me." I stepped forward and curtsied.

"And this is Mary and Ana," Mama stood forward with the girls in front of her.

"Where's the one named Berta?" the captain frowned.

"She's not coming."

"What seems to be the hold up?" Elder Barnett came through the crowd and stood next to the captain.

"There'd be no problem if the passengers would get on when their name is called." The captain gave a curt nod and checked our names off of his list.

We grabbed our few belongings. With Mary and Ana in hand, Brother Rasmussen followed behind. Papa's farm equipment had been transferred directly from the train.

It was nearly evening before all of the passengers boarded the steamship and the *Aurora* made its way from the harbor. Mama and Papa took my sisters below to get them dry and settled. I stayed outside, leaning against the ship's railing, and watched the ever-changing shoreline. It brought me comfort to stay outside and memorize my homeland, yet, my breathing came in shuddering gasps.

"Your parents are waiting for you below." The sound of Brother Rasmussen's voice startled me. I hadn't seen his approach.

"I know I should be helping, but I just can't make myself leave." I rubbed my cheeks to settle myself, feeling silly that he'd seen me fret.

A warm jacket once again graced my shoulders.

"You don't need—" I began.

"Nej, it's chilly out and your parents wanted me to bring this to you." His shoulder lifted in a shrug.

My jacket. I pulled it around me, not having realized until that moment that I was indeed cold.

"It is too bad that we aren't traveling north." Brother Rasmussen peered out across the Øresund Strait.

"Pardon?" My brows furrowed. Why did he wish we were traveling away from our destination? We were headed south to Kiel Germany tonight. Tomorrow we would go by train to Hamburg where we'd board a ship headed to England.

"I say this because Helsingør lies toward the northern tip of Sjaelland. Have you been there?" He leaned against the rail beside me and gazed toward shore.

"Nej, this is my first time leaving Fyn." I saw a windmill on the distant horizon, and thought of home.

"It would be a fitting farewell, don't you think, to say goodbye to Denmark by way of her most famous castle?" The corner of his mouth quirked into a lopsided grin.

"Have you?" I felt strangely nervous at the attentions of this older gentleman. "Have you been to Helsingør and seen the Kronborg Castle?"

He shrugged, "Indeed. I have travelled much since my wife passed on."

I glanced up and then looked away at the mention of his departed wife. He didn't look upset. Perhaps she hadn't passed on recently. Still, I hardly felt comfortable discussing a subject such as this one with a close friend, let alone the stranger who stood beside me. I took the coward's way and remained silent.

Having learned about Helsingør and Kronborg Castle in school, I knew it hadn't been a royal residence in a hundred years and presently stood as a military base and prison. I'd also learned how an English playwright named William Shakespeare made the castle famous in one of his plays and had called it Elsinore.

Biting my lip in concentration, I tried remembering the name of his play ... well, it didn't matter, really. I'd never have the opportunity to see the play, nor would I ever have the opportunity to see the castle. I had seen a picture once.

Built against the Øresund Strait as a fortress, it had looked magnificently formidable silhouetted in the glow of an evening sun with its battlements reflected in the water.

"It is the final resting place of Holger the Dane," I said, breaking our silence.

"Yes, Holger rests there—I feel a bit akin to him." He placed his hand over his chest.

"You don't mean ..." I eyed him critically. Was he making some declaration toward his health?

"No, no." The corner of his lip lifted. "I only mean to say that we've both traveled extensively and both have always longed for home."

"But we're leaving our home, forever." My words choked in my throat. "Holger traveled away from Denmark, and then came back to the home he loved."

"My home is now in Zion." He sounded paternal. "And that is the home I will love."

"How you could say that?" The words came out more shrilly than I anticipated, but I continued. "I could never call anyplace but Denmark my home. How can you know you will love it in America?"

His eyebrows rose and he tilted his head forward.

Realizing my childish outburst, I took a deep breath. "Thank you for your kindness and for your company." I curtsied, yet didn't dare meet his gaze. "I fear the hour is late, and I must rejoin my family."

Chapter 7

"Return to your berth, each of you." A sailor stood at the hatch guarding our only way out.

A storm had gathered during the night. Frightened, we had all tried leaving the belly of the ship. Confusion ensued.

"What is happening, Papa?" It was pitch black. I could barely see him.

"All is well and good. These are simple orders to follow." Papa turned and carried Mary back toward the crowded sleeping area. Mama followed with Ana.

I ran along behind, bracing myself against the walls of the rocking ship, trying for answers and getting none. We had arrived in Kiel early that morning, traveled to Hamburg, boarded the ship to England, and had made it nearly to the North Sea with nary a problem. But before we completely escaped our southern neighbors, a storm broke out.

"Are we sinking?" I stopped to peek through the porthole, my heart palpitating. Clouds roiled in the sky—angry, accusatory—their blackness belied the morning hour.

"We are not sinking." Papa gave me an impatient look, and then I realized my error in speaking near Mary and Ana.

Their eyes were wide with fright. Mary began crying.

"We're headed to port." Elder Barnett stood on the steps that led to the outside world, addressing us. "Let us all pray that we make it safely to shore."

Were we to die only a day's travel from Denmark? The storm pitched the ship up, down, from side to side. The sea thundered in my ears as it crashed against our vessel. We huddled in the darkness like frightened mice, listening with trepidation to noises from above deck. Shouting, anxious footsteps and sounds I did not recognize mingled with the rumbling of the storm.

We prayed for our safety, prayed for the storm to end, and after what seemed like hours, the hatch opened. Torrents of rain fell through the opening and I heard someone clamoring down the steps.

"We've made it!" Elder Barnett's voice boomed above the gale. "The captain has instructed us to exit the ship in an orderly fashion. If those closest to the hatch would kindly come with me, and then follow in order."

At Elder Barnett's word we stood in large, thick lines. We made our way onto the deck, fighting to stay standing against the tossing of the ship. The scene turned to chaos as we scampered about like wet and frightened sheep—everyone rushing and struggling to disembark without being thrust into the stormy waves below.

Finally, and after great effort, we each made it off the ship and onto the dock. The storm continued raging and blasting us with icy pellets of water. Mama and Papa held Mary and Ana fast inside their overcoats as we ran.

"Whoa!" My arms flailed about and my feet slipped on the saturated ground. Brother Rasmussen was there in an instant holding me upright. I glanced at him briefly, offering a smile of thanks. Then, like a school of fish, we made our way as one huge group to an immense building.

The sheets of corrugated metal forming its walls shook in the wind. The roof rattled, lifted and banged under the gale's determined influence. I thought we'd witness the building's destruction on the spot where we stood.

"We'll stay here until the storm relents," Elder Barnett shouted above the tempest. "Once we get to safety, we will thank the Lord."

When we would actually feel safe, I did not know. We filed into the aging warehouse. It surely didn't look sturdy enough to keep us safe in a storm of this magnitude, and I felt certain we were rushing to our doom.

"I'm c-cold, Mama." Mary and Ana complained in unison. Their voices went nearly unheard as a rush of wind howled through the metal sheets. The walls and roof clattered again and then slammed with a loud bang. Mama and Papa hugged the girls tighter. I ducked and followed close behind, my heart pounding.

"Where are we?" I wondered aloud. "Does anyone know?"

"We're in Cuxhaven, Germany," Papa said. "We will stay here to bide out the storm."

"We're still in Germany?" I made a face.

Why would we be punished so? Weren't we trying to obey the Lord's will? Germany, our greedy southern neighbors, haggled over our borders, and won. We Danes, though fearless, were not nearly as large and had been forced to relinquish a good portion of our land. Did the Lord have no mercy putting us here in their care? "Perhaps I'll take my chances on the ship," I replied. I was merely tired from the constant travel, but I crossed my arms, frowning.

Mama frowned back at me. Papa put his arm around my shoulder and guided me farther into the trembling warehouse. "We're all God's children," he said firmly.

I found no humor or comfort in his words.

"We're hungry, Mama." Mary and Ana, I believed, voiced the opinion of everyone, though they didn't know it. I knew I was hungry, our food was long gone, there were no food vendors here, and the chances of the town's market being open in this weather were doubtful.

We spent the remainder of the day sitting, standing, or pacing the width of our gloomy metal prison, ducking for our lives when thunder shook the building, and waiting for the storm to pass. It didn't.

Several lanterns were lit, casting long, ominous shadows. The frequent flashes of lightning that occasionally shone through the walls only added to the somber mood.

Elder Barnett instructed several of the women to lead us in singing hymns while many of the men, including Papa, were called away. I watched Brother Rasmussen and the redheaded young man rush to join them. I didn't feel like singing. However, after Mama gave me a disapproving stare, I smiled falsely and mouthed the words.

"May I take Mary for a walk?" I asked before another song began. We could see well enough to make our way, and it would get me away from Mama's irritable gaze. She allowed me to do so, and as we walked, Mary chatted endlessly beside me.

People, blankets, and travel bags nearly covered the cold cement floor. Several families huddled together for warmth, some mingled with their immediate neighbors. Mary and I stepped over and around many with their blankets spread on the floor as we distanced ourselves from Mama.

My mind wandered to Isaac, but I discovered that although it hadn't yet been forty-eight hours since his angry goodbye, Isaac was barely more than an unhappy memory. So much had happened since then. Why hadn't he just read the Book of Mormon? If he had ... well if he had, I wouldn't be in this miserable place. But, given his outburst, I had to confess I was glad that I wouldn't become his bride.

"Hello, miss."

The young man with flyaway blond hair kept pace with me, and I tried to force down the warmth that wanted to steal into my cheeks.

"My name is Lars Hansen." He tipped his woolen cap.

"Catherine Erichsen." I paused and curtsied, feeling like I'd never talked to a young man before. His dimpled grin must have been one of amusement at my awkward state, for all of a sudden I felt like a clumsy oaf.

Mary tugged, reminding me of her presence. "This is my sister, Mary," I muttered stupidly. We both curtsied, and I hoped mine improved on my second effort.

"I'm not sure if you noticed, but we've been traveling together since Fyn."

Not wanting to confess that I had indeed noticed his presence on our journey, I merely said, "Oh?" My eyebrow lifted as if in surprise.

"Do you mind if I accompany you and your sister while you walk?" He bowed elegantly. "I find that I'm not much of a singer, either."

I loved to sing, just not while my teeth chattered, but I nodded nonetheless. We began our walk again with Mary between me and this Lars Hansen. I discovered myself enjoying his company. He was twenty-five, had ambitions to become a banker in America, and missed his parents, who, I discovered, couldn't afford the journey and had stayed behind.

Why hadn't he shared some of his obvious wealth so his parents could join them? The thought made me wonder, but perhaps he wasn't wealthy, and had merely spent his last money on new traveling clothes. Lars made no mention of his redheaded travel companion, and I didn't broach the subject. Perhaps they had merely met along the way.

A bright flash of lightning illuminated the building, and the metal roof rumbled and clattered. Thinking the roof was caving in, I crouched down, hovering over Mary to protect her from harm.

Lars extended his hand to help me up. His lips curved in an amused grin. "This will prove quite a night. Don't you agree?" Lars lifted his eyebrows in apparent disapproval of our surroundings.

I did have to agree. Rising to my feet, eyes unable to leave Lars's, my hands felt a delightful warmth from our brief contact. I rubbed my fingers in my clenched hand wishing to retain the feeling.

"I wonder at the wisdom in having our little throng stay the night under such unseemly circumstances." Lars smirked. It was odd for him to voice a complaint against Elder Barnett and the others who presided over our journey, but I disregarded it given our miserable circumstances.

Mary tugged at my skirts again, prattling on about something, and growing irritated.

"What is it, Mary?" I asked impatiently. Couldn't she see that I was busy?

"I'm hungry, and I'm cold, and I want to go back to Mama." Mary frowned and stamped her foot.

This wasn't what I wanted at all. "Just let me say goodbye," I whispered, not wanting a fuss in front of Lars.

"Perhaps you wouldn't mind if I accompanied you back to your family." Lars touched my arm. The tingling I felt must have been from the cold.

I nodded, hoping not to seem overly anxious, and once again placed Mary between us. The warehouse was large, but we were a group of hundreds—each with eyes for watching and tongues for wagging.

When we neared Mama, Lars tipped his hat once more. "A pleasant evening to you, Miss Catherine, and to you as well, Miss Mary." He smiled at me. "I hope we meet again."

"Thank you." I curtsied and then maneuvered Mary and myself the remaining steps to our family.

I watched as Lars retreated toward the fiery-haired young man who seemed to be looking my way. While I couldn't imagine why Lars's tall travelling companion would look at me with such an entreating gaze, I also couldn't find it within myself to glance away. It felt as though I knew him.

It was ridiculous. I shook myself out of my trance. The only thing I knew about this young man was that he didn't have the flyaway blond hair or pleasing blue eyes of his friend. Yet, I twisted a lock of my hair as I remembered his sparkling green eyes.

Lars approached him then and appeared to speak to him. What he said couldn't have been kind, because the redheaded man's shoulders drooped and he looked away.

"Come and eat some supper," Mama said. "The men went into town for us at great peril to their lives." The walls vibrated loudly in the wind as if to confirm Mama's words. "The locals here were very generous in helping them to provide nourishment for us." Her eyebrows lifted.

I nodded. She was right. I'd been too quick to judge. Mama encouraged us with a simple meal of bread and smoked herring, along with fresh milk. We were hungry after going without all day and it tasted like manna—or as satisfying as I assumed manna would have tasted.

Papa returned to us not long after. I snuggled Mary into my lap, and Mama held Ana. We did our best to keep warm while Elder Barnett talked of the Lord's love. I would never have confessed it to Mama or anyone, but I was feeling a bit doubtful of the Lord's love just then.

After Elder Barnett finished his discourse, the soulful sound of a violin echoed through the frigid building. My doubtful heart took comfort as we joined in singing, *Come, Come Ye Saints,* after which, the room fell silent for an evening prayer.

With Mary snuggling into his arms, Papa lay down and rested near Mama. She held Ana like a mother hen would her baby chick, with me lying near. I had no idea how we could sleep. The floor was cold and hard, and our woolen blankets though they were made from the exceptionally warm Faroese wool, were not warm enough or soft enough to make the floor feel any better.

"If the storm still rages in the morning, Elder Barnett suggests we have a fast." Papa whispered.

I knew what that meant. We had no food. Captain Klein of the Aurora had only enough provisions to see us safely to England—if the ship didn't sink. Our stay in Germany was at our own peril. Would we starve before the storm relented?

"How long can the others hold out?" Mama whispered to Papa.

"I don't know." Papa lifted his cap and brushed his hair back. "If the tempest lasts much longer, I'm afraid that some will have to turn back."

"Can we help?"

"Nej. There are too many." Papa surveyed the warehouse. "If we have any money left at the end of our journey, it will be used to help build the temple."

Mama nodded.

Mary and Ana, exhausted from their day, soon fell asleep. I wished I could be so fortunate. My nose was cold, and I ducked my head under the blanket.

With the crashing thunder and flashes of lightning accompanied by the creaking and moaning of overextended metal—how could anyone sleep? The scratching sound of small creatures scurrying, rats probably, carried through the sounds of the storm—I shuddered, and said a silent prayer.

Chapter 8

I jerked awake, my heart palpitating, my mouth dry. Where was I? A burst of light shone through a crack near the ceiling. "Oh," I groaned as realization dawned. We were in the warehouse.

A thunderous boom rippled the tin walls. I squeezed my eyes shut and put my hands over my ears, my teeth chattering. The gale forced its way through the metal sheets of the roof and beat upon the building with fury. My bones hurt and my ears were cold. How had we stayed safe through the night?

Elder Barnett broke into my thoughts. "Brothers and Sisters," he began, "it seems we've hit a snag in our plans. Captain Klein of the *Aurora* says storms like this one can last for a week or more." Elder Barnett paused amid gasps and moans. "We've wired Captain Thomas in Liverpool and explained our delay. However, we cannot expect him to hold his ship for us indefinitely."

Through the muted light of morning he looked around the room, his expression grave. "I implore each of us who are physically able, to begin a fast. I will start with prayer. I hope that you will all join me in fasting until this weather has cleared, that we may once again begin our journey to Zion."

We hadn't eaten a full meal since the eve of our departure. My stomach growled. Would we be in hardship from lack of nourishment the entire journey?

"What will we do?" I overheard a woman next to me ask.

"We have sold our home," someone responded. "We have nothing to go back to."

I shivered and pulled my blanket near. What if the storm didn't relent? Would we make it to Zion? As much as I had complained, I realized that I did not want to go back. The Lord wanted us in Zion, so to Zion we would go. Without worrying who watched, I bowed my head and prayed that the storm would cease.

When I finished my prayer, I felt much better and wondered what we could do to pass the time. I thought of home and the things we did there to pass time during seasons of poor weather. We darned socks, baked, worked on crochet, mended clothes, and cleaned the eggs. I would give anything to have a few eggs.

My stomach growled again. A woman on the other side of me whose name I didn't know glanced at me with a smirk. I shrugged my shoulders, embarrassed. Ester stepped forward then. "Don't mind my friend. Her stomach misbehaves every time she's a little bit hungry." She curtsied.

My cheeks warmed. "Sh!" I said.

Without acknowledging me, she turned to Papa with a sweet expression. "Can Catherine accompany me to the front?" asked Ester. "I think we are meant to pass the day in song and joyful meditation."

Papa consented, and Ester took my hand. She led us to a place near the other end of the warehouse.

"I know that you're recovering from a difficult time with Isaac, but there's no reason to choose hastily," she said.

"What?" I must have misunderstood. "I do not wish to discuss Isaac." Ester knew that.

The whole congregation was joined in singing, *Nearer, My God, to Thee*. I sang along, ignoring my friend.

"It was quite a trick you pulled in København." Her lip quirked up. "It did not work for you though."

"It was no trick." I frowned at her, and then continued singing.

"You had every unattached man in the area searching for you. Some of the married men as well," she persisted. "Why let the old gentleman rescue you?"

"He did not rescue me." My voice rose in denial. Several people looked at us. I lowered my voice and muttered, "When I came back, Brother Rasmussen opened my way to the front. That's all."

"If you say so," she said. She didn't look convinced.

"I do." I folded my arms across my stomach.

"I am only trying to tell you there is no need in choosing so soon." She elbowed me "Think of when we arrive in England."

"Ja." I nodded. I wasn't planning on choosing anyone any time soon. Upon remembering Mary's words, I added, "But we're not getting younger, you and I."

"You are impossible," she said and walked away.

Ester was the impossible one. Why would she think I couldn't be friends with anyone, regardless of their age? I turned my attention to a man testifying of the Savior and the rightness of our journey.

My heart swelled with the strength of his words.

After the meeting, I went back to Mama and Papa, pulled out a thread and needle to mend my stocking, and sat down. I'd sewn the last stitch, knotted it, and had the thread in my mouth to sever the end when Brother Rasmussen approached and bowed to Papa. "Brother Erichsen, do you mind if your daughter, Catherine, joins me for a short stroll around the warehouse?"

I chewed through the thread with haste and put my stocking and shoe back on. I wondered, had Ester put him up to this? I searched her out, and saw her standing with her back to me. She would tease me for this, but if I refused, every man would think me unapproachable and snobbish.

Papa gave his consent, and Brother Rasmussen extended his elbow in a comfortable, yet formal way. We were acquaintances. Nothing more.

I joined him and we began our walk in the semi-darkness amidst the sound of crying children and the constant thunder of rain rattling the metal roof—not the most agreeable of circumstances.

"Are you well on this fine day?" He asked. He navigated us

around huddling groups and families with ease.

"Ja, ja. Thank you," I said. "Though you could hardly call the weather fine."

"Miss Catherine." He glanced down at me. "I know that I promised a stroll." His eyebrows lifted. "However, I feel compelled at this moment to join with you in reading the Holy Scriptures. May we?"

"It would be most agreeable." We weaved through the other immigrants and I greeted them, relieved, having doubted that Brother Rasmussen and I could find enough common conversation to occupy the time.

We stopped near a lantern in the middle of the room, and read out of the Book of Mormon in First Nephi.

We were in a similar situation, crossing the ocean because of our love of God. Nephi and his family left their home, as we did, and traveled to America. The Lord hadn't made it easy on them either.

"It brings great relief knowing that we'll be on our way again by morning," he said, closing his book of scripture and patting the cover. "Don't you agree?" Several people on neighboring quilts murmured their accord.

"How can you be so sure we'll be leaving by morning?" I tilted my head, hoping he could answer. Although I desperately wanted to believe—how could he know it as fact?

"Have faith, dear Catherine. Have faith." He reached over and touched my hand.

Because of his word and his faith, mine strengthened. It gave me hope for the morrow and I felt better. "Thank you," I said.

"For what?" He tilted his head, smiling.

"For helping me to see and for sharing those verses of scripture with me." I had needed that reassurance.

He paused in thoughtful reflection, and then he held out his hand and helped me to my feet. "Shall we continue our walk?"

Time seemed to stand still as we maneuvered in and around the others. While we walked, he entertained me with stories of his travels around Denmark. He had seen museums in

København, and had even eaten at an expensive restaurant.

I particularly enjoyed his story about the Domkirke in Roskilde—an imposing church made of Romanesque-style architecture. This was where the royals married and were buried when their lives were over.

"There are special Royal Sepulchral Chapels adjoining the Central Nave." His eyes lit up with the memory. "The tombs there are magnificent, and the sepulchers are like nothing you've before seen."

He told of elegant white statues adorning crypts covered with filigree, some trimmed in gold, others made of pure white marble. I had grown up hearing of the Domkirke, but it always seemed more fable than truth.

"Even the Domkirke priests are entombed there. Their crypt speaks volumes as to the particular priest's popularity or wealth." He shrugged. "All are shrines to the people's lives, and most are contained within the walls of the church to safeguard them against the elements."

It still seemed an almost unbelievable story. In my part of Denmark, everyone was buried outside in the cemetery, including the priest.

"I fear it is time to return you to your family lest we set some tongues to wagging." He extended his arm. I took a step forward and beheld we were directly in front of my sisters. So enraptured was I in his story, I hadn't noticed our arrival.

"Thank you for an enjoyable time." Feeling embarrassed, I curtsied, and turned to my family.

Mama had packed several of Papa's handkerchiefs and they now gave the appearance of ragdolls as Mama had twisted them into knots. Mary and Ana sat playing house beside her. I pulled Berta's handkerchief from my pocket and toyed with the stitches, but wouldn't twist it into a doll. I couldn't.

"Come play with us, Catie," Ana pled.

I sat between the girls, and Mama gave me her doll. Papa took her hand, and when he looked at Mama, he had a happy sparkle in his eyes. I hoped someday to find a man whose eyes sparkled for me.

"Mama and I are going for a stroll. You'll keep watch over the girls, ja?"

"Of course, Papa."

I joined the girls on the floor and Ana, at nearly three, squealed with delight. Although they weren't old enough to share secrets and be close friends like Berta and I were, I enjoyed my little sisters and they looked to me as a type of second mama.

We played dolls until they became restless. We stood then, and, joining hands, I had them twirling in circles and giggling. Then I sat Ana on my lap and told them the story of The Ugly Duckling.

"Let's play dolls again," Ana said when we finished. She picked up the ragdolls, and I wondered if we'd have to play dolls the whole way to Zion in order to keep her happy.

And then two worn shoes stopped in front of us. I looked up. The young man with hair the color of red embers stood before us.

"Hello, my name is Josef Hansen." He tipped his cap.

"Hello." I smiled. "My name is Catherine Erichsen."

Despite the cold, beads of moisture prickled around his hairline. He didn't speak again right away but held his gaze to mine.

The heat of a blush started to warm my cheeks. I looked away and said, "These are my little sisters, Mary and Ana."

"What beautiful names." Josef knelt beside them. "May I join in your game?"

"Ja, ja," they cheered. Josef glanced at me uncertainly.

I nodded and indicated the floor beside us. "Which one shall we give our new friend?" His hand grazed mine as he took a ragdoll, and my heart skipped a beat.

Hansen was a fairly common name, but it seemed too coincidental for Josef and Lars to travel together from similar points in Denmark and not be related. A cousin, perhaps? It wasn't polite to ask, so I resigned myself to enjoying our new acquaintance.

Mary and Ana were more than happy to supply Josef with

continual chatter. He appeared comfortable playing with them and answering their questions.

"Do you like my doll best?" Mary asked.

"They're both equally nice," replied Josef. "I shall make a friend to join them." He took out his handkerchief, twisted it into knots then showed it to the girls. "Here, do you like this?"

Ana made a face. "Nej."

"You've got it all wrong," said Mary. "You have to tuck in the corner at the head, like this." She took the doll from him and tucked the pointed corner into the knot and then gave him the doll back.

"Ja, ja, I see how it goes now." He turned the doll in his fingers, smiling cordially, and then flounced the doll forward in a pretend walk.

Watching the three of them interact filled me with contentment. The girls liked him, and I wanted to get to know him better, so I sought a subject that would set him at ease.

"What part of Denmark are you traveling from?" I asked.

"Otterup." He set his makeshift doll on the floor. "Mother and Father couldn't afford the journey, and insisted that my brother Lars and I travel first. We will make a home for them to come to and they will join us in a year."

They were brothers. "What will you do in Zion?" On the evening before, Lars had regaled me with a number of his hopes and dreams for the future. If Josef was like his brother, this topic could keep him talking through the night. I straightened my apron and waited for him to begin.

"I will be a farmer in America, just like my father is a farmer." His green eyes intensified as he spoke. "I love the smell of the earth after a good rain, and I enjoy helping things to grow."

These were things that I also enjoyed. I hoped that when we got to America, Mama would teach me her secrets for growing beautiful roses.

"It is enough about myself." Josef smiled at Mary and Ana. "I much prefer talking about you and your family. Is it the five of you then, or do you also have family left behind?"

Not expecting our conversation to take this turn, my eyes

suddenly stung. "I have another sister," I said, not meeting his eyes.

He touched my arm. "She is very precious to you."

I nodded and bit my lip. While I tried mustering the strength to speak without a quivering voice, Mary spoke up.

"Berta stayed home to marry Jens, but I told Catie that Jens can't marry her." Mary shook her head, "Nej—"

"Enough of that, Mary." I put a finger to her mouth. "You know what Papa says about how we should behave in public." I gave her a fiery look of warning that worked so well when Mama used it.

Mary lowered her head and nodded. "Good children should be seen and not heard."

"Now, if you and Ana can play quietly while I visit with Brother Hansen, I shall take you exploring later."

Mary's face brightened. She took the doll from my hands and turned to play with Ana.

"My sister, Berta, has stayed in Denmark to care for our aunt who is old. Since our uncle died, she has had a hard time." I glanced at Mary to make sure she would remain quiet. "Berta also likes a young man and has stayed in hopes of marrying him."

"Your aunt is very lucky to have family to help care for her." Josef sat beside me. With his chin resting on his knee, he offered me a crooked smile.

I must say that I rather enjoyed the sight. He was handsome when he relaxed and behaved naturally, and he was the only gentleman who had taken the time to play with my sisters and learn about me and my family. This gave me immense satisfaction.

A rush of wind swept through the corrugated metal with a banging clap, reverberating its way from one end of the warehouse to the other. I lunged toward Mary and Ana to protect them from the falling roof. But it didn't fall. When I began to sit up, I realized that Josef had positioned himself to protect me, and a pleased flush warmed my cheeks.

Josef laughed and sat back. "It looks as though we have both overreacted. Ja?" He extended his arm to help me straighten, and I took it. When our eyes met, I felt a giggle inside of me that I didn't want to let loose. But then he smiled.

Against my will and better judgment, my giggle surfaced, and we were both laughing.

When the laughter subsided, I didn't know what else to say, and Josef once again behaved awkwardly. I tried my best to make conversation but could not get him to answer more than a yes or no.

After a few minutes, he stood and swatted unseen dust from his breeches with his cap—his face red. "I must leave now. Elder Barnett has asked the men to help secure food for an evening meal." He glanced around, took a step away, and looked again at me. "Good day, then." Josef smoothed his hair and replaced his cap. "Mary, Ana, pleased to meet you."

"Good day." My eyebrows pinched into a puzzled frown as I watched him maneuver the crowd and make his way toward the door. Why had he left? The men were not yet gathering.

Moments later, Papa walked Mama 'home' as they called our woolen blanket, and he joined the men who then left the warehouse to find food in the nearby town.

"Mama, I promised the girls that I'd take them exploring." Ana clung to my skirt and I picked her up. "May I?" When she gave her consent, I took Mary and Ana on their promised walk around the warehouse, letting them explore every nook and cranny. They made friends with several other children their age and it did them good to run around.

Before breaking our fast that evening, Elder Barnett called on the Lord asking for agreeable weather in order to assist our further travel to Zion. He had located several more lanterns, and we enjoyed eating under their glow.

Lars appeared once we got things cleaned up, and we strolled around the massive warehouse. The wind continued pounding against the building. The rainwater had seeped under the front wall and was pooling there. The families who had taken shelter nearby now crowded inward. I caught a movement from the corner of my eye and looked just as a mouse scurried past my feet. I let out a little scream, flung myself away and into Lars' arms.

He grinned broadly.

I pushed myself away and straightened. "I'm sorry," I muttered, rearranging unseen strands of hair. "I'm scared of mice and rats."

"I must confess I didn't like them either." Lars winked. "Until tonight." Mischief twinkled in his eyes.

My face warmed. "I must return to my parents." I gazed at the concrete floor, humiliated.

"I apologize." He bowed as though greeting the queen. "Please forgive my manners and let me continue escorting you."

He seemed sincere, and so we continued our walk. Lars talked about his family's poor circumstances and how he never intended to have dirt underneath his fingernails again. He didn't mention Josef. I found this disturbing at first, but Lars was charming and I soon forgot about his brother.

This day, after having garnered the attentions of three men, gave me hope. Perhaps Mary was wrong about my becoming a spinster after all. And, as Ester had said, there were many eligible young men traveling with us, and we were meeting a larger group of Saints in England.

However, only Lars had flyaway blond hair and the deep blue eyes that I'd prayed for—only Josef made me feel as though he could see into my soul.

I shook my head. There was plenty of time, and I certainly felt no desire to choose poorly again. I thought of my goodbye with Isaac, and shuddered.

"A penny for your thoughts." Lars' mouth quirked up.

What did he mean by this odd remark? Did he intend to pay me to talk to him? My mouth opened to respond, but I didn't know what was appropriate. Luckily, we neared my temporary home where Mama was preparing the girls for bed.

"Good night." I hurried to Mama's side.

After Lars was out of earshot, I tapped Papa's arm. "What does, a penny for your thoughts, mean?"

Papa chuckled. "It's a silly saying, isn't it? It means that person is wondering what you are thinking."

"Oh." I nodded. That made sense. I had been deep in my thoughts when Lars said this.

"Papa, can we go home?" Ana said. "I do not like it here."

"Hush now," Mama said. "Come lay with Mary and go to sleep."

"I want my bed." Ana frowned, hands on her hips.

"So do I," Mama mumbled quietly.

Mama never complained. I looked at her, surprised. She went about her business as though nothing had been said.

"Be a good girl and lie down beside your sister," said Papa, "and I'll tell you a story."

"Hooray!" The girls cheered and settled onto the woolen blanket. I helped get them situated. I always loved listening to Papa's stories so I snuggled next to Ana while helping to keep her warm and waited for Papa to begin.

"Once upon a time." He started as he always did. "A family of princesses lived in a magical, wonderful kingdom."

"What kingdom, Papa?" Mary asked.

"Denmark, of course."

Mary snuggled into Mama's arms with a dreamy look.

At the mention of Denmark, my mind filled with visions of green alfalfa fields, cows chewing their cud, and a sky that always wanted to offer rain—a land of storks, and of our white stucco chimney that housed the grand nest of one of those graceful creatures.

Lanterns still lit the warehouse when I awoke to the sound of a different male voice—someone talking to Papa.

"I've been reduced to feeling like a teenager," said Brother Rasmussen.

This stilled me, and I strained to hear the conversation. Why would Brother Rasmussen be confessing something so absurd to Papa?

"Ah," Brother Rasmussen groaned.

Curious as to the cause of his anguish, I almost sat upright, but clenched my teeth together and remained on the floor. Then I heard him say something alarming and wished I had mistaken.

"I might as well come right out and say it," he murmured. "You have a beautiful daughter. Never since my Sena died have I felt so at ease with a woman."

I strained to hear more, but Brother Rasmussen must have lowered his voice because I only heard pieces of the rest.

"... a lot of spunk... also very charming... your permission..."

Oh, I wished to scoot closer. They were talking about me. I wanted to hear. Papa's permission? For what? My whole being froze with anxiety. Some Danish families still arranged marriages for their daughters.

I had been previously betrothed of my own accord, but

I hadn't chosen wisely. Papa wouldn't take it upon himself to choose my husband now. Would he? If so, he surely wouldn't choose someone Brother Rasmussen's age when there were so many good choices closer to my own.

I waited, straining to hear Papa's response. Perhaps I was wrong. Perhaps I overreacted. It seemed an eternity of waiting. I desperately wanted to give up my guise of sleep. To demand an explanation. Yet, if I did something that rude, the whole company of Saints might turn their backs on me.

When Papa spoke, he had lowered his voice as well and was facing away from me. I barely made out anything he said.

"Catherine... Seventeen..."

This was good. My heart took courage. Papa merely stated the obvious. I was too young for Brother Rasmussen.

But then I heard Papa say, "... desired her to marry... a good man. ..."

I knew then that my life was over.

Chapter 9

Streams of sunlight peered through cracks in the metal walls of our two-day cage. True to Brother Rasmussen's faith, the storm had died out during the night. The building was abuzz with excitement.

Brother Rasmussen stepped forward. "It's a beautiful day, don't you agree?" He smiled with the satisfaction of a cat that had just caught a mouse.

I glared at him and said nothing. His brown hair bent and poked and looked like an unruly weed patch. I rolled my eyes. Had he rushed so quickly to claim me, his prize, that he didn't think to groom himself? It was ridiculous. How could Papa do this to me?

The Aurora blasted her horn in the distance, beckoning us to enter and be on our way. This did nothing to lighten my gloomy mood. I felt angry and betrayed and had not slept well.

We gathered our things together and walked out of the warehouse feeling perhaps like gophers peeking from their earthen dungeon on the first of spring. We squinted against the brightness and huddled in blankets. Our breath froze into white clouds, but the storm had passed.

I huffed a sigh, wishing to rid myself of the pain in my head and the ache in my heart. An arranged marriage? I looked from Mama to Papa hoping they would tell me it was a mistake.

"Maren." Papa slipped Mama's hand onto his arm. "Girls,

you remember Brother John Rasmussen? We first met him while in København." Papa stared pointedly at me.

I eyed Papa, nervous. Dare I question his authority on the matter of an arranged marriage?

"Since Brother Rasmussen travels alone, I suggested he join our family." Papa patted Brother Rasmussen on the back.

My nightmare was real. Why didn't Papa just come out and tell everyone what he'd done? Why didn't he tell me? "Papa?"

"Do you mind if I join you?" With eyebrows raised, Brother Rasmussen smiled pleasantly.

Mama and Papa looked at me, waiting for my answer.

I glanced sideways at him, not daring to look him full in the face. Remembering my manners, I curtsied and replied with as little venom in my voice as I could muster. "That would be most pleasant." Some men, it seemed, needed very little encouragement.

"Well then, on to England." John took my travel bag and slung it over his shoulder. As we began our short trek back to the Aurora, I noticed that his leather shoes sloshed—probably from going out in the storm for our food.

Lars and Josef strode past, tipping their caps as they made their way onboard. I gritted my teeth. My life was hopeless. Not feeling that I had any other options, I walked beside Brother Rasmussen and entered the Aurora.

The wind seemed to be at our backs during our voyage to England, for we made the trip in record time according to the captain. We cheered only days later at the first peak of land on the horizon.

It was strange being on the crowded train that carried us to Liverpool. As part of our preparations to immigrate, the missionaries had come to our home regularly to teach us English. After a year's instruction I thought I knew the language well, but the workers on the train didn't speak at all the English we'd been taught. I chewed my lip in worry.

Brother Rasmussen continued to shadow my family, or rather me. I found myself ungrateful, and needing the Lord's constant forgiveness. After all, I had prayed for a man in good standing with the Lord. I just hadn't expected a man near Papa's age.

"You've made me feel so welcome," Brother Rasmussen murmured, his head tilted toward me. "I feel like a part of the family. Thank you."

When he didn't say more I looked up and caught my breath at his nearness, startled. "Brother Rasmussen, I'm sorry, I …" At a loss for words I felt heat creep up my face and neck.

"No need to apologize." His silver-grey eyes twinkled. "And, no need for this formality. Please call me John."

How could I ever call him John? I stared out of the train's window across the aisle from me. England and Denmark were similar in regard to the landscape with their rolling hills, farms separated by thick lines of trees, and light splashes of rain alternated with the sun's peeking through the clouds. This wasn't Denmark, though. Nothing would ever be the same or familiar again. We traveled through a strange land—wanderers.

I pulled my gaze from the landscape and looked at my family. They appeared peaceful as they slept. Brother Rasmussen slouched against me in sleep, his hat over his eyes, crowding me.

Ester touched my shoulder. "Catherine, will the whole trip will be this dull?" She knelt in the aisle beside me.

"It's terrible, ja? We will be tempted to sleep the whole way to America."

"When we board the *John J. Boyd*, at least we'll be able to work on our embroidery."

"Ja, ja." I faked enthusiasm. "We will have plenty of time for that." I would rather be on the farm. It was time for planting.

"I wonder how many others will meet us in Liverpool. I hope they are all available, handsome men." Ester's shoulders lifted and her eyes sparkled. "Did you look at the sailors on the *Aurora*? I wish they were going with us to America."

"How could you say such a thing?" Sometimes Ester shocked me with her fresh mouth.

"Don't scold, Catherine." She nodded toward Brother Rasmussen and whispered, "Is he still breathing?"

"Oh, stop it." I whispered back. "He's actually quite nice."

"To each her own." Ester smirked. "You'll need to keep plenty of warm milk on hand." She stood and returned to her family. I watched her take her seat, and shook my head as she turned around and started chatting to a young man behind her.

I leaned back and looked across the aisle and behind me. Lars caught my gaze and winked. He then pulled his cap down over his face, mimicking Brother Rasmussen and leaned onto his brother, Josef, who shoved him straight. When this happened, Lars lifted his cap and wiggled his eyebrows. I couldn't help but smile. It all seemed so silly. Lars crossed his legs and then closed his eyes. I gazed at the brothers for a while before settling down and closing my own eyes.

The day seemed an eternity, but finally I heard whispers around the train that we were in Liverpool. Brother Rasmussen sat up straight and stretched. He glanced at me impishly. I had already forgiven his leaning against me. We traveled through a section of the city with tall narrow buildings each sporting soot-blackened chimneys and separated by even narrower streets.

And then I caught sight of the sea—it joined the sky almost seamlessly. Masts and sails reached from sea to sky, seeming as tall as the earth itself and guarding our entry.

When the train stopped, Brother Rasmussen took hold of my elbow and guided me forward. He was a good man, a gentle man. Once again I forced myself to count his good qualities. He was faithful to be sure. Because of his travels, he could tell interesting stories of Denmark and other places.

Not even Ester could deny Brother Rasmussen still had his good looks. He had a handsome face and dark brown hair similar in color to mine except his held a wavy curl that mine did not, and his silver eyes often sparkled with good humor.

There. I admitted it. Papa could have chosen worse than Brother John Rasmussen. Although, when I saw Lars and his brother Josef, I admitted that it was also possible for Papa to have chosen better.

"What are you waiting for?" Papa stood beside me, his voice pulling me out of my thoughts. "Let's get going." He motioned for us all to walk as a family to our ship.

"May I help you with your bag?" Brother Rasmussen looked all too eager to help. However, I felt suddenly tired of his constant attention.

"I can manage." I glanced across the sea of Saints bustling about gathering their belongings and saw Ester and Lars talking. "Mary and Ana might appreciate the help, however." A mischievous smile etched my lips as I took my place near Papa. My little sisters had become quite fond of Brother John Rasmussen and leapt into his arms as one.

"I need help barking," Mary squealed.

"Me too. Me too," said Ana.

"That's embarking," I said, and started toward the dock.

When curiosity got the better of me, I glanced back, amused at the sight. Brother Rasmussen held Mary and Ana in his arms and struggled to carry his luggage. He was quite a spectacle.

"You girls get down and walk." Papa's eyebrows pinched together in disapproval. "Brother Rasmussen does not need such a burden."

"I don't mind, honest."

"Not today, John," said Papa. "The girls need to learn their manners."

To their dismay, Brother Rasmussen let the girls down, after which he hurried to my side and tried making conversation. I didn't attempt to reply over the din of voices.

The congested harbor seemed to go on forever in both directions, and I'd never before seen such a sight—clipper ships, sail boats, steam ships—the variety and grandeur of vessels amazed me. I wished we could sail on a steamer. We'd heard such a vessel could get us to America in a matter of weeks.

We were directed, however, to the *John J. Boyd*. In truth it was a merchant's sailing ship not built for speed, and a large American flag waved from one of the tall masts. I swallowed, wishing instead that I'd seen our beloved Dannebrog flying in its place.

Hundreds of Scandinavian and English Saints were already boarding. It was a thrilling sight, to be sure. What would Berta think? Then, remembering her fear of sailing across the great sea, I felt rooted to the spot. Would we live through the voyage?

"The Lord will guide us safely to our new home." Brother Rasmussen laid a gentle arm on my shoulder and urged me forward.

"Ja, ja." I hurried along, unsure yet grateful for the comfort of his unfailing faith.

Elder Barnett stood on a wooden crate motioning. "Let us gather in closer." As we did so, a hush fell over the crowd of Saints.

Another man, a reasonably dressed, older gentleman stepped up beside him. Elder Barnett shook his hand. "This is Elder Clark. He will preside over our group, and I will assist him for the duration of our voyage."

He nodded and waved to the crowd. "We are joined by many

others today with a total of seven-hundred Saints waiting to immigrate to America." He paused as a murmur ran through the crowd. "However, there is a matter that needs resolved before we go any farther." He encouraged a man to step forward. "This is Bishop Iversen. He and his small flock thought they paid their immigration funds to a reliable contact and discovered they laid all their money and trust into the hands of thieves."

The bishop hung his head.

"All is well in Zion, dear Bishop." Elder Clark patted his back and turned his attentions to our group. "We won't go into detail, only to say these good Saints each believed they had paid their passage, yet only now have discovered Captain Boyd has no record of them. I have wired church headquarters and their passage fare is guaranteed, yet we've no funds or time to gather the required provisions, nor is there room for such."

A cumulative gasp and the buzz of chatter kept Elder Clark from finishing his business. He waited patiently for the group to quiet.

Elder Barnett stepped forward. "What can we do to help these, our brethren and sisters?" He indicated the impoverished group with a flourish. "They also dream of living in America and traveling Ato Zion. Would we turn them away? Insist the captain leave them alone in a strange country? Or will we make the Lord proud and share our provisions?"

"We will share our sea biscuits," someone called.

Elder Barnett and Elder Clark conversed privately for a moment. Elder Clark then stood forward.

"It is proposed," said Elder Clark, "That we share our rations—a portion of our sea biscuits with these more unfortunate brothers and sisters. All in favor please signify."

I raised my hand in agreement. How could this have happened? Hundreds of others joined together, raising their hands in assent.

"All opposed please signify."

I stood on tiptoe, but saw no one oppose.

"The voting has been unanimous. We will share our sea biscuits." Elder Clark stepped back as he took note.

"In truth, it will be crowded," Elder Barnett said. "We will long for the comforts of home, for the comforts of land where there's room to stretch and walk about. But we are Saints and not heathens, and we will make the Lord proud."

When they finished, Elder Clark directed us toward the gangway spanning land and ship where we took turns by family in boarding.

I saw the captain directing passengers aboard from a distance and thought nothing of him. When we got close, however, I gasped.

Chapter 10

The captain's strong odor of lavender-water and spice laced with the acrid scent of tobacco tormented our noses when we stood a wagon's length away. I shuddered involuntarily. Ana clung to me, whimpering as we neared. He wore a captain's uniform made of heavy black wool. It bore the mark of extended wear.

Although his graying, shoulder length hair was pulled back in a neat ponytail, I was not accustomed to seeing men groomed thus. The small part of his face that showed under his pompous beard looked tough and wrinkled. None of this was cause for alarm.

It was his eyes.

Black and unfeeling chunks of coal, they surely held no light. His eyes bore down on me, regarding my presence with a wink.

My heart skipped a beat and I stepped back. This was not a man to be trusted, though none of us had a choice except to depend on him for our very lives. I didn't step forward, didn't breathe, but only stared apprehensively.

"What are you gawking at, missy? My feather?" He was an Englishman, yet spoke in broken Danish. "It's a beauty, I know. I wrestled this here plumage from a rather large parrot on a recent trip." He pulled the hat off his head and fanned his hand affectionately across the blue and yellow feather.

We stood, horrified, not wishing to listen to his tale and yet unable to move on until he checked us off his list.

"Aye, a terrible beast that bird." He continued, "It kept sqwakin' all hours of the morning when I was trying to sleep. I'd been up all night drinking and performing my manly duties, if you know what I mean." He winked again. "I grabbed him right quick and pulled his head clean off." He made the motions as he talked and then laughed a booming laugh. "That bird never gave me a lick of trouble after, and I slept in peace the rest of the day just like a little babe." His grin revealed brown and decaying teeth. His breath smelled of fish and ale, and I thought I might be sick. Mama pulled me back to stand beside her and Mary.

"Oh, did I go upsetting you fine, sensitive ladies?" He laughed again.

I wanted to shout at the captain and let him know how I felt about his boorish behavior. Yet, pressing my lips together, I resolved to remain silent.

Papa tried gaining the captain's attentions in order to cross our names off the passenger list. The captain ignored him.

Brother Rasmussen stepped forward, placing himself between me and the captain. I felt much safer with two honorable men as our champions. "I'm John Rasmussen." He reached out and shook the captain's hand. "This is the Erichsen family, and I'm traveling with these fine people. I'd appreciate it kindly if you'd cross our names off now, so that we might board the ship together."

"Hmph!" He glared at Brother Rasmussen and shot Papa a frown.

Once again, my thoughts returned. John is a good man, a gentleman. Feeling repentant for my childish behavior, I resolved to call him John, as he had asked me to do on numerous occasions, and try to make the best of my situation.

"Ana, sweetie, are you cold?" John's eyebrows rose as he questioned her.

She nodded and snuggled into me with her cold nose on my neck.

"May I?" John waited to put his coat around her shoulders and mine. I had my own jacket, but Ana was chilled, so I agreed. He buttoned Ana and me together securely in its warmth.

I glanced up at him. "Thank you, John."

His eyes glistened with pleasure at my use of his given name. He turned away then and sneezed.

"Nej, you are cold. Do not give us your coat." Feeling guilty, I tried to wriggle loose. "What shall we do if you fall ill?"

"Nurse me back to health again." He smiled crookedly, and I felt myself blush. John took my free hand, which I had put through the sleeve of his jacket, and helped me onto the ship. Indeed, it was nice having someone dote over me. Isaac never doted, it wasn't in his nature.

"Are you sick, Catie?" Mary asked. "Mama, is Catie sick?"

"No, Mary, I'm feeling perfectly fine." I glared at her, wishing for her to quit this conversation. She ignored me.

"Why's Brother Rasmussen need to help you into the ship then?" Mary smiled sweetly and looked at me, her eyes wide with question. I wanted to hold my hand over her fresh little mouth.

John reached down, picked Mary up, and gave her a squeeze. Then he held her on his arm as he spoke. "With young women, it's polite to help them in every way possible."

"I'm a young woman, you said so yourself just yesterday. You didn't help me into the ship, and I almost tripped."

"It's an oversight, I promise," John made a big X over his heart. He then pulled a handkerchief from his pocket and coughed into it. "Will you forgive me?"

Mary answered with a big hug around John's neck. "I like

you. You're nice." She jumped from his arms and started to run off.

"Hey, now, don't be chasing off." Papa grabbed Mary before she could go very far. "We need to get settled below and set sail before you or your sister do any exploring. Let's all help Mama get our temporary home set up."

Before we went anywhere, the captain breezed past and disappeared into the crowd.

"All singles, men or women, need to go to the third deck below." Elder Clark met us on the ship. "Families are on the second deck below."

"John, perhaps we'll see you for supper," Papa said. John tipped his hat and descended the companionway stairs.

Papa led us to the second deck below. On the bottom step, I put my sleeve to my nose to breathe. My eyes stung with the smell of putrid air. Did they not clean the ship between voyages? People bumped into me from behind when I stopped to survey our living quarters.

The second deck below was a small, foul smelling village. Rows of wooden berths, two bunks high, took up the sides and the middle of the narrow ship, none offered much privacy. Our new home consisted of a wooden berth similar in size to Mama's armoire at home.

Inside the box-bed was a slender mattress made of cotton-tic so worn and soiled that I worried it housed bed bugs. I scratched my arms and shuddered. The Lord will provide. I remembered Papa's words and hoped they were true, for it seemed as easy to perish on the way to America as to make it safely there.

It didn't take long to set our things in place. As soon as we did, we and hundreds of others clambered up the steps, racing for a breath of fresh air.

After everyone boarded the ship, the heavy ropes were

pulled loose from the dock and the anchor was raised. The crew rushed around tying ropes and climbing poles. I watched, amazed with the ease in which they set our ship to sail.

Yet, they looked iniquitous, like their captain, and I knew I should not want to meet any of them alone. Of course that wouldn't be a problem as long as we were on this ship. We stood nearly shoulder to shoulder.

Worried they'd get lost, Mama and Papa kept a tight hold on the little girls. I found a crate, stood on it, and watched as the harbor became a distant memory, leaving us a small floating speck upon an infinite plate of blue.

The captain called everyone together. Since we were from several Scandinavian countries and England as well, the captain spoke in English. We divided into groups according to our language, and missionaries from each country translated. The captain then gave us the rules of the ship, which mostly meant that we were to treat the crew and captain with respect. The captain had the final word on anything regarding his ship and its sailing, or any other thing he felt was his business.

"... The final matter I'll be laying before you is what I'm to be called aboard ship," he said. "Captains need their due respect, and though I know most of you were snubbing your high and mighty noses at me as you boarded, I've been captain for a good many years, and it'll be me and my crew that get you to America safely." He stopped and regarded us with a scowl.

I shuddered.

"I prefer being called Captain Boyd." He waved his hands grandly, showing off the ship. "Because of my love for this beautiful lady, I've taken on her name. It's the best marriage I've ever had."

Amid murmurs and the shock that accompanied the captain's last remark, Elder Clark addressed us.

"We shall do all we can to keep up morale, for life aboard ship can become extremely tiresome. A strict schedule of worship every morning and evening shall be adhered to, accompanied by songs of rejoicing and prayers to the Almighty in supplication for our continued safety. We shall also have dances and the opportunity to socialize in a most pleasant manner every night, with Sunday nights being the only exception."

Bishop Iversen came forward and shook hands with both Elder Clark and Elder Barnett before turning to the gathered Saints. "The Lord is proud of you this day for you have truly proven yourselves as saints. My monies were also stolen by those demons professing to arrange our immigration, and when we arrive in America, I vow to do all in my power to bring those unholy men to justice." He bowed elegantly. "I thank you all from the bottom of my heart."

He stepped into the crowd and embraced many of them—possibly the Saints he had shepherded here.

Elder Clark clapped his hands, quieting the crowd. "May I continue?" He asked, and began again. "Given the amount of disease that is wont to run rampant through immigrant ships," he said, "Elder Barnett and I have devised a plan that will hopefully alleviate the problems usually accompanying such crowded and dirty living conditions."

He lifted up something that looked like a large, flat rock. "The brethren will scrape the floors each day with a holystone and other tools provided by our crew, thus keeping the floors clean and free of filth."

We were divided into groups or wards according to nationality and the language we spoke, missionaries translated as necessary, and the men were entreated each to do their share.

Elder Barnett came forward, announcing that upon our arrival in America, his mission was over. "I have been away from my family for a long time, and I am most anxious to reacquaint myself with my children," he said. Several Saints rushed to Elder Barnett, hugging him and shaking his hand.

After the meeting, the men lingered for assignments. Mary and I gained permission and walked to the ship's railing. Together, we looked across the vast ocean to the distant horizon. Would we make it to the western shore? I couldn't help but wonder what hardships awaited us as we journeyed.

Life aboard ship soon became routine. Our main task was to keep up our morale—a difficult directive considering our limited ability for accomplishment. We were an industrious people, and the lack of actual work quickly became tiresome. The men had it best only because their ugly task of scraping the floors clean kept them slightly more occupied during the long and dreary daylight hours.

Although there were many different languages spoken aboard ship, we easily formed new friendships among those who spoke our native language, even among those who we might not have considered for friendships in our homeland.

The children often formed small groups of play, and the women gravitated to one another to visit while doing their needlework. Some of the men took straw from below where the ship animals resided and made shoes. They did it for a lark, and it preserved their more sturdy shoes for their arrival in America.

I was sitting near the sterncastle helping Mama entertain Mary and Ana two days later when my friend, Ester, flounced down beside me, crying.

"My grandmother's pendant is gone!" She put her hands over her face.

"Did you lose it somewhere along the way?" I patted her

back and hugged her. It could have fallen off her neck without her even knowing.

"Nej. I had it locked away for safe keeping until we arrive in Zion." Ester looked up at me and dabbed the tears from her eyes. "I take it out every morn and kiss it, and then I put it back." The tears started flowing again. "It was there yesterday— and now it is gone!"

"Have you talked to Elder Barnett or Elder Clark?"

"They think that I lost it, ja. I'm always losing things, I know. But I did not lose this." She put her hand to her neck and felt the empty space where the pendant would have gone. "Mama and Papa are very angry with me."

I calmed her by promising to help look for the pendant. Mary, Ana and I made a game of it, retracing all of her steps and asking everyone around us. It was to no avail.

That afternoon, at Ester's suggestion, we formed a small circle of friends that included Hanna Jensen and Kirsten Olsen, two girls that Ester had become fond of. The four of us would meet each afternoon to visit and embroider. "It will help us pass the time," she said. By then, I was ready to try anything to keep from going stir crazy.

A commotion interrupted our chat. We put our needles down, looking for the source of the upheaval.

A man ran past us shouting, "*De scrimshaw kniv som min stora-farfar. Det sak nas!*"

"See. I am not the only one." Ester's lips pursed together.

"You understood him? What did he say?"

"My mama is from Sweden." Ester frowned at me, and I remembered her telling me this once before. "The man said that his great-grandfather's scrimshaw knife is missing."

Not two minutes later, another man followed in his path, visibly upset, and shouting, "*Jeg kan ikke finne mitt gull klokken!*" Bishop Iversen walked with him, trying to console, but the man seemed beyond comfort.

He wasn't Danish. Was he Norwegian? I glanced around our group hoping someone could translate. Ester's tears had returned. She picked up her things and hurried away.

"The man cannot find his gold watch," murmured Hanna. "This is the captain's fault."

The others nodded their heads in agreement.

"He is stealing from us and we cannot do a thing about it." Kirsten put her things in her bag and stomped away.

There were thieves among us—how could anyone do such an evil deed? We had already lost so much and were traveling like veritable paupers on an overcrowded ship. The greedy captain had stuffed every inch of the ship with immigrants and with crates of merchandise to be sold in America. Why steal from us too?

I ran to my bunk. Feeling violated and mistreated, I searched my belongings to see if anything had been touched. A sound soon stopped me, and I listened. Barely loud enough to be discernible, someone was whimpering. It sounded like a young child so I stepped down and went to investigate.

"What's the matter?" I knelt beside a young boy huddled in a corner, possibly around ten. His shirt was tattered, and his breeches patched. My heart went out to him.

He shook his head but didn't look up, so I tried a different approach.

"My name is Catherine Erichsen. What is yours?"

He wiped his nose on the sleeve of his shirt and looked at me with doleful eyes. "Nikolaus Møller."

"How old are you, Nikolaus?" I smiled, hoping to ease his burden.

He scowled. "I am nearly twelve. And if you think I'm crying like a baby, I am not."

"Of course I don't think you're a baby." I kept my expression serious. "It is very tiresome on this ship, ja?"

He nodded once. "I am very tired of always being hungry." Nikolaus sat with his elbows on his knees. "The owner of our home and land was very cruel when he learned of our joining with the Mormon Church. He made it difficult for father to make a living. Finally we sold everything we still owned to come to America." He had an expression of bitterness on his face that I'd not seen in one so young. "It wasn't enough. Father had to stay behind to look for work, and now we find our money has been stolen."

"Do you know who took it?"

"If we knew who took our money, we could tell the authorities, ja?"

"I am so sorry." I touched his shoulder hoping to comfort him, but I knew it was very little comfort if any. "I will bring you a bite of my supper tonight." Whatever we were having was better than nothing, and I couldn't bear the thought of this young boy living on hard biscuits until we reached America.

Chapter 11

"I feel very fortunate this day," Lars said. His eyes glistened and his mouth quirked, just a bit, as though trying not to laugh.

"How so?" My eyebrows lifted.

"I've been seeking ever so long for an opportunity to obtain your companionship. We can take a stroll around deck." He extended his elbow.

I looked around the vessel. It was more crowded than the warehouse. We'd have to step over and walk around hundreds of people just to make it half way.

I turned to Mama. "May I?"

I saw her eying Lars with strict regard, but at last Mama nodded her consent. I'd been helping her keep Mary and Ana entertained with the handkerchief ragdolls.

"Thank you," I whispered. Taking hold of Lars's offered arm, we walked away. Before we'd gone too far, we came upon Bishop Iversen talking to someone.

"Dear Sister, don't despair. Send your prayers to heaven. The Lord will hear." He handed the woman a handkerchief.

When we'd walked out of earshot, Lars said, "That poor bishop. He is such a good man, and then to have something like this happen." He shook his head.

"Ja, ja," I agreed. The bishop did seem like he was born to nurture and console. Each time I saw him, he was counseling with someone. I thought of his poor flock, robbed of their immigration funds, and reflected on Nikolaus and his family, the poor souls. Their clothes were inadequate for travel, and I had no idea how they'd get to Zion wearing rags.

"Is Brother Rasmussen ill?" Lars interrupted my thoughts, his eyebrows lifted in question. "Other than today, it seems that he is constantly by your side."

I stared downward, not wishing to discuss the matter of my relationship with John.

"He is merely a friend, a traveling companion to your family, ja?" Lars stopped near the railing and took my hand in his. "Please, don't tell me you're betrothed." He rubbed his thumb across my knuckles.

"I ..." Not knowing what to say, I glanced up, but Lars winked at me. I covered my face with my hands, feeling embarrassed with his teasing. Isaac was not a flirt like this.

He took hold of my hand and patted it. This encouraged me, and looking into his eyes, I started again, "I ..." but my mind was a blank. I could not form into words my exact relationship with Brother Rasmussen for I didn't know it myself.

"Hm." Lars grinned. "My heart gains courage. Has he not asked you for your hand?" He rested his forehead against mine. Although it felt nice, his behavior was too forward and I eased away.

"He has not." My response surprised me. "Nor has he implied that he might do so." Lightheaded with relief, I couldn't hold down a slow smile.

Indeed, neither John nor Papa had given any indication of a betrothal. His feelings for me must be more like an affection toward a family member. He did say that he felt like one of the family—an older brother perhaps. John helped to guide my thoughts toward the spiritual, was a perfect gentleman, and was as kind to Mary and Ana as he was to me.

"Does this bring you sorrow?" Lars asked, taking both of my hands in his.

"Nej." I looked down at my hands in his with mingled pleasure and optimism. When I looked into his eyes, I felt the chains of an arranged marriage slip from my soul to leave me free. Free to choose for myself.

"Your words give my heart reason to hope once again." Lars bowed with a flourish. "I shall seek every opportunity to gain your favor before someone less worthy snatches you away."

His conversation and behavior were flattering to be sure but were acted with grand exaggeration. I barely succeeded in keeping a laugh from bubbling from my lips, and yet his look was one of deepest sincerity. I forgave his silliness at my expense, for I truly loved to laugh.

During our walk, Lars discussed at length his plans to seek my companionship that very night at the social. Not long after, he brought me back to Mama's side.

When he walked away, I wiggled my hands in the air, too excited to hold still. Then I fell to my knees and gave Mary, Ana and Mama a quick embrace. "I love you. I love you. I love you!"

Mama eyed me, head tilted, but didn't speak a word.

I didn't care anyway. I could skip around the whole of the ship and still have enough spare joy to do it over again. I was free to choose for myself!

"I'm hungry," cried Ana.

"Princess, there is no food until evening. Come here and let's have a story." Mama pulled Ana onto her lap. Mary snuggled against her side.

For our noon meal, we were set to have sea biscuits. However, since we voted to give them to the less fortunate on our ship, we went without anything during the day while our fellow Saints ate them rather than starve. They soaked the nearly flavorless biscuit in their coffee or tea to soften it and make it more palatable.

Even now, at the beginning of our journey, many of them had drawn, pale faces. They huddled together on deck, lethargic in their misery.

When I realized that this was also why our ship was

overcrowded, my heart went out to them. Evil men had done this to us all. I wished I could help them more. If we were at home, we could give them milk and cheese and fresh baked bread.

I thought of my new friend Nikolaus, and my stomach growled. Surely my hunger was not greater. I would sneak him a portion of my dinner tonight as well.

Papa approached Mama, his face weighed in sorrow. "Grandfather's watch is gone. It was in the bottom of our bag."

"Are you sure?"

He gave a curt nod in response. Mama stood and took him into her arms, consoling him.

My legs faltered, I clasped the railing for support, and then rushed to him. "Oh, Papa!" I put my arms around them. "We should offer a reward—give them our money. Anything," I sobbed. "It is worth everything to have it back in our possession."

"Nej, daughter. It is gone. I will not offer money to thieves." His voice cracked, and he hugged tighter to Mama and me, drawing in ragged breaths.

Who was doing this? Could he be one of us, or was this thievery done at the captain's hand? Mama and Papa were still arm in arm when the distressing cry of a sister rang out. "My mother's brooch has gone missing! Someone must catch this thief!"

Was Elder Clark aware of our situation? I had to know and crept away, searching the crowd for a glimpse of him. He was headed toward the quarter deck.

Would Elder Clark accuse the captain or demand he set this right? I followed to see for myself, hoping the captain would confess either his misdeeds or that of his crew and put an end to this. They met on deck near the navigation room. I stood behind the mainmast, watching and listening, though they didn't see me.

"Captain Boyd, I know we discussed this yesterday, but it

has come to my attention that more of our things are missing today. We would not steal from ourselves; your crew must be responsible." Elder Clark held his hands behind his back. "If you would search the crew's billet and oversee the prompt return of our precious mementos, all will be forgiven."

Captain Boyd stepped away. "Mr. Clark, I handpicked the crew myself. I know they look a bit rough around the edges, but if something's gone a missing from your things, perhaps you might be looking at others of your own group." He glared at Elder Clark. "Or maybe they didn't bring those particular items at all. Perhaps your self-righteous Saints just wanna stir up a bit of trouble with my crew."

"Captain Boyd." Elder Clark bristled. "I assure you of my people's absolute honesty."

In my eyes, the captain was either guilty or perfectly aware of the thievery going on. Not wanting to arouse suspicion, I moseyed to a wooden crate. If Elder Clark and the captain finished their conversation suddenly, I wouldn't have them think of me as an eavesdropper.

"Well, Mr. Clark, it seems we're having a bit of a disagreement then." Captain Boyd sneered. "Our lot, we spend months at a time away from our loved ones and family, all for the likes of you. It's the same every time. You come around thinking you're all high and mighty, thinking just because you're Christian that you're better than the rest of us. I'll not be upsetting my men just because of some hollow accusations. Bring me proof, then we'll talk."

"Captain Boyd," he protested, "we've all paid a fair amount for our travel. You should see to the safety of our belongings and do a thorough search of the ship. That way no one is accused."

"I'll not be doing any more than originally promised. We're taking you to America, and with rations the Queen herself would proudly eat. Don't be trying to weasel more out of me than that." The captain took a pipe from his pocket and lit it.

"My crew and me, we've got a ship to sail. We don't have the time nor the stomach to be babysitting a bunch of grown men." Captain Boyd puffed his pipe, took in a deep breath and then blew the accumulated smoke into Elder Clark's face.

He fanned the smoke away and stood his ground.

"If my crew finds things just laying about not being taken care of, it's only natural to be a picking it up. You'd do the same. So here's the deal I'll be making with you, keep a hold of your own and I'll be doing the same."

"I see." Elder Clark gave the captain a curt nod. I stood and forced myself against the crate. He swept past me without a glance.

Anger roiled inside of me. Papa's watch was stolen. We wanted it back. It's not like it wasn't still somewhere near. The thief couldn't go farther than the ship's edge, making a search easy, if the captain would allow it.

That evening during worship, Elder Barnett addressed us, and then before the prayer, Elder Clark spoke. "We've given a thorough examination of our situation regarding the heirlooms and other items gone missing from among ourselves and have come to the conclusion that we must set guards below to ensure that no further items disappear."

"Here, here," I murmured. If only this action had come sooner.

"Our things are still on board," an older gentleman said. "Search the crew to discover the guilty party and then return our valuables to us."

"I agree," I said. Mama shot me an impatient look and I clenched my teeth to keep from uttering more.

"We are doing our best to look into the matter," said Elder Clark. "However, until the day we discover who is responsible, no one else need fear." He gestured toward the companionway. "Now I implore you to socialize this night and give the matter no further thought."

The issue of thievery was far from resolved. I wanted to speak up, to shout out my frustration. Papa's watch was missing! Did no one care? My hands balled into fists.

"Come, princess." Mama put her arm around me and guided me away.

I looked back at Elder Clark as I walked, somewhat begrudgingly, to the social. Did he understand the importance of Papa's watch or of Ester's locket? Would he behave differently if it was his special watch missing?

Then I remembered Elder Clark was our spiritual leader on the ship. My face burned with shame that I'd thought such a thing of him. I would do better. I would be better.

Violin and harmonica blended harmoniously, their music wafting throughout the ship. I set my mind on the night's possibilities, my whole body tingling.

The large room on the first deck below where we prepared our food, ate, and socialized soon filled with cheerful movement. I peered through the room, hazy from lamplight, and saw Lars talking to Hanna. Josef played the harmonica beside a violin player whose name I did not know.

I watched the Saints all dressed in custom for their region—some men in knee-length breeches with silver buttons on each side—others in long, baggy breeches that met their shoes. Most of the men wore vests with double rows of silver buttons down the front. Their hats varied from simple caps, to billed caps to tall, black hats.

The women were also dressed in great variety. Some wore white pinafores over their dresses, and others wore different colored aprons tied around the waist. One woman had a beautiful lace collar over her dress that came nearly to her waist. We all had our hair pulled back. Mama and some women wore bonnets with a long-tailed bow in back. Others, like me, had bonnets with shorter, tied bows. Some women merely covered their head with a scarf.

Many women, including Mama, had great skill with a needle and had begun embroidering their bonnets, aprons and even the hems of their dresses as a way to fill the long hours.

The pleasing sound of wooden shoes accompanied some, while others danced in comparative silence with black leather boots to the knee or black leather shoes. I should like to have some of those leather shoes after settling in America.

John talked to Papa. Mama stood a short distance away playing with the children. I pushed my way through the throng of Saints to Mama's side and took Ana's hand.

"Let's dance, shall we?"

She squealed with delight.

I picked her up and danced with Ana in my arms along the edges of the room. Before we twirled too far away to see, I watched Mama, Papa and Mary join the group.

Lars stepped around a nearby couple and stood before me. "May I have this dance?"

"You may." I curtsied.

Having no room for a circle dance, we varied the Danish line dance, and thus I was able to keep Ana with me. After the music ended, another song started, and Lars kept us by his side.

"If I have my way, we shall be partners for the evening." Lars tipped his cap and winked.

My heart skipped in delight. "That is all well and good," I said, working to keep the silly grin from my face. "However, it is close to Mary and Ana's bedtime and I suspect Mama will want me to get them there."

Upon the mention of bedtime, Ana began whining. She did not want to leave the fun even though her eyes were beginning to droop. If she had her way, she would sleep in my arms while I danced. However, after holding her for two dances, my arms were ready to give way.

At the end of our third dance, Ana and Lars both protested

as he escorted me to Mama's side.

"I fear it is time to put the little ones to bed." Mama took Ana from me.

"Ja, ja," I agreed. Curtsying and thanking Lars, Mama and I turned and went to our little wooden home. I started to snuggle in beside the girls, thinking to tell them a story and keep them warm.

"I would like you to go back." Mama put her hand to my shoulder. "You are young and should meet the others your age."

I started to argue, knowing that surely Mama would like some help, but then remembered Lars, and brightened. "Thank you Mama," I said, and went back to the social.

Only a moment passed and a young man approached.

"Hello." He bowed. "My name is Jørn Petersen. May I have the pleasure of this dance?"

"Ja, ja." I smiled and curtsied. "My name is Catherine Erichsen." As we joined the dance, I saw Lars across the room. Expecting me to be gone for the rest of the night, I presumed, he had taken company with another young woman. I had noticed her in England with her honey-colored hair and silken voice. They seemed to be having a good time. He had her smiling and laughing as I did in his company.

Two dances, three dances and Lars had yet to notice me. I danced every dance with a different young man, yet I felt disheartened by Lars's lack of attention.

"May I have this dance?" John stood before me and gave an elegant bow.

I sighed in relief, curtsied, and took his proffered arm.

John was tall. Lars would notice John and then see me dancing with him.

One dance led to another, for John and me as well as for Lars and his partner. Why did Lars not come?

"You are very good." I added lightness of foot as another of

John's good qualities, and then smiled as I remembered I need only worry about his friendship.

"It's something I picked up." He tilted his head. "My Sena and I danced at home on every occasion."

The mention of his deceased wife made me uneasy and I avoided his gaze. Having considered my hand given to him without my permission, I had simultaneously tried to appreciate him and his good qualities while also rebelling against the idea altogether. Since Lars had helped me realize there was no betrothal, my new relationship with John puzzled me. I didn't quite know how to act.

It was unheard-of to spurn a worthy suitor merely because of age. However, this position of uncertainty gave me cause to hope in a different future, for my heart could not accept being chosen for, but rather needed to do the choosing. Thus far, although I admired John, my heart refused to choose him as a mate regardless of his redeeming qualities.

I considered myself therefore sinful.

"You seem distracted this night. Would you care to go on deck and seek out the stars?" John's eyebrows rose in question as he awaited my reply.

Mama and Papa expected me at the social. They didn't like my wandering the ship alone. Although I wouldn't be alone, people would probably talk. As I glanced around, I saw Ester and Kirsten looking our way. Their tongues would wag for sure. Yet, I ached for a change of scenery, if just for a moment. John had ever been the gentleman in my presence and I knew to trust him.

"An evening stroll would be delightful." I nodded politely and took his elbow. As we ascended the stairs I peered over my shoulder and was satisfied that Lars saw me leaving.

We were far from alone on deck, I noticed, as John escorted me to the railing. Dozens of people seemed to have the same idea.

"It's magnificent," I whispered. The water stretched out unhindered before us in every direction—a vision of indigo—the night sky reached down to touch it with the stars and the rising moon reflecting playfully in the rolling waves as flecks of silver and gold.

My teeth chattered in the chill air, and I pulled my shawl up around my ears.

"We shouldn't stay out here long—it's too cold." John turned and sneezed. "But I couldn't miss the opportunity to witness God's miracle in the sky." With his arms resting against the railing, John peered across the sea.

"What do you think of the Saints' missing treasures?" I blurted it out before I had time to change my mind. It was bold to ask, but John was a Brother after all. Surely he would feel the same as I did regarding the thieves' discovery and punishment.

"It isn't anything you need concern yourself over." John took my hand and squeezed it. "Remember the Mormon Creed."

I frowned and pursed my lips together, but then I couldn't hold in my thoughts. "The Mormon Creed says that I should mind my own business and let others do the same, but I can't imagine that includes leaving thieves to their own devices." I pulled my hand free from his and folded my arms tightly in front of me. "If someone found Papa's watch and the other missing heirlooms, I wouldn't need to be concerned. And what about those Saints who are starving aboard ship? How did this happen?"

John shouldn't think of me as a busybody. He shouldn't imply that I was wrong in showing concern for my fellow immigrants. I left him and walked toward the fore side of the ship.

I disliked the idea of being stolen from, and I disliked the captain even more for not insisting on a thorough search of the ship.

"Catherine, let the men worry about such matters." He

caught up to me and secured my shawl around my shoulders lingering just a moment longer than I thought necessary. The warmth felt nice, but he wasn't to be forgiven so easily.

"If each of us worried more about our fellowman, things would be righted much sooner." I pressed my lips together.

"Catherine." John took my shoulders in his warm hands. "Although the ship is over-full with Saints, don't underestimate the opportunity for disaster should you stick your nose where it doesn't belong." He gazed into my eyes with such ferocity and determination that I was unable to look away.

"You are right, of course," I agreed, after finding my voice. Then at his smug look of victory, I continued. "It is too cold to be out. Can you please take me back? Mama will worry."

He gave a curt nod. Taking my arm in his, we walked in silence.

Elder Barnett and Elder Clark were both wary of implying anyone's guilt or innocence, yet in my heart I knew the crew was guilty and not one of our Saints.

Bishop Iversen and his flock had also been wronged and deserved restitution. Glancing carefully about, I noticed fewer of the crew on deck, and the captain nowhere in sight.

Perhaps Captain Boyd would not allow the crew's billet to be searched and Papa would never see his watch again.

How could we live with that? Someone needed to intervene. If no one else would do it—I vowed to be that someone. I could keep a watchful eye on the crew's comings and goings and still keep myself perfectly safe. When the time was right, their guilt would be made known.

Chapter 12

"Isn't Elder Christensen adorable?"

"I absolutely love Jørn's nose. It's so straight and masculine."

Kirsten and Hanna sighed with longing. I wanted to go to the edge of the ship and relieve myself of my recently eaten meal—their syrupy conversation made me ill. Yet, I sat unmoving with a growing group of friends trying to force myself to enjoy their silly conversation as Mama wished me to.

"We saw you talking to Lars," Hanna said.

"And dancing with him," added Ester.

They looked at one another, smiling and amused.

"Isn't he gorgeous? I'm sure you're glad you came with us now." Kirsten finished an embroidery stitch and looked up. "I mean, your last beau—Isaac was it—anyway, he couldn't have been nearly as handsome."

"But I saw her on deck last evening with Brother Rasmussen." Kirsten's friend, Bodil Poulsen, clipped her thread. She had a neat row of blossoms across the bottom of her apron. "They looked very cozy." Bodil smiled wryly, her eyebrows raised.

"He's old enough to be her father." Anna Grette Mikkelsen, a recent acquaintance, frowned at the others.

"Are you courting them both?" Ester's eyes were round with amazement. "I have underestimated you, Catherine Erichsen."

They looked at me like cats hungry for a mouse, waiting for me to answer their questions.

Anything I said would be fodder for their gossip. My throat constricted, my hairline warm with beads of denial.

"I am not courting anyone," I muttered.

The five girls stared at me, unbelieving. Then they all began chattering at the same time about me and Lars and about me and Brother Rasmussen.

"I don't care if you believe me or not." But I did care. Gathering up my embroidery threads, I shoved them into my pocket and stood. I did not wish to hear how they delighted in dancing with Lars, nor did I wish to discuss my feelings for him—or any other man, for that matter.

None of them paid any attention as I walked away. Of course not. They were too busy gossiping about me.

The whole morning's activity had evaporated after only an hour—disintegrated in the ashes of idle chat. There were still hundreds of daylight hours to fill, but I would not go back and re-join myself with those silly girls. From now on, I would avoid them, I decided, and took my sewing things below rather than risk being poked by their needles.

The weather had taken on an unusual chill, and in my mind I pictured Nikolaus' worn shirt. Did he have a coat?

I grabbed my woolen blanket, and then went on deck to the place I usually found Nikolaus when the sun was out. He was huddled against a wall with a woman I assumed was his mother.

"Hello, Nikolaus," I greeted. When they looked up, I handed him my blanket. "It is terribly cold this morn. I thought you might use my blanket till this eve."

"Oh, thank you, thank you, Frøken." The woman took my blanket and wrapped it around herself and Nikolaus. Embarrassed with her gratitude, I curtsied and hurried away.

With nothing better to do, I sauntered to Mama and spent a little time helping her instruct Mary on how to embroider.

They appreciated my company much more than Ester and the others. Ana's little fingers were still too clumsy to hold the needle properly, although by guiding her hand I helped her with a simple pattern.

The girls soon tired of their needlework lessons. I grew cramped from sitting and stood, resolving to forget the Mormon Creed and to put my nose exactly where John didn't think it belonged. I would prove him wrong about my helping—I wasn't interfering—and everyone would thank me later.

John and Papa were below scraping the floor with several others, keeping guard over our meager belongings.

"A good morning to you."

Completely lost in my thoughts of intrigue, I startled and turned. "Oh, Josef!" I clutched my heart. "A good morning to you, too."

"Will you allow me to show the girls something?" When I nodded, he kneeled to their height. "I have something very special to show you, ja." Josef's red hair had a slight curl to it under his cap and his face bore freckles from the sun.

Mary and Ana were more than happy to have someone relieve them of my inattentive company and eagerly took Josef's hands. He led them away with me hurrying to keep up.

"Look here." Josef picked up Ana and Mary and rested them on his hips so they could see over the ship's railing. In the water floated mountains of ice.

"Catie, look!" said Ana.

"There is ice in the water and someone painted it blue," Mary said.

"Those are called icebergs," I informed the girls. "They're not really blue, but merely look it." I spoke to my sisters but never glanced away from the amazing sight before me.

"They are blue. I can see them right there." Mary would not be convinced they were not exactly as she saw them.

"They do look a wonderful shade of blue, don't they?" Josef readjusted the girls on his hips. "It's a wonderful, magical trick God created just for our enjoyment."

Absorbed as I was in my mystery, I would never have noticed the icebergs on my own. Josef had provided us with a rare treat indeed.

"Thank you." I glanced into his green eyes. "It is so kind for you to show us this wonderful sight."

"I hoped you would enjoy it." He smiled. "I am so glad you did."

I noticed the happy creases in his cheeks and looked down, feeling pleased with his company.

A gust of frigid wind blew in our faces. "We must get the girls back," I said.

Josef carried both Mary and Ana. With his coat open and stretched across them, he walked us to the innermost portion of the deck near the mainmast where Mama sat embroidering with several other women.

Mama looked up from her sewing. "Are you done so soon with your walk?"

"Josef showed us the ice curds," Mary explained. "They're floating in the sea."

"Ja?" Mama quickly tied off her thread. "You must show me."

Josef helped Mama to her feet. Since Mary and Ana refused to stay behind, we all went to show Mama the wonders of the icebergs. I thought Josef a most valuable friend.

Not an hour later, Ester grabbed my arm. "Kirsten, Hanna and I miss you. Please come and sew with us," she pleaded.

I hugged her, feeling the warmth of her friendship. "I need to get my things," I said. "I'll be right back."

I raced down the steps to the second deck below. "Hello," I greeted the guard, Brother Jacobsen.

"Miss Erichsen." He nodded.

"I have come to get my sewing thread," I said as I hurried past.

When I neared our berth, a sound surprised me, low and suspicious, not too far away. After slipping my shoes off, I crept behind the wooden partition that began another set of bunks. I peered around. My heart beat wildly at the sight. Two men, one sailor and one of our own stood near what I assumed to be the man's bunk.

"We two are alike, you 'n' me."

"Don't flatter yourself, Pierre. I'm nothing like you."

My heart beat rapidly. These men were conspirators. I stood flat against the wall trying to control my breathing. Were these men responsible for our thievery? I dared not assume.

"We're more alike than you care to admit—we can both be bought for a price. There's no denyin' the coinage we found among your things."

I peeked again, needing a better look in order to reveal their identity to Elder Clark. They were both in shadow, but the one looked familiar. The hair on my arms and neck prickled. If he could only just change his stance a little to the left, a hazy beam of light would fall about his face. I couldn't accuse this man unless I was positive.

"How dare you! My indiscretions are for a noble purpose, to start a new life in America. If I find anything missing ..."

"What? You'll what?"

"You dare test me? Why, I'll go down to the crew's billet and get what's mine, and a bonus or two besides."

"Not if ye know what's good for ya."

"There's a particular gold watch—it'd fetch a good price in New York City."

Papa's watch. I pressed myself back against the wall, my breathing rapid and shallow, and then I peeked around the corner once more, hoping to identify him. The way he stood, the shape of his body. It had to be him.

They took a step in my direction. I sucked in a breath and ducked into the shadows.

Did he see me? Did he recognize me? The answer to these questions I had yet to discover, but I ran to the nethermost corner of the second deck below. How could this be so? How could this man, of all people, be involved in thievery?

I waited in the shadows for the death knell to toll for me. Five minutes crawled by when no one discovered me, nor did anyone pass by in an effort to search me out. I breathed more easily.

These men's crimes could all be brought to light on this day. I should only need to gain the nerve. I frowned down at my stubborn and immobile feet trying to convince them to move, to take me down one more deck and to the crew's billet.

A few minutes, that's all I needed and I could have Papa's watch. If I went to Elder Clark now, with no proof of anything, it would give the thieves time to hide the evidence. If that were the case, we may never see Papa's watch again.

I needed tangible proof.

After waiting a while longer in the dark recesses with no sight of the men in question, I took several calming breaths and made my way to the stairwell. The thieves would be in custody by nightfall.

Upon descending, I walked along the narrow corridor. My eyes began to water from the fetid air. It was the smell of old urine, rancid clothing and unwashed sailors. I was getting closer to the billet. I put my apron over my nose and mouth in order to filter out the stench.

The ship creaked, which it was often wont to do, but so nervous was I that I very nearly cried out. With one hand over my mouth, I placed the other over my chest, feeling my thudding heart. The door ahead was closed, but hopefully unlocked. I sneaked forward.

If someone found me here, I could not explain my presence. I would be in terrible trouble. Mama and Papa expected me to live the Mormon Creed, to mind my own business and allow others to do the same. I put my ear to the door and listened. All seemed quiet. All except my heart. It beat loud enough to wake a sleeping babe.

I tried the door. It opened.

The brief ray of light revealed the empty room. Taking courage, I moved in and closed the door behind me. I had seen an upright barrel in the middle of the room, probably for playing their games or for use as a table. Blackness lay heavy in the room, and even though I knew I needed to be quick lest one of the crew get off duty and find me, I waited for my eyes to adjust so that I didn't trip. Even after waiting, the room remained completely dark.

My hands became my eyes as I searched for the wall and groped my way to the nearest hammock. I fumbled through the bedding and tried to discover anything that might be amiss.

The worn and dirty blankets were clammy and thick from the humidity and salt air. I hated touching them. But determined to discover the stolen treasures, I searched from hammock to hammock.

Scritch. Scritch. Scritch. Something scurried across my foot. I screamed, and then threw my hand to my mouth. I needed to be quiet, but a whimper escaped my lips. I jumped around like a simpleton trying to thwart the creature from crawling up my leg. I outright feared those pointed claws and sharp little teeth.

When I kicked out, my foot connected with something hard. Hoping my erstwhile enemy had scampered far away, I knelt. My eyes had finally adjusted completely, and I made out a shape under the hammock. A sea chest.

It was locked.

One chest meant there were many. I moved to the next hammock. True enough I discovered another chest. Locked. Anything stolen would be in the chests, of course. Not in the hammocks. Desperate to obtain my goal, I rattled the latch in hopes it would come loose. It remained locked.

I pounded on the chest. How could I open it and reclaim Papa's watch? But there were many locked chests. Every sailor was not a thief. Yet, I had come too far to leave empty handed. What else could I do? I stood to leave, and then shivered involuntarily.

A dim ray of light came from the now open door.

"What do ya think yer doing, missy?" Two sailors sneered at me from the doorway.

A scream pierced the air. It was me. When I realized this, the sound quieted. "I—I'm lost," I lied. Knowing they would not take my false story, I fumbled behind me searching for a post—something—anything. I needed strength.

There was nothing.

"Yeah, we see how lost ye are." The door closed, and the leering men were hidden from my sight. "Going through our trunks, are ya. Tryin' to steal our meager belongings, are ya." I heard them step into the room.

"N-nej." Steadying myself against the side of the ship, I tried inching away. "I came below to retrieve something for a friend."

If they thought someone might come looking for me, or that I was on errand, perhaps I could convince them to let me go. I thought of Ester and Hanna. Would they worry since I hadn't returned? Would they come here to look for me?

I heard the sound of the sailor's soft shoes padding on the wooden floor. My heart palpitated. I didn't feel I could breathe. My thoughts were a jumbled mess.

"Truly, I must have entered the wrong room." My voice

sounded panicked and whiny. "Is this not the singles quarters?" I felt the bunk behind me for anything of aid, and latched onto a blanket. It wasn't much, but perhaps I could throw it over their heads and make a run for the door.

The wood floor creaked. The pounding of my heart throbbed in my ears. These men were not allowing me to leave peaceably.

No one would hear my screams. Mama, Papa and the others would search frantically. Nonetheless, no one would think to look in the crew's billet. They might think I fell overboard—these men might throw me overboard. But I feared I had a much worse fate ahead of me first.

"M-my friend will be after me in a m-moment if I don't return." I wished to sound brave, but failed miserably.

The men stepped forward again. They loomed between me and the only door out. This was the end. I couldn't escape them. They wouldn't let me live through their attack.

It was useless to try, but I couldn't give up. I needed to fight. It had been foolish to come here but it wasn't in me to willingly give in to their fiendish lusts.

The barrel in the middle of the room might be my only hope. In an act of desperation I rushed forward, hoping to skirt around it and them and toward the safety of the door.

I should have found a tool of some sort and thrown it at the men. I should have had a weapon with me while lurking in dangerous places.

I shouldn't have come.

The men laughed. Each grabbed me by an arm and wrestled me to the floor. The blanket fell from my hands.

"Let me go! Let me go!" I screeched. I kicked furiously, yet my feet never connected with anything sharply enough to do any harm.

"Now why would we be a let'n' you go? We're just starting t' have fun." His hot breath covered my face.

My body quaked, and I clenched my teeth as I tried to wriggle free.

"Give us some light so we can see our prize," he said.

One held me fast to the floor. The other moved away from my side. I struggled again in vain. "Don't be afraid, missy." He touched my face, and I recoiled in disgust. The dim yellow glow from a candle then showed me the silhouettes of the wicked men who would soon be responsible for my doom.

Chapter 13

"Please! Please, just let me go." I wept and struggled against their unwashed bodies and filthy hands as I sent silent prayers to the heavens for my deliverance.

It was then I heard the rustling of the doorknob.

Were prayers answered this quickly? Surely not. My dilemma would soon worsen if sailors as vile as these two came upon us. I fought against their kisses and groping, my stomach twisting in knots, and screamed with all the strength left in me. A hand slapped over my mouth.

Someone banged on the door. "Catherine! Are you in here?"

Never before had I been so grateful to hear this voice. It was John! I bit one of the fingers that held my mouth shut. The man cursed and jerked his hand away.

"He—" Two chapped lips covered my mouth making it impossible to continue.

"Hey! Lemme at her," the other one groused. He threw the first man to the ground and had his foul lips over mine before I could catch my breath to cry out.

He sat and put a finger to his lips. "Not a word." He snuffed the light out. They both released their hold on me and clambered to their feet.

The door burst open and slammed against the wall. John charged into the room. His angry face, to me, was that of an angel—come to save me from the depths of hell. I got up and rushed into my savior's arms, sobbing.

"What is going on here?" he demanded. Pulling my shaking frame closer, he rubbed my back in an effort to soothe. The dim light coming from the door provided a vague outline of the sailors.

"The little wench was tryin' to break open our chests." The dark-haired sailor dusted his breeches. "We was just defending our property."

"John. You have to know that is not true." I clutched his vest.

"Caught 'er right here by our chests, we did." Both sailors stood in the middle of the room, unrepentant. "We didn't mean no harm to 'er." He winked. "That won't stop us from goin' straight to the capt'n if she comes here again."

"You can't believe them," I pled. They meant very well to harm me.

"Tell him now, missy, we didn't do ya no harm." The sailor with a long blond ponytail sneered.

I turned away from John and glanced from man to man, ready to give my indignant response. They each held a knife at the ready and looked anxious to use them. Their clothes were filthy and tattered, and although the men were slender to the point of looking undernourished, they'd proven themselves quite strong. They sneered with their weathered faces, daring me to accuse them.

John tensed, guiding me behind him and toward the door. "Go get Elder Clark," he murmured.

I wouldn't complain. I couldn't. My shoulders drooped.

If I left to get help, they would fight. John would be hurt.

"Nej, John," I murmured. "It is as they say, they've done me no real harm. They just frightened me, that's all." I placed my hand on his arm.

He stepped toward the men, staring them in the eyes. "This

woman and her family mean a great deal to me," he said, pulling me tight. "I don't think I could be held responsible for my actions if something serious were to happen to any of them. Do we understand each other?"

With malevolent sneers, they nodded. John led me out of the room then and down the hallway. The two men roared with devilish laughter behind us.

Once out of harm's way and into the area where the singles slept, John stopped and turned me to face him. "What were you thinking coming down here? Must you always worry your loved ones so?" He clutched me to himself again.

Feeling somewhat lightheaded, I rested my head upon his chest, taking note of his anxious heart. It nearly matched mine.

After a moment, I whispered, "How did you know to come?"

John shook his head. "I was on my bunk when I heard your scream." He drew back, cupping my face in his hands, and kissed me tenderly on the forehead. "It was the Lord's hand that saved you this day, for I'd never have heard you if I'd been on the second deck or above. I think we should offer Him a prayer of thanks for your safekeeping."

When I nodded, we knelt on the floor with our arms resting on the frame of his bunk, and he offered a short prayer of thanksgiving.

We stood, and he slipped his arms around my waist, pulling me closer. I felt so safe there I could not fathom being anywhere else for I had neither the strength nor the will after experiencing such peril. My tears soaked John's vest, but I could not stop them.

"Thank you for coming, for saving me from my own foolishness." I shuddered once more at the thought of what might have happened.

My heart at last began to settle into its normal rhythm, and after minutes of silence, John lifted my chin with his finger.

"You still haven't told me how you ended up in the crew's billet. I already have an idea, but I need you to tell me."

"I was being foolish, to be sure." Not able to meet his eyes, I stared toward the floor like an urchin being scolded, and dabbed at my eyes. When I saw that he wouldn't release his hold until I met his gaze, timidly I looked up.

John's grey eyes searched mine, and his dark eyebrows pinched together in disapproval. The heat of shame warmed my face and neck. I quickly looked away again.

"Don't make me confess it," I pleaded, "but only see me safely to my parents' side."

He regarded me for a moment before speaking. "I will," he said, "but on my oath, Catherine, if you even think of throwing yourself in harm's way again, I shall take you over my knee and deliver it myself."

Upon nodding my understanding, John escorted me across the width of the ship to the companionway. We walked in silence so thick and disapproving that I was tempted to kneel at his feet and beg his pardon once again for the worry I had caused.

At that moment several men descended the stairs. Holding me tight so I shouldn't lose my balance and fall, John stepped aside to let them pass. I assumed they were changing shifts with the men guarding the second deck. The man I thought I'd seen in the shadows was among them.

Overcome again with terror, I gasped and tucked my head into John's arm until they'd gone. Had he seen me? John patted my head and held me close. "There's no need to fear. That was only Bishop Iversen and some other brethren." We walked up and into the daylight.

"You don't understand," I whispered. "I heard him talking. He has the stolen money. He knows where Papa's watch is." I clutched hold of his sleeve.

"How did you hear such a thing, and when?" John frowned.

"Just now. It's why I was below."

"Bishop Iversen wasn't below." He tilted his head and gazed at me. "You've had quite a fright and aren't thinking clearly." He placed my hand on his arm and led me to the railing.

"You were in the billet. Catherine, two sailors were there with you, accusing you of thievery."

I shot him a panicked look. They were the thieves, not me.

"I don't believe their story." He patted my hands. "Unfortunately, you were somewhere you don't belong. If they choose to, they could have you arrested." John gazed at me with kind eyes. "You should let your parents know what transpired in the billet."

"You are right, of course." I frowned. "They will be angry with me, ja."

"If you don't tell them, you know that I must," he said.

My fear momentarily lifted as annoyance at his proposed interference seeped in. "Ah, Brother Rasmussen, you must kindly remember the Mormon Creed." I spoke the words lightly as a joke, yet my jaws set with determination and I folded my arms across my chest. I could not have him telling my parents before I'd had a chance.

"Of course." His mood darkened and he stepped away to leave.

"Please don't go." I grabbed his arm. "What if the sailors hurt me before I get safely to my family?" My heart pounded anew.

"They won't harm you in this crowd." He gave me a fatherly look. "Stay where you belong and you'll be fine."

"Nonetheless, could you please escort me to Mama before leaving?"

He nodded, silently guiding me to where my family waited, and then he disappeared into the crowd.

"Mama!" At the sight of her, my tears flowed once more and

I rushed to her side. "I love you so much!" My voice choked with emotion.

She looked at me, questioning. "Look at you—what has happened?" She gave me a quick embrace. "You are shaking."

"Mama." She knew something was wrong. I opened my mouth to confess.

"I saw you coming from below with Brother John Rasmussen." Mama glared. "Has he done something to you?"

"Nej, Mama. John is a gentleman." How could she think any differently?

"Well, I don't like it." Mama frowned. "I'll not have my oldest daughter disgraced by being below, alone, with a man."

"Nej, Mama. I will never do it again. I promise." And I wouldn't, yet not for the reasons that Mama thought. She assumed I'd been misbehaving with John. This disturbed me and I stepped back. John was right, I should tell. But not when she thought this of me. If the opportunity arose again, I would confess.

"The girls need some exercise." Mama put her sewing away in a rush. "It would be well for you to take your sisters, ja. Let them play with the other children."

"Mama," I began. I couldn't have her leaving me. I would confess now. "When I was below, I, the sailors ..."

Mama gasped.

My heart skipped a beat, and I was nervous to continue, but I started again. "The sailors stole Papa's watch." I gulped. "They have it and the other things that were stolen. And Bishop Iversen—"

"Did you see it? Did you see him?" She touched my arm.

"Nej." I shook my head. "Their trunks were locked. He was in shadow."

Mama gasped. "You were in the billet? Riffling through their things?"

"It's not like that, Mama." How could I explain?

"Oh! I cannot hear more of this. Not now. Catherine, how could you go down there? How could you be so irresponsible? If someone had caught you." She shook her head. "Such a thoughtless, selfish child." She clenched her jaw.

"But, Mama—"

"Nej. I'll not hear another word. You will watch your sisters. I have Relief Society business to attend to. See that you don't get into mischief."

"May we stay here? By you? We promise not to be a bother." I chewed my lip, hoping.

"Nej. I have other duties. Several have taken sick. Make yourself helpful by seeing these girls will sleep soundly tonight for need of rest." On her word, Mama left.

I glanced furtively for any sign of the yellow-haired sailor and his evil companion, and silently prayed again for my continued safety.

The prompting came that I should tell someone. I'd tried to tell John. He was there, but he still did not believe me.

He had wanted me to confess, to tell Mama. She hadn't taken my word either, and only cared that I'd been in the billet.

I surmised that John knew enough about the sailors. I trusted him. He would keep his word and allow no harm to come to me.

"Play, Catie, play." Ana tugged on my arm.

I searched the crowd looking for a friendly face. Papa was not to be found. My breath came quickly and the beating of my heart pounded anxiously once more. Would I find shelter from my fear?

"Catie, let's play," Mary begged.

With a sigh of relief, I found my safety in the smiling face of a redhead. With Mary and Ana both in hand, I walked hurriedly to his side.

"Josef!"

"Catherine." His handsome smile soon turned to awkwardness and he fumbled with his hands.

Unwilling to be left on my own, I persisted. "You will be at the social tonight, ja?

"I play the harmonica." Josef glanced at me then pulled it out of his pocket and showed me.

"Oh, that's nice." I struggled with something else to say, and finally asked, "Will you play for us?"

"I will play at the social." He stooped down and faced Mary. "You look very pretty today."

"Thank you, Brother Hansen." Mary beamed at his praise.

"Call me Josef, please. We're friends, ja?"

Mary giggled and nodded.

Josef stood. He tipped his hat awkwardly and excused himself. As much as I wanted to be in his company, Josef could barely speak to me. I frowned, disappointed.

Chapter 14

One day passed, and then two since that horrible day in the crew's billet. No one came forward to accuse me of thievery. I pried my memory, trying to recall their exact faces. It had been dark. Their faces shadowed in silhouette. I tried to put what I knew of those evil sailors—their eyes, their sneer, their stench—into each sailor I came upon. But no one seemed to fit the evil faces in my memory.

John was right. Why would they risk their freedom in order to harm me? It didn't make sense.

My parents were angry about me being in the billet. They were angry that I'd tried to find Papa's watch. "Have faith," Papa said.

"Things will work out in the Lord's due time," Mama said.

They wouldn't let me finish telling what had happened. I had no proof. It was gossip.

Ester, Hanna, and Kirsten were angry. They thought I had snubbed them so they snubbed me.

John seemed to pay more attention to Mary and Ana. Lars was busy, though his schedule hadn't been this demanding before. People that I knew and didn't know stopped talking and watched when I walked by.

My only constant was Josef. He had begun helping to entertain my little sisters for an hour or two each day, and they seemed to cling to him even more than they did John.

"Tomorrow, ja?" Josef stood to leave.

"Tonight." I smiled at him. "I'll see you at the social tonight."

Some unknown expression crossed his face, and I faltered. Had I said something wrong? I thought he enjoyed my company. Now I was unsure.

"Make him stay longer, Catie," Mary said. "He's more fun to play with than you."

"Now, Mary, you have a very nice sister." Josef gave Mary and Ana a quick hug. "Be good for her while I'm away."

"Thank you for your help." We had found common ground in talking about our parents' farms. I enjoyed the way his eyes lit up when he talked of farming.

"My pleasure." He tipped his hat and left.

I watched him disappear, and pulled Ana onto my lap. "Let me tell you a story before supper."

The evening social always started just after dusk and was not far off. Mama and Papa were zealous in attending all gatherings of the Saints. Since I had no intention of being cooped up in our little box of a home with nothing to do, I went below to use Mama's brush and make further preparations before accompanying them.

I sat on the bed and pulled out Mama's bag from underneath. No sooner had I found the brush than Papa sat near me. Instead of speaking right away, he fiddled with his fingers.

I glanced at him and then removed my bonnet.

"Things are progressing nicely between you and John Rasmussen, ja?" Papa's face wrinkled in thought.

My heart skipped a beat. "Progressing?" I raised my eyebrows and tilted my head.

"You call him by his given name." Papa's expression hinted

that I should know what he was talking about. In truth, I didn't want to know. His hands stilled and he watched me, waiting.

I looked down at my fingernails, short and uneven. "Ja, Papa, I do call him John." I worried my bottom lip and watched Papa's expression for any hint of his wishes. "It is because he asked me to. He says we are like family." Did he mean to tell me that my hand had been given to John? My stomach twisted.

"He would make a good husband." Papa stood, took his cap off and ran his fingers through his hair like a comb. "He would help you to grow up and mature."

Papa acted casual, so I replied casually, drawing in an uneven breath. "Is it my choice, Papa, or yours?" With shaking hands, I let my hair down to brush it.

His eyebrows rose. "It is your choice, of course."

My heart thumped its relief but I kept my expression even. "Then I will choose someone younger. John is like my brother." A spiritually worthy older brother.

"The way he looks at you is not the way a brother looks at his little sister."

"I cannot say how he looks at me, but tonight you will see that he treats me only as a friend."

"Perhaps," Papa said and remained quiet.

With fumbling fingers, I plaited my hair and reattached my bonnet. What if Papa spoke the truth? The desire to attend the social left me. All the dancing, all the socializing, it sounded too wearying.

However, I had told Josef I would be there. So I went. I heaved a sigh, releasing my frustrations from my talk with Papa, and looked through the crowded room. Josef accompanied the violin with his harmonica, as he did each night. A feeling of relief washed over me. I smiled and waved. He looked handsome.

The tune was over, and he smiled. He took a couple of steps forward. I hoped for his company. Perhaps we could dance as friends. I stood on tip-toe watching his approach, but he stopped. His shoulders slumped and he turned back.

Someone tapped my shoulder.

"My fair maiden, come to relieve me of loneliness." Lars bowed deeply as though I was the queen.

I laughed. "You didn't look so lonely the other night dancing with Anna Grette." I looked over at Josef. He had started playing another tune, his expression even, so I turned back to Lars. "Or when you danced with Bodil, or even when you danced with those other women." I enjoyed seeing his uncomfortable squirm and forgave his inattention of the past few days. In truth he loved flirting.

"Any girl on this ship is second to you." He took my hand and led me into the dance. "Nevertheless, you appeared to be enjoying the company of Brother John Rasmussen. Do I have cause for concern?"

"He is a good dancer and a good friend." It was my turn to squirm under his scrutiny.

By unspoken agreement we decided to behave. We danced one dance after another while enjoying one another's company. His cheerfulness and over-exaggerated charm made me laugh.

Lars hadn't made a show of meeting my parents like John had. I wondered what Papa thought of him. To me, Lars seemed quite debonair, sophisticated, exciting. I knew I wasn't alone in thinking he would make a perfect beau, and at a future time, a perfect husband. He had grand ideas of being important in whatever community he lived in and, I was sure, would make a respectable provider.

The music died out, and we chatted amiably. Lars loved philosophizing, and giving his views on what he thought should be done regarding the thieves aboard ship. His views, I felt, were a little harsh. So engrossed in our conversation, we hadn't noticed John standing before us. Had I moved, I might have bumped right into him.

"Brother Hansen." John tipped his head.

"Brother Rasmussen," Lars reciprocated.

"Miss Catherine, may I have the pleasure of your hand for the next dance?" John turned to me with a formal bow.

"It would be my pleasure." I curtsied. Although I still preferred the company of younger suitors, I had much reason to be thankful for Brother John Rasmussen and let him lead me to the line of dancers as the music began.

"I trust you've been able to keep out of mischief these past few days?" The corner of his mouth quirked into a grin.

I knew he meant to tease, but my face heated just the same.

"Miss Catherine, crimson is a lovely color on you." He gave me another charming smile, and my face heated all the more at his flattery.

"Brother John." I raised my eyebrows. "I see you are without your armor tonight."

"Ah," said he, "you think me a knight—you flatter me. Yet, I hope in your eyes to always be the white knight."

"Always, sir, always."

I liked this silly side of John. He was full of cordiality and the elegant graces of a true gentleman. If in England, he surely would be a knight. He would devote his life to saving others as he had saved me.

Lars waited at the sidelines, hoping for another dance I presumed. However when the music finished, John escorted me in the opposite direction.

As I had with Lars, John and I danced several dances enjoying one another's company. "Would you care to join me on deck for a look at the stars?" he asked. As the music quieted, he extended his elbow.

"Are you sure?" I loved seeing the stars but the weather had turned cold again. "Josef predicts a storm, and you have a cough."

"Your concern is sweet." He placed my hand on his arm and started toward the stairs.

An icy gust of wind greeted us on deck. I wrapped my shawl high over my neck and ears. I should have worn my coat. The wind from the moving ship, combined with the breeze of an unsettled sea, made it difficult to walk.

"This is not a good idea." I scrunched my face against the cold.

"This is a fine place to talk." John pressed forward.

When we reached the railing on the starboard side of the ship, John removed his jacket and wrapped it around me.

"You are already coughing." I turned to go back. "I don't want you to catch a fever." My frosty breath blew away and disappeared.

"It is you who I am most worried about." He placed his coat around my shoulders.

Already freezing cold, I relented, smiling my gratitude.

He drew close to me to share the warmth of his jacket but I didn't mind as it made me feel less guilty for having it. At the same time, he pointed out the Milky Way through the clouds. Although I knew it and many of the constellations, I never tired of finding them in the night sky.

The black clouds in the horizon worried me a little, but other than our time in Germany we hadn't fallen prey to inclement weather.

"It's too cold to remain outside much longer, but you may know what is on my mind." He paused, looking somewhat nervous.

My mind went to the incident with the sailors. Had he found something out? "You caught the thieves?" I placed my hand on his arm, hopeful.

"Nej." His brows wrinkled in a look of puzzlement which

slipped into a frown. "However, I don't mind saying that you scared me to death the other day."

"Ja, ja." I didn't want to talk about this again, tell him what Mama had thought, or that she and Papa were angry but didn't care what I knew since I had no proof. Nor did I care to ask why he'd made himself scarce since that day.

Shivering with cold, I started to turn away once more. I would go to bed and hopefully warm up.

"You misunderstand." John held my arm.

I shook my head, unconvinced.

"Catherine, you helped me put life into perspective."

I stopped mid-step and turned to face him. John sheltered me from the wind, yet a bad feeling churned inside me. He didn't speak right away—as though he was searching for the right words.

"We need to go in," I said. "Mama and Papa will be worried and we will catch the death of cold." I continued silently, pleading for him to take me inside.

"Ja, ja." He knelt on the icy wooden surface.

At first I thought he had lost something. Then he pulled me onto his knee and looked into my eyes, with my freezing hands in his. "My parents had an arranged marriage and lived in bliss all of their days."

John's mention of arranged marriages sobered me instantly. I feared moving or even breathing, and then remembering Papa's words, wished I'd never been so foolish as to come outside with him.

"Catherine Erichsen, will you be my wife? Not out of arrangement, yet with the Lord's help we will grow to love one another more fully."

I gasped, pushed myself up and turned away, horrified. This wasn't how a proposal should be. This was abrupt. Unexpected—unwanted. I didn't want to marry someone who needed the Lord's help to love me.

At my silence, he stood behind me with his hands on my shoulders and continued. "I gained an interest in you when we met in København. While in Germany, I asked your father if I could court you. He, of course, said you could use your own mind to decide." John turned me to face him. "I came to discover this truth. You do have your own will." He lifted his eyebrows as he took my hand and kissed it. His lips were icy.

"John." My teeth chattered. "We need to go in."

"I thought I should live the remainder of my life alone," he murmured, almost as if talking to himself. "But the episode in the crew's billet showed me that until I return to my dear Sena, I can have purpose in my life. And you certainly need a protector." John shook his head with an amused smile.

I, on the other hand, was not amused.

"Catherine, you are so full of mischief, and seeing that you stay out of trouble will keep me young. I will be a good, devoted husband."

I needed to say something, explain to him how I did care for him as a brother or dear friend. My mouth opened and shut.

As if trying to convince me, or himself, John straightened, drew me into his arms and put his lips to mine.

Startled, I tried to pull away, but wrapped as I was in his coat, he didn't seem to notice. His kiss gently caressed, yet showed the strength of his commitment. When he lifted his head from mine, his eyes gleamed. Our kiss had shown him something good.

"Nej. This is not right." I bolted from his grasp and ran for the hatch.

In my rush to get below, I failed to drop his jacket. I would have to face him again on the morrow.

Chapter 15

My stomach felt queasy. Someone was rocking my bed. I took hold of the slats on either side of my bunk and tried sitting up, but was thrown back. The world swirled around my head. Moaning, I tried once more to gain my bearings. I felt like I was in the top of a tall tree during a terrible windstorm. Nej. We were on a ship. We must have sailed into the storm during the night. Josef had been right.

Elder Barnett latched shut our hatch to the outside world, and then descended the stairs. "Captain Boyd wants us all to remain in our berths until he deems it safe for us to move about the ship once more." He descended the next set of stairs and repeated the warning to the third deck below.

It was a welcome command. I wished for nothing more than to remain abed for the entirety of the day. My head ached, my ears rang, and my nose had turned into an unstopped spigot.

"Catie, are you not feeling well?" Mary patted my cheek.

I groaned, wishing her to let me be.

"Mama, Catie isn't well."

Indeed I wasn't. Usually of a stout nature, I had never been so miserable. Undeniably, it felt as though our milk cow had rolled over on top of me. Mary and Ana stirred beside me, and then their little warm bodies slipped away. Mama gave me her healing poultice to apply to my chest and neck.

I lay like a limp rag inhaling the strong herbal aroma while she covered me tightly and wrapped my apron about my head and neck. If I'd felt well, I'd have worried about how silly I appeared, but as it was, the combining effects of the poultice and the apron comforted.

With the girls gone, Mama lay beside me to keep me warm. It wasn't an angel's voice I heard then while I slept but that of my own mama as she alternately sang and hummed some of our favorite Danish tunes.

We had no food or water that day. I didn't feel deprived. Many of the Saints were also sick from the violent pitching of the ship and, like me, could not have held anything down. Tossing and turning in my miserable abode, I thought briefly of Nikolaus and his mother, wishing them well. Babies and small children were crying and sick. Perhaps there were adults crying too.

It pained my heart to hear their unhappiness and added to my own. Silently, I raised my cries to heaven, pleading for salvation from the storm and from the effects of the chill about me. I did not want to die in this infernal pit.

Trunks, crates, and anything not tied down slid back and forth with the rocking ship. Due to the dangers, they cancelled our evening worship though few were well enough to care.

The men were not able to scrape the floors clean, and the stench accumulated during the day, turning the stomachs of the most stout. Because of this, many sank into despair.

However, it comforted me that each time I awoke, I heard Papa's soft tones as he entertained Mary and Ana with stories, while Mama stayed by my side, nurturing, calming, warming.

Because of the hazards in lighting a lantern, the night's gloomy fate enveloped us in darkness. We, a band of over seven hundred Saints, were helpless. Others felt it too. Their despair haunted me, and a tear rolled into my hair. Would we be swallowed by the sea?

Then out of the blackness and barely audible at first, a man began to sing. Everyone quieted. Even the babies were calmed by the hymn—one of my favorites—and certainly fitting to our current situation.

"O God, our help in ages past, our hope for years to come, our shelter from the stormy blast, and our eternal home. Within the shadow of thy throne, still may we dwell secure. Sufficient is thine arm alone, and our defense is sure...."

The words touched my heart, and the shining ray of God's love dissolved my anguish. All would be well. Shedding tears of gratitude, I listened as Mama and the others joined in singing, and silently I joined in the last verse.

"Be thou our guide while life shall last, and our eternal home."

"Amen," whispered Mama.

"Amen," I agreed.

I dozed off again soon after, but not soundly. That night I dreamt of Berta—and of loveless marriages. I awoke restless and worried. What had I dreamed? What had it meant? All I could recall was the image of my sister—she seemed sad. I rummaged for her handkerchief, clasping it to my chest. All was not right. Yet how could I know except by the Lord's still voice? Not wanting to wake Mama, I folded my arms and began a prayer in Berta's behalf.

He was the only one who could help her now. I pled for her safety and welfare. She deserved peace and happiness. Once again I thanked the Lord for my deliverance from evil and asked that he bestow the same mercy on a most beloved sister.

It was still dark in the ship, and I wished I knew the hour. Unable to return to sleep, my mind became burdened with worries, and I rejoiced when Mama stirred beside me. She reached over and felt my forehead.

"I am well, Mama," I assured her.

"I think we shall all be well this day," she replied. "Feel the ship?"

"The storm has quieted." We were safe, and I sent a prayer of thanks to Heaven.

Mama helped me dress, and as a family we made our way onto the deck, squinting, with our arms protecting us from the sun as though we'd spent weeks underground instead of one day and night. This bright new world was welcoming, familiar.

Only a few puffy clouds reminded us of our ordeal. The women stayed on deck clad in shawls and blankets. I was wrapped in my wool blanket. The men took on the miserable task of cleaning the floors below. Afterward, we celebrated the calm sea with food.

Bishop Iversen's Saints huddled under thin blankets and looked pale and sickly. He brought them biscuits and water, doting over their every need. He seemed to truly care for them, and they for him. Had I misjudged him?

Mama stayed by my side and watched the girls run and play with the other children. They were happy to be outside. I slept off and on, regaining strength from my brief illness.

When the vision of a black eyed, dingy-haired sailor disturbed my sleep, I opened my eyes with a start. A shadow passed over my face. I looked up, relieved to see Lars' silhouette between the sun and me.

"Sister Erichsen, may I have the pleasure of Miss Catherine's company for a walk about deck?"

All of a sudden I felt a bit better. A walk would do me good.

Lars took my hand and helped me up. Then he led us away from my baby sisters' pleas to come along. We walked in amicable silence for a time, yet all wasn't silent. Fellow passengers everywhere were busy talking, playing, sewing, and weaving—in all ways showing gratitude for their salvation from the storm.

I worried briefly about encountering John. Would he want to talk again? Would he be upset? Those worries were quickly forgotten as I glanced sideways at Lars and enjoyed the warmth of my arm twined in his. What might it mean?

"Do you play the harmonica?" I asked, thinking it a harmless question.

His eyes grew stormy.

"It's a bad question, ja?" I shrugged my shoulders. "Josef plays every night."

"You know Josef is my brother?" He shook his head.

"Ja, of course." I'd known since Germany. "Should I not?"

"My brother has no ambition." He flicked his hand outward as though shooing a fly. "I don't want you thinking we are alike."

We continued walking, but his demeanor gave me reason to pause. Since I loved and missed one sister dearly and cherished my other two, his behavior didn't make sense.

Lars soon snapped out of his surly mood with an endearing smile. "Please forgive my behavior." He clicked his feet together and bowed. "My goal for the day is to escort a beautiful woman around the entirety of the ship's deck. I hope to accomplish it with more merriment than that with which we first started." He pulled from his pocket a coin. "Watch this."

With a few waves of his hand, Lars made the coin disappear. I hadn't gotten over the shock of it when the coin magically reappeared in my ear and he pulled it out to show me.

"Do another." I laughed and clapped my hands together in delight and didn't care that I acted like a schoolgirl. His magic tricks amazed me, and I found myself enjoying his company once again. However, still not entirely healed from my illness, I began to tire.

"May we sit and rest a bit?" I hesitated, looking for a place sheltered from the constant breeze. "I was ill yesterday, and I fear I'm not yet recovered."

"Of course." Lars led me aft of the ship. "That was quite a storm. If I were captain of this ship, I wouldn't store cargo in the passengers' living quarters." We sat on some crates and continued visiting.

Before I rested completely, I saw a couple of sailors standing near the mizzenmast. Were they the ones I'd seen in the billet? It had been so dark then, their faces dim with shadow. Yet, these men's actions seemed peculiar to me.

"Do you see those sailors over there?" I pointed, trying to block the view with my other hand so they couldn't see me pointing them out.

Lars looked and shrugged his shoulders. "What about them?"

"They keep staring over here." I looked again, trying to see them more clearly.

"And?" he asked. "There are sailors everywhere. We're on a ship."

He was right, of course. There were a hundred people between these sailors and me. Why was I worried? I watched closer. One sailor nodded to the other as though making some sort of agreement. They started walking toward us. My heart pounded in alarm.

"Let's go. Quick!" Surely they wouldn't accost me in broad daylight. I jumped up and grabbed his hands, pulling. I didn't want to take any chances. "We must hide from them," I murmured angrily at his stubbornness.

"Why are you playing this silly game?" With an eyebrow raised, he offered me a sideways grin and patted the crate. "I thought you were tired."

"I'll rest after we are safe." Frantic, I tugged on his arm once more. He stood reluctantly and walked while I tried running and holding on to him at the same time.

"Catherine, you're being ridiculous. What are you doing?" Lars pulled me toward him.

"The sailors," I whispered. "I think they mean to do me harm. Look at them. They're following us." I tugged on his arm. "Let's hide."

"Ah." His eyes twinkled. "It is unusual for sailors to be walking on a ship. Let us hide over here." He pulled me through the crowd of Saints and we walked until he discovered a hidden niche which was near the hatch. "How's this?" He smiled and wiggled his eyebrows.

Ignoring Lars's ridiculousness, I peered around him looking for the suspicious sailors. I didn't see them anywhere. "Ja, it's good."

"And how long shall we stay here?" He pulled me close and nuzzled my neck.

"Are you not a gentleman?" Affronted, I stepped back and swatted him on the shoulder.

"I am a gentleman, as all who know me would attest," he said, though he continued his embrace.

"Sir, I tell you now that a gentleman would never take advantage of a lady in distress." I folded my arms against him and looked the other direction. It was clear that I could not confide in Lars. He would laugh at my foolishness and I couldn't bear it.

"Catherine, my beautiful lady." He nuzzled me once more and kissed my cheek. "You seem completely naïve of your charms."

"Stop it. I'm serious." I pushed him but he didn't let go.

"I'm serious as well."

His eyes sparkled with amusement, yet I would not be amused. Did he mean to make light of my fears?

"Oh, I see." He sobered. "You don't believe I'm serious." He loosened his grip, but patted my hand and kept hold of it.

"Catherine Erichsen, I've never been more serious than with you."

I began to fear the direction of our conversation. Would he spout flowery sonnets of his love and adoration while completely oblivious to my distress? Biting my lower lip and trying to force away an angry tear that had surfaced, I turned away, frowning. I was angry and didn't want to give heed to his flattery.

"Look at me, please." He tugged at me, trying to get me to turn around.

Reluctantly, I complied.

"I mean to make a name for myself in our new country. I will be a banker, and hopefully one day I'll even be mayor of a town. I deserve a beautiful bride."

My chin lifted under the guidance of his fingers as he sought my gaze in earnest.

"I intend for you to be my American bride. I shall not ask today for I see your vexation," he said.

Was he proposing? This was such a sudden change from his earlier silliness. I turned away once more, in order to process his mood.

"Catherine, give me the chance to apologize more fully, for I shall spend the rest of our voyage making amends if need be, and shall ask after I am more sure of the answer."

With the shock of this near-proposal I turned to face him yet again, but still unwilling to forgive, I stared at the deck before speaking. "Lars, you are so full of teasing and flattery. How do I know when you are sincere? Perhaps you are merely trifling with me." I waited for an answer and studied his expression.

"It pains my heart that you would consider me thus." He removed his cap, and his blond hair rustled in the breeze. I took note of his eyes—the intense blue of a Danish sky in autumn. My heart melted at last and I spared him a smile.

"There is hope!" Lars flung his cap in the air and clasped

his chest. The wind took his cap away. "I'm sorry," said he, shrugging, "it's my only one," and he rushed after it.

I trembled with a feeling of aloneness at his absence, yet the suspected sailors were nowhere in sight. It seemed odd that they would want to harass me nearly a week later. I had overreacted. Still, I stepped from our nook ever watchful for the two fiendish men, and made my way toward Mama.

Sitting down with a flump, I put my hand to my chest, feeling wheezy and exhausted.

"You've exerted yourself." Mama pulled her container of poultice from her apron pocket. "Where is your gentleman?" She handed me the salve, and I rubbed it on my neck and under the top of my frock. "And why did he not see you safely back?"

"His cap flew away, and he chased after it."

"Tsk, tsk," Mama mumbled. Shaking her head and pursing her lips together, she took my apron from me and once again wrapped it about my head and neck.

"Mama!" Mortified that anyone should see me this way, I hid my head in my hands. Just as I had worried, Lars appeared from the crowd at Mama's back.

He winked at me. "I'll see you tonight," he said. Tipping his cap, he turned and walked away.

"You most certainly will not." Mama scowled at his retreating frame.

I wanted to set Mama's heart at ease. Because Lars hadn't escorted me all the way back, she had decided to not like him now. If I explained his charm, and how he had nearly proposed, she would understand. Lars was a man not to tire of, for he was at once serious, at times playful, or arrogant and prideful, or humble and even childlike, but always religious. Mama would like him if she knew him better.

Yet, so exhausted was I, that sleep soon overtook me even

amid the sunny day. Hours later, I awoke right where I'd fallen asleep on the bare deck near the sterncastle. People stood nearby, and I listened to the sound of Josef's gentle voice as he played with Mary and Ana. Opening one eye and then the other, I saw that Josef sat right beside me.

Chapter 16

"You're awake." Josef glanced my way. "Do you feel better?"

I tried to smile, but upon remembering the dark-eyed sailor from my nightmare, I fear it appeared more of a wince. In truth, sleeping on the deck of a ship made my back ache. The bed, however, wasn't better. My bones hurt and my head throbbed. I would've endured all the pain of sleeping on deck and borne the stench in the berth for the rest of eternity if only I could take back my being in the crew's billet.

"I came hoping to show you something."

"What?" Remembering my apron, I slipped it from my neck and tied it to my waist. "Where's Mama?"

"She is helping Sister Thompsen. I volunteered to watch over Mary and Ana while you slept." His eyes sparkled at this admission.

Mama felt it her duty to help the Relief Society president each day if possible. It helped her fill the long, tiresome hours aboard ship. While hiding a yawn with one hand, I lent Josef the other so that he might assist me in getting up.

"Where are we going?"

"I'm not sure if they're still there." He nodded his head toward the railing. "Let's give it a look." Just as he had the other day, Josef escorted me to the side while carrying Mary and Ana. For a brief second, a thought or feeling entered my being; it felt as though we were a family. It was odd, to be sure, and I shook the feeling away.

My relationship with Josef wasn't complicated as it was with John and Lars, and I felt glad that we could enjoy one another's company. Men and their strange behaviors puzzled me. Why did John act as my brother when he desired more? Why did Lars act like a great bird strutting his feathers when I knew he was more sensible?

"Are we looking for ice curds?" asked Mary.

"We are past the ice bergs," replied Josef. "I think you'll like this even better."

"A mermaid?" asked Ana

"Nej, not mermaids."

"Look!" Mary pointed into the sea.

It took me a moment to see what she saw, but then they appeared not a kilometer from the ship.

"Oh!" My hand went to my mouth in amazement. Berta would have loved seeing this. I gulped back sudden emotion and felt for her handkerchief in my pocket.

"Atlantic white-sided Dolphins," Josef said.

There were hundreds of them. Their backs were blackish purple, and they bore a cream white on their underbelly with a graceful combination painted along the sides in large wavy strokes. As we watched, they moved closer, their effortless movements like a dance. Some of them began showing off, chattering, swatting the water with their tails, and doing flips before disappearing below.

"More, more!" squealed Mary and Ana. They clapped and laughed and wiggled.

"Watch out," said Josef, "there's no telling what the dolphins might do if you fall into the water beside them."

The girls giggled their delight. "I could be like Little Tiny," said Mary, "and instead of riding on the back of a bird, I could ride on a dolphin."

"That's much too dangerous." I shuddered at the thought of either of my little sisters falling into the sea. They could get swept under the ship—it was too dreadful to think of.

"You're cold." Josef fussed with my jacket, lifting the collar so it covered my ears. "We need to get you back."

His concern pleased me. However, I was ill. He was being

nice, but my heart flip-flopped at his brief nearness. It puzzled me, and I scolded myself for my foolish reaction.

Josef was my friend. He was also kind and thoughtful, like John. I could not make my life with Josef confusing. I enjoyed too much our easiness and kindred spirit.

"I'm not too chilly," I insisted. Josef's eyes were green with little gold flecks that matched the color of the few freckles on his nose.

"Would you have your mother angry?" He frowned with a look of pure stubbornness. I smiled at this as he had ever appeared the lamb previously.

"Nej." I conceded, knowing full well the tongue lashing he could get from Mama should I appear even the slightest chilly upon her return. Mama's disagreement with Lars proved that.

The icy air blowing past no doubt caused the slight blush appearing on his cheeks as he placed my hand on the crook of his arm. The sudden warmth I felt at his touch was merely coincidence. I gave a brief curtsy, feeling at once awkward as we returned to my family.

"Take us for a walk, Josef," begged Mary.

"Do you feel up to it?" He asked me, his brows lifted. He looked for Mama's permission. She nodded, and he gave his attention to me.

"A walk will be good." What else could we to do on a ship? I certainly didn't feel up to embroidery.

Josef's mannerisms were so dissimilar to Lars's. No strutting, no exaggeration of emotions to simulate flattery. Lars liked to make me laugh, and his silliness did just so. Josef was thoughtful and quiet, never prone to a pretended self-importance.

"I have a young friend I'd like to check on, if you don't mind?" It had been days since I'd seen Nikolaus.

"It would be my pleasure." He motioned for me to lead the way.

Along the way, I explained to him about Nikolaus. We found him lying across his mother's lap. Both seemed too dejected to go all the way to America. It made me worry. I did not fare well in times of death and sorrow, having locked myself away for a week upon Grandmother Erichsen's passing. I gulped.

"Nikolaus," greeted Josef. "We came to take you for a walk." He extended his hand.

Nikolaus made no move to get up.

"Come now, we need your help." Josef bent down and took his hand, helping him rise. I went to Nikolaus' left, and together Josef and I led him away.

We headed downstairs to the infirmary, something I'd not thought of doing.

"This young lad and his mother could use a cup of broth," he told Sister Thompsen.

She took a look at him, and poured Nikolaus a cup, which he drank thirstily.

"Here is a little something for his mama," she said, offering me a tin cup half full of broth. "If they get worse, bring them back, though I don't know what else can be done."

When we returned to Nikolaus' mother, she drank the broth. "The Lord has shined His light on us through your kindness," she said. "Thank you. I know we shall make it now. Either way, it is as the Lord wills."

"It was nothing." Josef tipped his cap and turned away.

I hurried after him. "Thank you. You are so kind." I looked into his eyes and felt an unwarranted blush. Whatever was the matter with me, behaving so with a friend?

However, Josef was handsome when he smiled. I encouraged his smiles by talking of our Faroese horses at home until he returned me safely to Mama.

Mama looked at him in approval and nodded. "You have good manners, Josef Hansen. Thank you for attending my daughters so thoughtfully." She turned to me. "Tell the young man thank you."

"Thank you, Josef. I have enjoyed your company very much." I curtsied, embarrassed.

"My pleasure. Truly." He tipped his cap, red-faced. "Good

day," he said and turned toward the crowd.

The small amount of time spent with Lars in the morning, and then the time spent with Josef in the afternoon only helped to highlight their differences. I wondered how two brothers could be so dissimilar.

"Mama, how much longer will it take before we're in America?" I stood beside her and a group of other women, wishing to be walking on dry land again.

"We're barely out of port. It hasn't yet been two weeks." Mama looked surprised. "We'll be another month at the earliest."

The other women in Mama's group turned their faces to their embroidery, sewing faster, pretending they weren't listening. I knew they were.

"How will I survive another month of this?" Stretching out my arms, I emphasized our crowded conditions and the relatively small size of the ship and contrasted it mentally to our farm back home. "There are so many things to do at home—milking, gathering eggs, working, planting our garden, reading." I could think of a dozen things, but I remained silent on the main thing I wanted to do at home—laugh with Berta. I missed her so much.

"Catherine, it's a sin to want what you don't have and to not be happy with your lot in life. We had it good in Denmark, ja?"

I nodded. This was the whole point of my conversation after all.

"There were many who didn't have it as well. Many on this very ship were starved away from their homes after joining the church."

I thought of Nikolaus and hung my head.

"We have it good on this ship as well." When I remained silent, her eyebrows lifted. "We are not the ones going without food."

When I frowned and glanced up, she continued.

"Many immigrant ships are filled with disease—nearly whole ships dying of measles and the like. Our Elder Clark has seen fit that we're not plagued with such atrocities, ja?

"Ja, Mama."

"When we get to America, will we have it good there?"

Mama put her hands on her hips and pursed her lips waiting for me to give the correct answer.

I didn't want to answer that question. I crossed my arms and chewed my lip.

"Catherine, how can you remain silent after all the Lord has blessed us with?"

"Mama, I don't feel blessed." How could anyone feel blessed while sitting on this pile of wood in the middle of the Atlantic? The Elders had said our way would be hard, but we'd felt full of purpose and faith. However, with people starving, thieves stealing, and no way to help, I no longer felt sure.

Mama stepped back, surprised as though I'd slapped her. Then she took my arm and led me to a more private place. "Catherine, what is the matter?" She patted my hand and had me sit with her.

There were too many reasons for my sour mood. I didn't know why, but my experience in the billet kept ticking at the back of my memory. But Mama and Papa didn't want to know more. John, though he thought I'd been too traumatized to remember correctly, felt that I was in no danger. I needed to trust him.

"I know the Lord guided us to immigrate." I bit my bottom lip and turned away. "So, why did Berta stay?" I dabbed my eyes with her handkerchief, heaving a sigh. "I miss her so much and I am lost without her."

Mama hugged me to her. "My dear child," she whispered. "I am not without feelings. I miss her too, as does your papa."

My breathing was shaky, and I struggled for control. "Without Berta, I know nothing. I'm unsafe and alone." If we were together, my problems would seem smaller.

Mama took my face between her hands. "We all miss Berta,

but you have me, you have Papa and Mary and Ana. And we have the gospel." Mama regarded me. "How much do you need before you can call yourself content? If Berta was here, what then? What would you require then—a grand castle with maids? Catherine, turn to the Lord. He is all you need." She stroked my cheek with her fingers.

"Ja, ja, Mama, you are right." I gave her a quick hug. "Mama, I have something else to say."

Her brows wrinkled in concern. "What is it?"

"That day, when I was below." I gulped at the sight of Mama's impatient look. "I know I was wrong to be there. But I think Bishop Iversen is the one responsible for stealing the money."

"This is a serious accusation." Mama frowned. "Have you any proof?"

"Nej. But, Mama, Bishop Iversen mentioned a watch."

"Everyone knew Papa's watch was also stolen. Could he have been questioning the sailor?"

"Possibly." But I didn't think so.

"You need to stop this foolishness." Mama placed her fists against her hips. "Do you understand?"

"Ja, Mama." I hung my head and turned away.

During supper, Mama was tense. I sat between my sisters and helped Ana. Saving a portion of my meal for Nikolaus, I wrapped it in my handkerchief and tucked it in my apron pocket. Then, after taking him this meager portion for which he was most thankful, I went down to my berth and began preparing for the evening social.

Mama stopped me by putting her hand on my arm. She shook her head. "You will stay with Mary and Ana this evening." Mama pulled the poultice from her pocket. "You are not yet well, and I'll not have you getting consumption. Rub this on your neck and chest again." She handed it to me. "You will also learn to control your curiosity," she whispered, displeased.

So I stayed.

"Girls." Mama knelt in front of Mary and Ana and talked in a serious tone. "I need you to stay here and keep Catherine still tonight. She isn't well enough to socialize. You will be very helpful if you let her tell you some stories." She held Papa's hand and they walked away.

"Hooray!" Mary and Ana climbed into the bunk with me. I made them scoot against the wall so they wouldn't fall out and tucked them tightly under the covers.

"Once upon a time, there was a young mermaid...."

The girls listened with rapt attention, but after only two stories, they fell asleep. I remained under the blankets, listening to the sounds of the ship. The faint lowing of the cattle could be distinguished among the ship's creaking. I wondered what it would be like to be a cow on a ship such as this and providing milk for the infirm. The poor thing must have been terrified during the storm.

I heard the music and envisioned Josef playing his harmonica, Lars waiting for me, and possibly even John. Having not seen John since three nights ago, I wondered if I'd wounded his heart or his pride. Surely neither, I decided after giving close consideration to the exact wording of his proposal.

When I considered Lars's near proposal I wondered if he put as much stock in beauty as he seemed to. Perhaps nerves caused him to say such silly things.

I heard a creak nearby. It sounded peculiar, like a person's step. I listened with bated breath and heard the noise again. My heart raced as I searched the room through the dim lamplight for the cause. A hand reached out, extinguishing the lamp. I gasped. A hand went over my mouth, stifling my scream.

"I hear you're ailing." He had a raspy voice. I sought desperately to remember someone aboard ship who sounded like this.

"I came at the suggestion of my friends, Pierre, and Louie. The two sailors you met down in the billet. They're curious, as am I, how much you know about their affairs." He started to lift his hand from my mouth.

"Who are you?" I asked, hoping he didn't feel me tremble.

He put his hand over my mouth again. "I'm the one asking the questions," he said. "Tell me what you know." He lifted his hand a space above my face.

What was the safest thing to say? I didn't know anything concrete. But would he believe me? These scoundrels didn't know what truth was. However, if I told them I knew everything, they may feel threatened enough to leave me alone till we reached shore.

"Wrong answer," he said of my silence. He put his hand back over my mouth, and leaned forward until his lips touched my ear. "I said, what do you know."

I glared into the darkness trying to identify him and squirmed, trying to free myself, but Mary and Ana stirred beside me and I stilled.

"If you wake your charges, it'll be over for all of you. Now I suggest a little honesty. What do you know?" When he mentioned my sisters, I almost didn't dare breathe. He lifted his hand from my mouth.

I blinked at the tears that fell to either side of my face and a sob escaped my lips. He slapped his hand over my mouth. "Tell me, or my friends will have a go at it. They have ways to make young girls talk. Believe me, I'm the better option."

I heaved a shuddering breath, and, closing my eyes, I nodded almost indistinctly. His hand lifted away.

"You and your friends stole the provisions money and the heirlooms. John Rasmussen knows as well. If you bother me any more he'll go straight to ..." To whom? I didn't know if Captain Boyd was trustworthy. "He'll go straight to Elder Clark."

I hoped that sounded convincing enough. Would he take my threat to heart and leave me alone? Breathing as though I'd just raced across our field at home, I chewed on my fingernail.

"You have two darling little sisters," he muttered in his gravelly voice. "I'm sure you'd hate for any harm to come to them, and you shan't have Brother Rasmussen to protect you."

I peered into the darkness trying to get a glimpse of him. Who was he? How did he know I had spurned John's proposal? "What more do you want?"

"What I want is for you to be a good little Mormon girl and mind the Mormon Creed. If that can't happen, other arrangements will be made."

I remained silent, not daring to inquire what he meant.

"Since you know more than you should, and certainly more than we wanted you to, it's rather convenient for me and my friends that your Brother Rasmussen will soon meet his eternal reward—and rather inconvenient that you shall not. At least not yet."

His eternal reward? His words shocked me. I tried to sit up, but he pushed me back. Trying to swallow my apprehension, I finally asked, "Why do you say such vile things about Brother Rasmussen—he is a good man."

"So neither your mama nor your papa has informed you about his condition?" The mask in his voice slipped a little. "I thought he was close to the family."

I'd heard this voice before. Where?

The rasp in his voice returned when he spoke again. "Well, never mind. I'll leave that pleasure to them. Remember, your family is under close watch till we meet shore. If you appear to even want to snitch, either you or one of yours will learn to regret it."

He slipped away as quietly as he'd come. If I'd previously given notion to sleeping during the night, it was all forgotten.

Chapter 17

"Papa, is something the matter with John?" I hadn't been concerned with his absence since the night of his unexpected proposal, but after last night I realized that I hadn't seen him anywhere.

"He is very ill and may not make it." Papa was weaving straw.

"Why didn't you tell me?"

"You were sick yourself. We didn't want to upset your recovery." Papa braided a few links then looked up. "Besides how did we know if there was something to tell or not?"

Mama and Papa were always so pragmatic and it frustrated me that they had kept important information such as John's health a secret from me. Well, they hadn't kept it a secret so much as hadn't bothered to tell me before they knew one way or another how his health would turn.

"Papa, take me to him. I shall nurse him to proper health like Mama did for me." I grabbed John's coat from under our berth, bent, and rummaged through one of our travel bags in search of Mama's healing ointment.

"It'll do no good. He has already had a priesthood blessing and is not improving."

"Papa. Please." I knelt beside him. "John will want to see me." I hoped he would.

"Every measure has been taken for his health." Papa remained stubborn to the idea that my presence could help him recover. "It's in the Lord's hands now."

I knelt and rested my chin on his knee, gazing at him, waiting until he stopped his work to consider me. "Shall everyone on the ship be allowed to pay their respects to Brother Rasmussen, save me?" I touched his hand. "Please, Papa."

He nodded once, stood, and took me to the place where John lay ill. To avoid the spreading of disease, the infirmary was in a secluded area. Only one person occupied a cot. His hair lay tousled and greasy looking, his face, pale and gaunt.

Was this John? I stopped, suddenly hesitant to go further. Papa nudged me. A trembling sigh heaved from my chest and I hastened to his side.

"John?"

He opened his eyes. "I'm not long for this earth," he whispered.

"Don't say such foolishness." I dabbed my tears and took his hands in mine, translucent skin over bones. "I only just heard or I'd have come sooner."

He nodded slightly.

I kissed his hands. "I shall nurse you back to proper strength."

John didn't argue. Perhaps he knew my will and my strength in accomplishing the task. Brushing the damp hair off his forehead, I felt his hot skin.

"Does no one except me know how to rid the body of fever?" I complained, and then I looked at the women who had faithfully cared for him. "I apologize," I said to Sister Thompsen, and Sister Johansson. "I'd like to take a turn helping, if you don't mind."

"Ja, ja." Sister Thompsen nodded and beckoned Sister Johansson to follow after her.

Taking the rag, I dipped it into a nearby pail of water, wrung it, and then applied the cloth to John's forehead. When the cloth became warm, I repeated the process. But his fever did not break.

I stayed the day with John, speaking soothing words of kindness to the man who thought to be my husband, tending to his every need, and never feeling discouraged at his lack of response. He would be better, I knew it.

Although I still only felt a sisterly love toward him, I would consent to be his bride upon his recovery. John was right, he always was. I would grow to love him better as time went on.

Darkness eventually descended and overcame the small bed. In order to spare the fuel, I lit the lantern only enough to keep the pitch black away. The low light, however, caused long shadows. That, combined with the creaking and scurrying noises abundant aboard ship, began to instill a fear in me that grew and strengthened with each sound.

John was sequestered away from everyone, and I felt alone. I was alone other than John. He was low with fever, barely moving and barely breathing.

I heard a noise from behind us. Was it Sister Thompsen coming to check on John?

"Hello," I said, and turned toward another noise. I saw nothing.

A shadow passed by my left. I gasped, my heart pounding. Out of the corner of my eye, I saw another movement and drew in a quick breath. Surely Sister Thompsen would send someone to check on us. I peered into the dim-lit area and saw a man's hand reach forward and snuff the lantern.

"I see—" he started.

I let out a tiny scream, my pulse throbbed. It was the same raspy-voiced man who had addressed me the previous night.

"—you're trying your best to restore poor Brother Rasmussen

to his proper health."

"Stay away from us, you foul beast," I hissed. Only when John groaned did I realize that I had taken too firm a hold of his arm. I released him, ashamed that I'd caused him harm.

"I'd like nothing better than to stay away," the man said. "However, your mama wished for me to find you and bring you back. She's worried that some unforeseeable harm might come upon you if you don't seek nourishment this instant."

My back tensed. "I'll not leave John here with the likes of you." I didn't move. Couldn't move. I wouldn't leave John under the direction of someone who would do him harm.

"Run along now like a good girl before your mama and papa worry. Or, perhaps if you test me, I'll give them cause to worry." The floorboard creaked as he stepped forward.

My knees shook, but what kind of person would leave a sick man alone with a monster? I finally found movement in my arms and dipped the rag in water, unable to control my trembling hands, and once again applied it to John's forehead.

"To show you how harmless I am, I brought him a drink reserved for the infirm." He placed a cup in my hands. "This milk should help revive your gentleman suitor's spirits."

I took it reluctantly—why couldn't I see his face when he was so near? Peering intently, I wished to identify him, but failed.

"Go," he said. "And don't worry. I wouldn't harm a man too ill to defend himself." When I still didn't move, he continued. "I brought him the milk didn't I?" The floor creaked as he took another step. "I'll take nearly as good a care of him as you would."

I felt his hand brush against my sleeve, and I jerked away, spilling the contents of the cup. The thought of his touch and what he might do, sent me running to the stairs.

When I got near our berth, Mama greeted me with a worried

frown. "I sent Bishop Iversen after you ages ago. Where have you been?"

"Bishop Iversen?" I was right. I placed my hand to my chest, trying to settle my heart. "Please don't send him after me anymore."

"You can't expect people to treat you kindly if you don't behave. Sometimes you are far too judgmental." Mama motioned, and I sat down. "You'll feel better after you eat something."

Sister Thompsen approached our table. "Catherine, we have regular schedules in caring for the infirm." She glanced at Mama. "If you take a turn, you need to stay until your replacement comes."

"Bishop Iversen came," I replied.

"You don't need to make up stories," her tone sweetened.

"I sent the bishop after her," Mama confirmed, her hand on my shoulder.

She frowned. "The good bishop is in a meeting with Elder Clark. A meeting I was compelled to leave when it was discovered that Brother Rasmussen had been left alone."

"But—" I started.

"No one's angry with you, dear. We appreciate that you stayed the whole day caring for him, but evenings are particularly critical. Just see that you pull your full shift next time." She nodded at Mama, and then left.

"You believe me, Mama. Don't you?" I asked.

She patted my shoulder. "Ja, ja. Of course. Someone was there. Was it the bishop?"

I frowned. "The light went out. I couldn't see him."

"You've heard him speak. Did it sound like the bishop?" Mama washed the dishes in a pail of water.

"Nej. His voice was deep and gravelly." I gulped. "I am sure he was the one I saw near the billet," I muttered.

"It couldn't have been the bishop then. He must have sent

someone after you."

"Ja," I conceded. "But he was threatening."

"How did he threaten you?" Mama sat beside me.

"Well, he said that I'd better mind the Mormon Creed, and if I didn't, something bad would happen."

Mama put her hand to her mouth and sighed. "This does not sound like Bishop Iversen, yet I've told you the same thing many a time."

"But Mama, it was dark, and I was afraid."

Mama hugged me. "I am sorry." She placed her hands on either side of my face and peered into my eyes. "All is well and good now. Ja?"

"Ja, Mama."

The pleasant sound of the violin and harmonica wafted through the air, the social had already begun, but I couldn't even think of laughing and dancing while John lay ill below. Mama and Papa had already prepared the girls and they only waited for me to finish eating and wash my dishes—which I did.

"Please don't make me go to the social tonight." I wouldn't be good company. "I'd like another opportunity to attend to John." But then a dark thought came over me—what if that man returned to John's chamber? "Papa, can you come with me?"

"Nej, you barely left his side all day, and the girls are both too excited for sleep." Mary and Ana played in circles around him. "Your mama and I will enjoy the social together. You are well enough to attend to your sisters and to help them use up some of this energy."

"Please, Papa. Can we visit him for just a moment?" Though I didn't understand the feeling, it was imperative to see him.

"You've spent enough time with him today that half the ship is wondering when you'll marry," Mama said. "If he means nothing to you, your attentions can wait till morn."

"Mama!" My exasperated tone made Mama's eyebrows rise and Papa's sank into a scowl. "I'm sorry." I lowered my head, contrite. "I will do anything, if only for a short visit."

"Perhaps it is a good thing to check in on Brother Rasmussen," Papa relented.

"Thank you." I squeezed Papa in a hug. "Thank you." I kissed his cheek.

"We shall not stay long."

"Only to see that he is resting properly." I took Papa's elbow and we walked toward the stairs.

"We shall meet you and the girls at the social." Papa looked over his shoulder to Mama as we disappeared.

As we got closer, my insides twisted in knots. Was John improving? I couldn't bear the thought of his being so sick. My attentions during the day had helped some, I was sure of it. Tomorrow I would make him well.

Sister Thompsen, our Relief Society president, sat nearby. Bishop Iversen was nowhere to be seen.

"How is our Brother Rasmussen doing?" Papa asked.

"Much the same, I'm afraid." Sister Thompsen lifted John's head and coaxed a little liquid down his throat.

I peered toward the dark corners for someone lurking there.

"He's a close friend of our family." Papa nodded toward me. "Catherine will like to check on him again after the morning's worship and after her other duties are attended to." Papa regarded me sternly, and I nodded my understanding.

When we arrived at the social, Mary and Ana were eager to dance with me, which we did along the side where others stood and visited. We twirled and skipped to the music. When one song ended, I sought out Lars and noticed straight-away that he was talking to Hanna again. Our eyes met, and I glanced away, not wishing to stare.

I couldn't help the fluttering of my heart when he excused himself from her company and walked my way.

"May I have a dance?" Lars extended his hand as he bowed.

"I hope you don't mind three partners," I said. "Mama put me in charge of Mary and Ana."

"If the only way to dance with the beautiful Catherine is to also take on her sisters, I'm game." Lars took Mary into his arms and I lifted a giggling Ana into mine.

After the dance, Ester approached. "Catherine." She curtsied. "It's been ages since you've joined our embroidery group." She turned to Lars. "Catherine's not one to enjoy such domestic pursuits." She touched Lars' arm. "Are you, Catherine?"

"Truly." I smiled sarcastically. "I'm not much for embroidery—or gossip."

"Humph!" Ester stuck her nose in the air and left.

"What was that about?" The corner of Lars's mouth quirked up.

"I have no idea." I watched Ester join with Kirsten across the room and wondered.

"It doesn't matter if you sew. My wife will have a personal maid for such mundane tasks." He lifted my hand to kiss it.

I glanced up. Josef was watching from the front of the room. I pulled my hand away.

Lars nodded and led us into another dance. The dancing and chasing around helped to wear out my little sisters. Since I'd arrived late, it seemed that the social ended rather soon, but it was enough to wear out the girls and give them some pleasure.

Once in bed I felt almost blissful, until one by one the lanterns went out. Would the intruder come again? I lay in the dark listening to every creak of the ship and wondering what each one meant. Rats were no longer the thing I feared most.

The next morn, I hurried through my chores while planning my day. I'd spend it with John. I'd encourage him to convalesce. Lars would seek my companionship but wouldn't find me. I'd also miss the opportunity to visit with Josef. It didn't matter. John needed me. Perhaps someone could help me bring him on deck to enjoy the sun's warmth. Surely that would help him improve.

After tidying our home, I went on deck for morning worship. Bishop Iversen spoke of keeping our inner vessels clean of sin. I listened, intent on his voice and mannerisms. He never looked my way. Didn't act guilty, and he didn't sound or act the same. This bishop could not be the same man who threatened me.

"Before going to John, you should spend time with the girls your age," Mama said.

My jaw clenched in rebellion, but I turned on my heels, silent. When I found Ester, Hanna and the other girls, I sat beside them.

"Hello," I said, hoping to sound cheerful.

"Catherine, it's been so long since you joined us." Bodil welcomed me to the group.

"From what I hear, she's been busy with Brother Rasmussen." Hanna took another embroidered stitch to her apron.

"As long as she spares Lars for me, she can have as many beaus as she wants." Ester glanced up and then continued her embroidery.

"I think Lars prefers my company." Hanna tied off a red-colored thread, and started with green. "He spent half the night with me after all." Her eyebrows lifted as she glanced at me.

"I must be going. I don't have my threads, and I think Mama is calling." What was Lars's relationship with Hanna? He had declared intentions toward me, though I wasn't yet ready for such a commitment. Perhaps this was his way of giving me time to choose on my own. I hurried to my family.

Mary and Ana were crawling over Papa when I returned. Before I had a chance to ask if I could leave and tend to John, Brother Pedersen, one of the Elders, whispered to Papa. He nodded for me to watch the girls, and then they left together. I settled down to help my sisters practice their sewing.

Josef strode forward bearing an easy smile. "You've been so busy lately, I didn't know if you'd be here." He pulled out his yellowed handkerchief knotted to resemble a doll.

"I've come to help entertain your little sisters."

"That's very nice." I took the doll from him and looked it over then returned it. "Mary and Ana are looking forward to your company. However, it is nearly my turn to help tend to Brother John Rasmussen. He is ill."

"Have you not heard?" Josef's face took on a serious expression that had me instantly alarmed.

"What? Heard what?"

"It is not my place, Miss Catherine." He shook his head solemnly.

If it concerned John's welfare, I had to know what was happening. Setting aside my responsibility with the girls, I rushed away leaving them standing with Josef as their attendee. I knew it was wrong to leave Josef to care for my sisters, but I couldn't help the panic I felt for John.

Apprehension filled me when I arrived on the third deck below—there were too many people near John's sick bed.

Mama came forward, frowning. "How are you here—where are your sisters?"

"What has happened to John?" I asked, pushing myself forward. I had to see him, but before I got to where he lay, Papa took my shoulders and stopped me.

"You mustn't go any further." Papa pulled me into his arms. "Brother Rasmussen has passed away."

"Nej! Papa, nej!" I leaned into Papa's chest while blinking at the tears blurring my vision. This couldn't be! I knew John—I cared for him! Why would he and his associations be taken from me? I needed his faith. I needed his strength. I needed John!

A sob escaped my soul, and Papa held me tighter, but I had to make sure. Breaking through the restraint of Papa's arms, I rushed to John's bed. Sister Thompsen and some of the priesthood brethren were nearby with a huge sheet. Mama was threading a large sewing needle.

My heart choked at the sight, and I threw myself over his lifeless form. "Why? Oh, why did you leave?" I felt, more than saw the crowd of others pull away from this good, honorable man who wished me for his wife. If only I had agreed to marry him, if I hadn't had his coat, he'd still be alive.

Mama's hands—so warm compared to John's—closed themselves on my shoulders. Gently she pulled me away. Hesitant at first, I threw myself into Mama's embrace, hiding my face in her shoulder, and sobbed.

Sister Thompsen went to inform Elder Clark of John's death. Mama sat me into a chair. Then she took a cloth, washed John's face and hands, and combed his hair. Papa straightened John's clothes and put his tie on. He then took the sheet, tore it in half and began to wrap his body. I stood unmoving and watched. My heart ached from guilt and shame.

A short time later, Elder Clark called all the Saints together on deck. He wanted John's funeral to be as grand as possible. I listened tearfully as we sang "Rock of Ages," and I tried to pay attention to Elder Clark as he spoke.

On this occasion, he talked of love and family and eternal life. John now had love. His death united him with Sena and his parents. No one knew if he had a living relative.

They brought his body forward wrapped in the white cloth. They placed John on a plank that straddled the ship's edge. I gasped. A gulp of disbelief stuck in my throat when they tied a rope around him and attached weights to his feet.

"Mama?" I couldn't bring myself to form the question.

She answered my unspoken query with a pointed glance and a nod directed toward the sea. My head shook back and forth in disbelief.

He was a good man and deserved a decent burial. But that couldn't be. There would never be a tombstone for John. No place for anyone to go and reflect on his goodness and no one to grieve his passing but me.

Their actions seemed slow, and I watched them tilt the plank. John didn't move at first. They tilted the plank higher. His body slipped soundlessly into the depths of the sea.

As though in a long tunnel, I heard a gasp from one, cries from others. Someone screamed. Life for me swirled in and out of focus. My knees wobbled as though no longer strong enough to hold me. Moisture beaded around my face. I thought I was sick. Perhaps I should call for Mama. My mouth opened. No sound came out. The world around me turned black and silent.

Chapter 18

"Catherine, Catherine."

A voice called to me, but who it was I did not know. The familiar sound swirled around, playing with my memory, and pecking at my brain like a magpie. Peck, peck, peck, "Catherine." The noisy little bird did its best to annoy.

My eyes fluttered open. I was in a wooden box. Why?

"Catherine, it's Mama."

Mama? Where was I? My chest moved up and down as I breathed. Opening my eyes once again, my wooden cage swirled into focus. I panicked and tried to break loose of my bands. Someone held me prisoner. Instead, I found myself wrapped snug in a blanket. How did I get in bed? I struggled for information that seemed just out of grasp.

And then I remembered Elder Clark talking about love and family. "What happened?"

Mama's anxious face hovered near mine. My mouth felt dry like straw. I feared her answer, but didn't know why.

"Princess, you gave us quite a scare." Papa was there, his voice strained.

Mama wiped threads of moist hair from my face. Had I fallen overboard?

"You fainted at Brother Rasmussen's burial."

"Oh." I felt the groan escape my lips. The burial at sea. John had died. I turned away from my worried parents and closed my eyes to the world once more.

"We will let her alone for a time," Mama said. Then I heard them walk away.

Blackness consumed me. Not because of nighttime but because of the despair in my soul. I couldn't shake it off, nor did I have the energy to try. It just was.

Would that no one could ever break my heart again, that it would be iron-clad. Two men I cared for were torn from me, one by his own actions, the other by death.

My unkind memory repeatedly tormented me with moving pictures of John and his attentiveness to me—in København— the time he saved me—his laugh. Two memories brought a wave of tears, our time in the warehouse in Germany, and lastly, the night he kissed me. Rather, I should say, the night I spurned his love.

The occasions of my bad temper played out more torturously—when I thought we were betrothed—all the times I avoided him. Honestly, I didn't deserve anyone's love. The memory of John slipping into the sea added to my torment—I knew for myself. He was gone forever.

Before I was ready for company, two small bodies pounced on me. They were too cheerful, too full of energy.

"Catie, Catie, Mama says you have to get up now." Mary pulled the blankets off my head and patted my cheek.

Although the shadows played long across the floor, I hadn't grieved near long enough. It couldn't have been more than a minute.

Shrugging the brats off, I pulled the blanket back over my head. I liked it there. With my eyes closed, I never had to face anyone ever again or be anything to anybody. I tried hunkering back into my abyss, but Mary and Ana continued pestering me.

"Come on, Catie." They pulled the blanket off my head. "Come play with us."

"Get off me now!" I glared at them but made no move to get up. They looked shaken at my outrage as well they should, the pests.

After only a moment's hesitation, they began again.

"Catie, Mama says you must get up." Ana pulled on my arm, trying to urge me out of bed. "It's time for supper."

"I'm not hungry. Now leave me alone before I throw you overboard!" I knew what was on deck. People. And I had no desire to be among them. Turning back toward bed I covered myself entirely, satisfied that Mary and Ana had finally run away, crying. They needed to grow up.

"Catherine!" Mama jerked the covers down with a flounce.

Moaning, I sat up. Hesitantly, I glanced her way. We weren't alone, of course. Never alone. Even in my bunk before bedtime there were others around. I felt their presence. This was the joy and curse of living with seven hundred others on my floating purgatory.

Mama had her hands on her hips. She looked angry. "How could you say such a wicked thing to your sisters?"

What had I said? I tried thinking back that far. "I only wanted them to leave me alone." I couldn't have said anything that bad. "I don't want supper. I don't want company either. Just make everyone go away." I shooed at the shadowed Saints as though they were pesky flies. No longer willing to support the weight of my body, I slumped back onto the thin cotton-tic mattress.

"Catherine, it's a fool's game you're playing, and it will lead to nothing but misery. Is that what you want?"

Tears beaded under my lids and streamed down my temples. "Nej, Mama. I do not want misery," I murmured tiredly. However, my life seemed destined for misery. I deserved misery. "Please, just let me alone till morning. I'll get up then. Promise."

"You've been here since yesterday." Mama brushed the hair

tenderly from my face. Her voice softer, yet still stern. "There'll be more for you to do on the morrow than merely getting up. You'll have to make it right with your sisters."

"Ja, Mama." I pulled the blankets back over my head. Once again, I let the welcomed feeling of despair fill my soul—the blackness seeped into every fiber of my being.

At first, I wasn't conscious of the silent sobs that escaped, but eventually, great wailing groans shook my grieving frame. Although everyone on the second deck below could probably hear my anguish, I closed them out. In my mind I was alone in an obsidian abyss where the sun would never shine.

Day came much too soon. I wasn't ready to greet anyone, didn't want to face my family, but knew better than to test Mama by staying abed. I wiped my hands across my face. My eyes felt puffy and my eyelashes were wet. I dried them on my sleeve.

The sun shone through the hatchway to the deck, it being left open each day to ventilate the lower decks. Wondering, but not really caring if morning worship had started or ended, I stepped onto the floor. My legs wobbled at first, and for a short moment, I wished that I hadn't been left so completely alone by my family.

The probable untidy appearance of my hair flickered across my mind, and I searched out the brush. I even went so far as to hold the implement in my hands before it fell unhindered back into Mama's travel bag, deeming it too heavy, the activity too tiring.

The sound of Elder Clark's noble voice wafted to my ear as I climbed the steps to where I would find an unwelcome throng of people—and my family. It was the singular threat of Mama's displeasure that kept me moving forward.

Disparaging glances greeted me, as I knew they would, from those unaccustomed to empathy. I should stick out my tongue at them had the activity not taken too much effort. The mere thought gave me ample satisfaction as I stood facing the backs of the Saints listening to the morning worship service.

"Brothers and Sisters, as we are gathered here together on this fine morning let us give thanks, for we are nearly half way toward our goal. There are but few who remain ill, and we can thank our Lord we've lost only one dear brother. Even in our sorrow we know our beloved John Rasmussen has gone home to his sweet wife and an Eternal reward...."

His words shot fire into my wounds and I couldn't bear to listen to another word. I didn't want to hear about only losing John. None of them felt his loss as keenly as did I. None of them knew the man as well as I. And, having abandoned him in the freezing weather while wearing his warm coat, none felt nearly as responsible for his death.

I didn't deserve to live. Yet there I stood alive, while John had been taken. Would I alone mourn the passing of someone so worthy of life? I cupped my face in my hands while trying to hide from my shame.

"... Brothers and Sisters, our probation here on earth is a time for learning, a time to experience all that life has to offer, including pain and the loss of loved ones...."

Did Elder Clark look directly at me? It appeared as though he did. Yet, how could he know my pain or my sorrow? He had a wife and children awaiting his return.

Had Berta been here ... we were such good friends. We always comforted one another. But I would never see her again. A sob escaped, but I stifled it before anyone noticed.

"... Let us remember our God and our Savior. Let us give thanks for our trials, allow them to stretch our faith so that we might become closer to our Father in Heaven. The great ones who have gone before us, even Noah, Moses and Abraham suffered afflictions at every hand and praised the Lord in the very act of their suffering.

"Jesus Christ died for us, and our own dearly departed Prophet, Joseph Smith, died at the hands of mobsters. He gave his life so we might know about the true and living gospel of our Lord and Savior. These next few weeks are only the start of our journey. Let us continue to travel these great waters with the spirit of the Lord, I pray, in Jesus name, Amen."

The sound of someone's sob broke the silence. Looking for the source, I saw many eyes filled with tears. Many of the Saints embraced one another. Elder Clark's poignant remarks stirred my soul into the memory of my faith. I needed the Spirit. I wanted to be strong—to give my all for the gospel.

Elder Barnett had once said that despair grew as faith diminished. I didn't want to despair. I wanted faith. But after losing Isaac, Berta, and John, it seemed nearly impossible. I wanted my conviction back, my strength.

The Holy Scriptures came to mind. I needed to start reading them again. I would be healed by the words of the Lord. But I needed to find my family first. I took a step forward and then another, searching for my parents.

When I first caught sight of Papa, Josef and he were talking. Papa nodded. Josef patted his shoulder. Mama said something and touched his hand.

"He was a good man, and will be missed." Josef tipped his hat and walked away.

When they saw me, I stood hesitant, almost shyly waiting as they opened their arms to me. "Mama, Papa." Their names choked in my throat. How I loved them! I hurried into their embrace. "I'm so sorry." I would be a better daughter, a better sister.

Mary and Ana darted behind Mama's skirts. They seemed almost afraid. What had I said to make them fear me so? Kneeling to their level, I peeked at them. Hoping they would forgive me, I extended my arms.

They gave only a moment's hesitation before rushing forward. I squeezed them tight and kissed each sister twice on the cheek. "I love you so much. Please forgive me for being cross yesterday."

"We love you too, Catie," said Mary. "Are you better today?"

"Ja, ja." I tried to smile reassuringly although I didn't feel sure. I looked up at my parents. "May I take them for a walk?"

"It is a good idea to keep the girls active." Papa picked up Ana and gave her a kiss, and he knelt to kiss Mary. "Run along with Catherine, and be good."

"Ja, Papa," they said.

"Let me take Catherine below first." Mama took me by the hand and led me below. She found the brush and brushed my hair. Then she fixed it into a braid, pinned it to my head and fastened on my bonnet. "I wouldn't want my daughter to be without her hair fixed."

"Thank you, Mama." I smiled—it felt good.

"Now let's get back on deck and count the Lord's blessings." We walked up the steps and to where Papa played games with Mary and Ana. Papa's twinkling eyes gave me an idea. "Mama, Papa, why don't you join us?" A family walk seemed like a good idea.

Papa gave a smiling nod and squeezed Mama's hand. "Elder Barnett is expecting me first. We have some matters to attend to."

"Later, perhaps?" Mama touched his elbow and I noticed her hand as it slid down the length of Papa's arm to where their hands briefly met.

Mama held Ana's hand and I held Mary's, and we walked

towards the ship's bow. Since I had helped Papa tend our land at home, I always enjoyed the outdoors.

Today there were plenty of large puffy clouds floating amid the blue of the sky, but an unusual lack of wind seemed to hinder the ship's current progress. It was odd, to be sure. Unconcerned, I looked overboard hoping to see more dolphins or icebergs but found none.

"Why isn't the ship moving?" asked Mary.

"There isn't enough wind," replied Mama.

"I feel wind." Mary held out her hand.

Mary was right, a nice breeze pushed past us. It made the obvious stillness of the ship disconcerting.

The tip of the ship rose as if on a great wave—except there was no wave. I grasped the railing for support. Another jolt caused Ana to fall flat on her bottom. "Stop it!" she said.

Chapter 19

"What is happening?" Mary stumbled and clutched the rail. Mama grabbed after Ana, and I took hold of Mama's arm to keep her from tumbling over.

I watched the confusion aboard our ship—shouting, running, toppling over—people grasping hold of anything to keep from falling overboard.

"All hands on deck!" While Captain Boyd barked out orders, the crew scrambled. "Mr. Clark! Someone find Mr. Clark immediately!"

"Let's try to go forward," Mama urged.

We were on the starboard side of the ship and by placing one hand over the other on the railing as though we were pulling a heavy rope, we made our way toward the quarterdeck. This was where Captain Boyd had first addressed us at the beginning of our journey.

"What is the cause of this disturbance?" Elder Clark rushed forward with Elder Barnett, Papa, Josef and several other men at his heels.

"Mr. Clark, get all the men you can gather. Go below straight away and bring back all the potatoes. Bring them to me now! Demand the rest of the passengers to come fore of the ship as close to the bow as possible!" Expecting immediate obedience, Captain Boyd turned his attention on the crew.

"Potatoes?" I gave Mama a questioning glance. She shrugged her shoulders.

What was going on and how would potatoes help keep us

from sinking? But, amidst the confusion, I began to hope that perhaps we weren't sinking. The ship, now that it was tilted, remained motionless. A silent prayer formed in my mind and I supplicated fervently for our lives.

"Yer not forward enough!" Captain Boyd complained. "Pinch in tighter."

We crammed ourselves forward to the bow of the ship, hoping to keep it afloat. Even when preparing to leave Liverpool, we were not as crowded as this. People whom I'd seen, but didn't know, had me pinned against the railing. I peered overboard thinking that it wouldn't take much movement to set me out into the sea. What was the cause of such an upset?

There, under the bow was the largest creature I had ever seen. A massive, grey-colored whale had lodged itself under the ship and had lifted us at least an arms-length into the air rendering us unable to continue our voyage. And, although it wasn't a hole in the ship or some other disaster, the whale held us in its power and was able to sink us at its will.

Papa appeared with the other men, each lugging a large sack, and pushed their way forward.

"Papa, look." I pointed toward the grey beast.

He nodded and frowned but didn't change his course.

"Oh, my!" Mama peeked over my shoulder. "Girls, let's fold our arms and pray."

"What's wrong, Mama? Why are we praying?" Mary asked.

Mama shushed her and helped Ana fold her arms.

The whale was large enough to destroy the ship without hurting itself. One swat of its massive tail—one snap of its jaws—and our lives on earth would be cut short.

"Fold your arms," prompted Mama. Then she uttered a short prayer for our safety.

"This here's a Humpback," said Captain Boyd. "They're curious critters, but harmless. She'll leave us alone after we feed her curiosity." He nodded his okay to the men who were holding sacks against the rail.

The one closest to the captain tipped his open bag and I watched with amazement and trepidation as our potatoes disappeared into the whale's large, open mouth as though they were nothing. When the bag was emptied, he moved out of the way and the next in line came forward, repeating the process.

"They're throwing away our potatoes! Make them stop," demanded Mary.

"They're feeding a whale." Knowing Mary couldn't see this fearsome creature, and thinking she would like to, I picked her up and leaned her over the edge to let her get a better look.

"Help! Mama, help!" screamed Mary. "Catie is throwing me overboard!" She kicked and thrashed. "The whale is going to eat me!"

It took all my strength to keep her in the ship. Everyone turned to look, and, mortified, I placed her down on the deck.

Just as the captain had predicted, when the last of the potatoes were poured into the whale's gaping mouth, it closed its mighty jaws and slipped into the sea.

"I was just trying to let you see the whale." I scolded. "It wasn't going to eat you, silly girl. It was eating the potatoes."

In anger of my supposed betrayal and unconvinced of my intentions, Mary took off on the run with the ship still rocking. She slipped through the congregated Saints and out of my sight.

"Mary!" I started pushing through the crowd, trying to chase after her. Before I made any headway, two sailors, one with a blond ponytail, jumped off of some rigging and followed in the direction she had gone.

"Mary!" Even as I screamed after her, annoying those around me whose ears caught the brunt of my concern, I had no rational thoughts as to why the sailors would pursue my sister.

"*Förlåta?*" "*Ursäkta mig?*" "*Tilgi?*" "*Undskyldning mig?*" I didn't understand the comments made by many of those whom I pushed, but assumed they were merely begging my pardon as

I forced my way through.

My heart beat in my throat. I rushed toward the place she had disappeared, wondering if I'd be able to make it to her in time.

Stopping on the larboard side of the ship, I bent to catch my breath while praying for any sign of my dear little Mary. I didn't see her anywhere. The ship, too small for our needs, seemed enormous when looking for one small person.

With a scream lodged painfully in my throat, I continued. This couldn't be happening. My sister could not be in any harm. This had to be a coincidence. I was being overdramatic. I kept trying to console myself, but I could not stop my searching as a thousand fears played through my mind.

Large crates and barrels, intended to make the captain more money per voyage, lined the center of the ship. Mary could be in any number of nooks or crannies.

"Miss Catherine."

My blood ran cold at the tone of Bishop Iversen's voice.

"Bishop." I curtsied stiffly, not feeling the least bit courteous at the moment.

"Now, Miss Catherine, whatever has you so cross?" He smiled in pretense of joviality yet his eyes remained unfeeling.

Could this be the man responsible for the near-starvation of over fifty Saints? I peered at him through narrowed eyes; no sound escaped my lips. Was he in league with the scoundrels who called themselves sailors? Shaking my head, I met his gaze with a scowl and tried to pass.

"I see. Has the cat got your tongue?"

Did he know Mary had run off? I searched his cool demeanor for a sign, but I didn't know how to read the faces of evil men. I tried to make my escape once again, and once again he detained me with the large frame of his body.

"Since you won't tell me, let me guess." He rubbed his chin in a mocking gesture of contemplation. "Are you missing a little sister?"

I felt the shock register on my face. He had her. But where? "What have you done with my sister?" I looked around and behind him but didn't see Mary.

"Don't be ridiculous. I don't have her. What am I, a nanny? No, I heard you screaming her name. Sad really. With poor manners like that, you're liable to put yourself and your sisters in real danger."

"Where is she?" I asked.

"Be gone with you." He flung his arm dramatically outward as though he had every power over me. "My advice to you, Miss Catherine, is to keep your lips closed and your sisters close. Everyone aboard knows those mischievous imps are your sisters—including the crew."

My heightened state of alarm was such that I hadn't the ability to move. My mouth opened. It was him. I stood glaring at him with raw fear as my cloak. Bishop Iversen took one step toward me, however, which sent me scurrying away like one of the ship's rats.

I ran. With tears blinding my vision, I ran. Would anyone believe that Bishop Iversen had Mary? If not, how could I find her? Pulling Berta's handkerchief from my apron pocket, I wiped my eyes and discovered myself on a near collision course with Lars.

"Catherine!" Smiling, he snatched me in his arms. We twirled around from the force of my movement, but I had no time for Lars's silliness.

"I can't visit. I'm looking for Mary. Bishop Iversen has taken her and won't tell me where she is. Will you help me?"

"But I just talked to your father. Both your sisters were with him." He took my elbow in an attempt to escort me on a walk, I assumed, but I'd have nothing of it and pulled away.

"I need to make sure she is doing well." I proceeded forward.

"I've missed you so these last few days." Lars followed close beside me. "There's no one aboard this entire ship who compares to you in beauty or wit. Will you at least promise to save a few dances for me this evening?"

"I don't know that I shall be attending the social this night." The thought of being there laughing and happy made me ill.

"You're not still in mourning over old Brother Rasmussen, are you?" Lars smirked.

I paused. What business was it of his? Just because he had promised to ask for my hand at the voyage's end, he hadn't asked for it yet. And even more important, I had no current disposition to accept a position as his bride, or any man's for that matter.

"Don't tell me you were in love with the codger?" He stepped back, blinking as though seeing me for the first time.

Not knowing a polite reply to his incredulous attack on my sanity, I started walking again. Then I stopped mid-step and glanced away, folding my arms across my chest.

"You were!" His eyes widened in disbelief. "Ha!" He laughed and slapped his knee.

I didn't appreciate his response at all and hurried away.

"It's not a problem." Lars, apparently recovered, walked once again by my side with his hands clasped behind him. "I love a challenge. Besides, I can't live without you, Catherine. And once I convince you of that, you won't be able to resist me."

When I saw Mama and Papa ahead playing with Mary and Ana, a sense of relief washed over me. Without another word to Lars, I rushed to greet them.

"Mary, I was so worried about you." I knelt to greet her, but she hid behind Mama's skirts. "I didn't mean to frighten you, and I am so sorry. What can I do so that you're no longer angry with me? I'm miserable." Peeking around Mama's skirts, I caught her bashful gaze. "Can we be friends again? Please?"

Smiling one of her best smiles, she ran into my waiting arms. I stood, still embracing her, and twirled her around so that her feet floated in the air.

"Do it again," she begged after I stopped.

I twirled first Mary, and then Ana, and became quite dizzy.

Grabbing the railing for support, I waited for things to come into focus again.

"How about we take that walk now?" Papa tipped his hat and Mama linked arms with him. They gazed at one another like they were the only two people aboard ship, and once again I wished for a love as sweet as theirs.

"Catherine!" Ester hurried toward me. "Did you see the whale? I nearly fainted at the sight of it." She put her hand to her chest.

"Ja, ja." I slowed a bit to keep pace with her.

"How do you have all the men staring your way?" Her face pulled into a pout.

I shook my head, disappointed, and started to walk away.

She held my arm. "I am serious. First Brother Rasmussen, then Lars—and I really care for him." Her eyebrows lifted. "Now you've got the attention of the sailors, too."

"What are you talking about?" I looked around me, but didn't see anyone staring.

"Even Bishop Iversen seems to pay attention when you're near. How do you do it?"

My chest constricted at the mention of his name.

"You like older men." Ester carried on unaware of my distress. "The bishop is unattached." She gave me a wry smile. "Then you could leave Lars to me."

I looked around, frantic. "I've got to go. Mama and Papa are leaving me behind." I hurried away from her.

"Catherine," she called. "You didn't answer me."

However, I did not go back. I ran to Papa.

"Papa, what do you know of Bishop Iversen?" I asked.

"I do not know the man, only to say that he makes friends easily." He patted my shoulder. "Why do you ask?"

"Well, I heard ..." Trailing off, I glanced ahead and around me. Was Pierre, or Louie, or the bishop nearby?

"Catherine. This isn't gossip, is it?" Papa regarded me sternly.

"I don't think so." I frowned in contemplation. Was it gossip if I didn't know for certain? "But, Bishop Iversen—"

"Perhaps you should make sure before you continue."

Papa tipped his head, nodding toward Mary and Ana, and again toward the nearby Saints. "There are too many ears around who might hear something they shouldn't, and then repeat it."

I looked over to the sterncastle and saw sailors on the rigging looking down at us. They were watching me.

Papa was right. Even if he let me finish, if I told him Bishop Iversen was bothering me, what could Papa do? It was my word against a bishop. I needed to concentrate on being a better sister. I vowed to be more diligent in keeping a constant eye on the little girls.

"Catherine?"

Sister Thompsen, the Relief Society president, approached.

"Ja, ja," I stopped and curtsied.

"May I talk to you a moment?"

Mama nodded her approval, and she and Papa took the girls and walked on without me.

"I need some help and wonder if you would be willing to help the Vestergaard family."

"The Vestergaards?" My brows lowered. "I don't know them."

"Your mama has been helping me to care for our dear Sister Vestergaard. She is due with a child any moment and she is not well, not well at all."

I tilted my head in question. I wasn't trained to deliver babies.

"They have two girls, Orla and Engla. They are similar in age to your sisters, and while praying this morning I got the impression that you are the one to ask." Her eyebrows lifted with hope. "You could care for them while they play with your sisters."

Chapter 20

The ship creaked. My eyes opened and I peered into the darkness, my heart pounding. Why did I awaken? I felt the rhythmic movements of our ship and listened to the sound of ocean thrumming against wood. It was nothing. I was safe.

My mind turned to the events that led me to this cracker-box in the middle of the sea. I wondered about America, and then I thought of that frightful whale. If there was one whale, there were others. Would the next one be bigger? More aggressive? Would another large creature take us into his jaws? We had no more potatoes.

My leg twitched. I suppressed a sigh and listened to the chorus of sleeping people. Daylight, long and monotonous when starting after the break of dawn, would be even more so when awakening this early. But, unable to stay still any longer, I got up.

"Mmf." Mama turned in her sleep.

Papa's snores joined with others in a bizarre mixture of snorts and wheezes. It was a wonder anyone was able to sleep in a ship as crowded and noisy as this. I dressed and then wrapped in my shawl. I did not want to disturb anyone, so I crept to the stairs in my woolen stockings. I would make sure there weren't any more whales around and then go back to my family.

Bishop Iversen would surely be sleeping. I climbed the

stairs and went on deck and noticed only a few sailors visible. None of them paid any attention as I walked to the railing. The stars were out and the sky cloudless. I looked up at billions of glimmering flecks.

The moon, close to the horizon, was preparing to make way for the sun. The air, though still frosty, had warmed now that we were done traveling with the icebergs. The sea flowed unhindered in every direction from our ship to the distant horizon. I would be grateful for the day when a vast continent broke up the monotony.

Being outdoors under less crowded circumstances was refreshing. My eyes closed and I inhaled, filling my lungs with the moist, salt air. I could think uninterrupted. I could feel however I wanted without criticism. Mama wouldn't allow me to grieve for John any longer. She said it was sinful to spend so much time worrying over someone who had gone to a better place.

I didn't feel sinful. I just wasn't as happy as Mama expected. Walking further down the rail, I leaned against it and peered into the black water. Reflections of the moon and stars shone as gold and silver on the tips of waves made by our ship's wake.

In this isolated setting, I could acknowledge my own feelings. The most poignant was my grief over John. Knowing he was with his wife and parents in Heaven didn't make me miss him less.

A tear slid down my cheek. His conviction strengthened me, his attitude cheered me. He had been an exceptional friend and the older brother I'd never had.

I missed Berta—I worried about her. If only I could talk to her. Tell her we were yet alive. Learn if she was happy.

There was no way, however, to send or receive such assurances. Another tear formed, and I blinked it away. The Lord knew my sister and would provide for her. I worried her handkerchief between my fingers not knowing how my world could ever be right again.

A sound startled me. I whirled around. Had the sailors, Pierre and Louie, started their shift? Holding my breath, I listened. The ship constantly creaked, but there was an extra, thumping sound. Was it of human origins?

A shiver crawled up my neck, and I looked about, trying to shake off the creeping feeling of someone's gaze boring into my soul and watching my every move. Yet I couldn't allow myself to be a scared little kitten that spent her life in hiding.

Well, hiding actually sounded like the perfect solution. I rushed toward the hatch and toward the safety of our berth. I lunged down the companionway taking the steps two at a time.

"Oomph." I bumped into someone and almost fell to the floor. I took a step back. Hindered somewhat by the darkness, and startled by the form of a man beside me.

"I thought I heard something." Josef rubbed his foot. I must have stepped on it. "What are you doing up?"

"I might ask you the same," I said, embarrassed that I'd been discovered.

"I'm on shift to guard," he murmured. "Why are you up?"

"I couldn't sleep." I tugged at my shawl and didn't want to say more.

"Does your papa approve of you sneaking about before dawn?" He sounded incredulous. "It's dangerous."

Would he tell Papa? I'd be in such trouble if he did, but it was too embarrassing to confess my fear of the whale. I remained silent and tried thinking of a witty reply. Nothing came, so I tried to push my way past. I'd go back to bed and then he'd have nothing to tell.

When our shoulders accidentally touched, however, I felt the same strange—well it was a tingling shock. Ja, a shock. And so unexpected. I stepped back and missed the step. My arms flew into the air in an attempt to stabilize myself. I would fall. I would be hurt. Before I gained my footing, and feeling certain of my impending broken bones, his arms were around me, saving me.

He drew me near and I felt Josef's warmth against me, his eyes searching mine. I shivered, though I didn't feel cold. With all danger of slipping past, Josef continued to hold me close to him with one hand. He stroked the hair out of my face with his other, his caress soft as he swept his thumb across my cheek and along my jaw.

I closed my eyes, tilting my head upward toward him, my lips parted. I felt him lean into me, his breath on my neck. This couldn't be happening, and yet for some unexplainable reason, in that moment I longed for his kiss and stood on my tiptoes, waiting.

His fingers lessened their grip. "It is time for you to get back to bed, ja?" He sounded irritated.

My eyes flew open and to my utter mortification, Josef turned me away from him and pointed me downward.

"I will escort you back to your family."

"That won't be necessary," I grumbled.

Humiliated and utterly confused, I tried to muster a thimble of dignity and I held my head up. While walking through the crowded makeshift housing on the second deck below and hoping to hide from my thoughts, I paid particular attention to the sounds of snoring, fussing babies and hushed tones of their parents' quieting. Although I heard Josef following me, I didn't say another word, nor did I turn around.

When my berth was in view, I heard him stop. Then, after rushing the last few steps, I turned to catch one last glimpse of him. He shook his head and retreated. I sneaked back into bed with Mary and Ana, angry with myself.

I frowned into the darkness, tossed and turned, and

wrestled with feelings of being disgraced. I must have slept some, however, because in the very next instant Mary and Ana were both patting my cheeks.

"Tell us a story, Catie."

Still tired, I moaned my displeasure of being awakened before ready. But then I sat up to tell the girls the story of The Emperor's New Clothes—a scandalous story—but one that always made them laugh.

The sudden flash of an early morning meeting appeared in my mind. More horrifying, I recalled my behavior toward Josef. I hoped against hope that I would be spared the embarrassment of bumping into him again. Maybe after a week or longer— maybe then I could face him once more. I touched my neck where I'd felt his warm breath.

What had I been thinking? Josef had never given so much as a hint that he wanted to be more than a friend, and yet at one touch I was eager for his kiss. What kind of person did that?

"Catie, why are your cheeks red?" asked Mary.

"They're not red, and I don't wish to discuss it." We could not have a story now. I jumped out of bed and grabbed the hairbrush, ripping it through my hair.

"Is something amiss?" Mama touched my arm.

"Nej, Mama." I glanced down guiltily.

After getting myself ready, I helped Mama get the girls dressed and ready for the day.

The sky was clear blue on this morn, and following my routine of the past week, my sisters and I sought out the Vestergaards after the morning worship.

"Hello, girls." I tried to act more cheerful than I felt. The girls themselves looked a bit glum. I knelt down to their level. "What shall we do today?" It was hard for them with their mama so sick.

Orla pointed to the crates near the sterncastle.

"Do you want to climb mountains?"

They nodded and clapped their hands.

"That sounds like fun," said Mary. She often liked to take charge of their games although she was the same age as Orla.

I helped each of the girls onto a crate, and then caught them one-by-one as they jumped down. After doing that several times my arms ached and I made them stop.

"Let's take a run around deck," I offered. They needed a more physical activity to wear them out, and I needed something to keep my mind off of Josef.

"Nej," said Ana.

"We could play dolls," suggested Mary.

"Ja, ja." All the girls nodded their heads in agreement.

"Let's get Josef," Mary said.

"Not today." I winced, once again remembering my humiliation. When I glanced up, I saw him pressing toward us. He made a habit of playing with the girls, but surely he wouldn't today. As he got closer, I looked frantically around for an escape. The ship seemed narrower and smaller than it had only a moment ago. My only solution was to pretend I didn't see him.

"May I join you fine ladies?" Josef asked.

Unwelcome heat rushed to my cheeks, and I kept my gaze down. How could he come here—did he think I had no feelings?

"Ja, ja, come," the girls cheered.

It seemed I was overruled. I closed my eyes and took a deep breath.

Mary and Orla jumped up and began pulling his arm, thinking to assist. Ana and Engla scooted over, both wanting to sit next to him on the crates. The problem doubled when Mary and Orla sat down. They pulled at him, each trying to get their way. All four girls wanted to sit right next to him, but since only two could fit, he remained standing.

"Wait, wait." I grabbed hold of Mary's arm and couldn't help but be amused at the bewildered look on Josef's face. He turned in a circle while they grabbed for his hand. "You are so popular today." The girls caused quite a stir and it dispelled my awkwardness for the moment. "You need to take turns. Younger girls first."

Mary and Orla whined their disapproval. Smiling in satisfaction, Ana and Engla took their places beside Josef.

He acted out the story of "The Little Mermaid," and of "Little Tiny" using our handkerchief-dolls like puppets. Those were two of my favorite stories, and I watched from the corner of my eye while pretending to ignore them.

Josef mercifully spared me as little attention as possible, for as soon as I got the girls settled into their routine of trading places—younger to older, older to younger—I became self-conscious again.

"Let's go for a walk, shall we?" Josef asked.

The girls jumped up and began disagreeing over who should hold his hand.

"Someone needs to hold Miss Catherine's hands," he said, stealing a glance my way.

My sisters came to the rescue, and this thing pleased me. I joined hands with them and the six of us walked around the deck. We were quite a sight, I was sure.

Mary and Orla began whispering and giggling.

"What are you girls giggling about?" I asked.

"Nothing." They giggled again, and then traded places. Taking their sister's hand, they ran ahead, leaving me alone with Josef.

"What is this all about?" Josef asked.

"I don't know." Yet, I feared that I did know. Mary was in for it when I talked to her later.

Orla came back, and, walking backwards while we walked forward, she took my hand in her left and Josef's hand in her right, and then after placing his hand over mine, she ran back to her giggling cohorts before we could complain.

Josef's hand closed around mine causing butterflies to flip in my stomach. I pulled away, barely making eye contact with him.

"I'm so sorry," I muttered, and rushed toward the laughing girls. "You girls have such sorry manners. I'm taking you straight to Mama." I grabbed Ana and Engla's hands, and we marched away.

Chapter 21

"May I have this dance?" Asger Madsen extended his hand to me.

"Thank you." I curtsied and took my place beside him at the end of the line.

Lars or John used to dance nearly every dance with me. It felt strange. John had passed on, and Lars was dancing with Mette. In truth, Lars hadn't yet asked me for even one dance.

After we danced, Asger escorted me back to the sides. "Thank you," he said, and walked away, choosing someone else for the next dance. Mama and Papa were dancing, and the girls were visiting nearby with Orla, Engla, Erik, and Christer. I stole a glance toward Josef playing his harmonica. He caught me watching, and his eyebrows pushed together. It was just as well. I deserved his scorn.

"Dance with us, Catie." Mary tugged at my skirt. I swatted absently at her hand.

I'd ruined my friendship with Josef. The past two days had been awkward. Shaking my head in remorse, I frowned. Although Josef still came around and played with the girls, it wasn't the same between us anymore. I felt an invisible barrier of tension. He couldn't help but think me shameless. I was.

"Catie, I asked you a question." Mary folded her arms, pouting.

"What? Would you like to dance?" I took her hand in mine but didn't move.

Lars spent time with me each day, but lately he seemed pre-occupied. I watched him as he danced with Hanna. Since ridiculing my feelings toward John, it appeared as though Lars had found other amusements.

"Mama, Catie is dreaming with her eyes open again." Mary ran to Mama and Papa as they walked near. Then I remembered that I was supposed to dance with the girls. Why had they just stood there?

"Let's go dance, shall we?" Papa picked up Ana. Mama took Mary by the hand and they walked to the middle of the room.

The music was lively, and I clapped in rhythm. It seemed that everyone had a partner. Everyone except me. Mama and Papa kept the girls on the dance floor for the next round. They laughed and danced and teased. Lars and Ingrid chatted and laughed as they danced. Everyone appeared happy. Except me.

Cheerlessness bore down upon me, and, unable to abide its increasing weight, I slipped away. Unnoticed. Invisible.

It didn't feel as though I had taken a breath the whole evening until I stood under the open sky. At last I deeply inhaled the salty air moist from the surrounding sea and then exhaled slowly. What would my life be like in that land called America? Could we live there and be happy?

My thoughts were interrupted by a sound. I stilled, listening.

"And no one suspects yer not a real bishop?"

Not a real bishop? Looking around me for an escape, I rushed to the crates and climbed between them just in time, for their voices got louder as they neared.

"What about the girl? We can't keep takin' chances."

I wanted to peek, but I didn't dare move.

"I don't think she'll talk."

It sounded like Bishop Iversen. The other men sounded familiar as well.

"Leave the girl to me."

"We all have an interest in the snoopy wench. We'll decide her fate together."

"Shh, I hear something."

"Yer always hearing something. I never seen such a superstitious git."

"I'm telling you, someone's coming. And if anyone sees us together, it'll be over for all of us."

The sound of the men scurrying away let me breathe a tad easier. It was a good thing I huddled into a crevice, for had I been standing, the sound of my knees knocking together would have alerted them to my whereabouts. I said a short prayer of thanksgiving for my safety. Then I waited a couple of moments more to give the men ample time and distance before I came out in the open again.

True enough, my legs wobbled like Mama's aspic as I made my way toward the stairs.

"I thought I saw you come out here."

"Aak!" I clasped my hands over my mouth so as not to draw undue attention from my venomous shadows. "You nearly scared the life out of me." I sighed with relief then at the friendly face before me.

"Miss Catherine, are you up to mischief?" Lars's lips turned into a conspiratorial smile.

"Nej, merely thinking." It wasn't wise to say more.

"Ja, ja, I was talking today with Bishop Iversen, and he—"

"Do you know him?" I couldn't help the deep furrows in my brow but made a conscious effort to smooth them out.

"We have grown quite close as of late." Lars slipped his arm through mine and proceeded walking. "He's quite a compassionate fellow. Why, just this afternoon he confided in me how worried he is about you since the death of Brother Rasmussen."

"Really," I said wryly. "I can't imagine."

"Ja, ja, and he has offered to take my place on guard several times."

The animated and devoted look on Lars's face as he talked of the pretend bishop let me know not to ever discuss with him the man's shortcomings. The idea of his probable thievery would completely baffle Lars. I looked about casually to see if the subject of our conversation stood nearby. The deck appeared empty.

"I thought you were enjoying the dance with Hanna and Ester." And Inger and Mette and Lene. "What prompted you to come on deck?"

"You're jealous!" Lars beamed.

"I am not." I turned away. There was a time when I would have been jealous, but I couldn't imagine it at the moment.

"Do not be jealous. There is no one compared to you." Smiling in spite of my denial, Lars led me to the rail. "It seems so lonely, doesn't it?" He glanced across the water. "We're so small, the ocean so big."

Didn't I feel the same way? I looked up at him, curious that he would have my same thoughts. He put his warm hand over mine.

"Do you think God is looking down on us now?" Lars looked out into the expanse of heaven. "And if he is, which of these stars do you think he's looking from?"

I loved looking into the night sky. To me, it was proof of a loving God in Heaven. Once, I had even convinced Mary and Ana that He had sprinkled diamonds into the sky. Lars shared the same feelings as those in my heart, and his comments made me feel a closer connection to him.

"Those are good questions," I whispered, mesmerized by the moment. "But I have no real answers. All I have is what I believe."

"What is it you believe?" Lars leaned toward me appearing

vulnerable, cupping my face with his hands. I trembled with the butterflies in my stomach.

"I believe that a loving God keeps a regular watch over his children," I whispered.

"Ja, ja." Lars nodded.

My heart rejoiced as I gazed into his twinkling eyes. I did have faith. My sister, Berta, would be well. John was in a better place, and good would always triumph over evil. This knowledge strengthened me and swelled within.

For the first time in a long while, I felt perfectly content. Neither of us spoke again for the longest time, and I wondered if heaven felt like this. But then I noticed the look in Lars's eyes—the same look I'd seen in John's eyes before he kissed me.

"Oh," I gasped, and pulled away. "I must go." This was not good. I did not want to kiss Lars.

"Please don't leave, Catherine." With his arm around my waist, he pulled me into his embrace. "You're shivering," he murmured, and drew me into his overcoat.

I needed to leave, but I could not still my trembling. If I didn't leave now, it would only make things harder on the both of us, but my legs didn't move. I was a little mouse hypnotized by her captor as Lars studied me, searching every part of my face, devouring me with his eyes.

My chest was on fire. My heart thumped. I watched, powerless to turn away as he leaned forward. Then I remembered—I had nearly kissed his brother only two days ago.

I was wicked.

Alarmed, and thoroughly ashamed, I broke his grasp and raced back into the ship. Clambering down the steps, I didn't stop running until I bumped into Papa. Like a wall, he stopped me.

"What's wrong, Princess?"

"Nothing's wrong." I gasped, trying to catch my breath. "I just realized the late hour and knew you'd be worried." I put my hand to my chest, wanting desperately to calm down, and hoped Papa couldn't see my guilt.

"Your mama and I have been worried." His face pulled into a frown.

"Are Mary and Ana tucked in bed?" I asked, lowering my eyes from his scrutiny.

"Mama is telling them a story. I left to come find you."

"I'm very tired." Still avoiding Papa's eyes, I yawned as proof. "Do you mind if I go straight to bed?" Before he could answer, I ducked underneath his arm and rushed to our berth.

"Mama, do you mind if I leave the lamp on so that I might read God's Word?"

Eying me curiously, Mama nodded and then joined Papa. They whispered together, occasionally looking my way while I gathered the holy book and began reading. I would read until I could repent of my evil ways.

The next morning when I awoke, my hand went to my sore cheek. I outlined the imprint of the Book of Mormon on my face. I hadn't read more than two or three pages before falling asleep. Mama or Papa had turned out the lantern.

"What's wrong, Catie?" Mary clamored to the edge of our bunk.

"I wished I'd read more last night before falling asleep," I confessed.

"Why?"

"Never you mind why." I felt suddenly cross. "Just know that I'll be reading more today to make up for it."

Mary glowered at me and then started to hop off the bed.

"Help your sisters with their hair, ja. It's almost time for morning worship." Mama handed me the brush and some ribbons. I pulled Mary back. After fixing hers and Ana's hair,

I braided mine and donned my bonnet before following Mama and Papa into the cool morning breeze.

Lars appeared to my left. "Good morning." He tipped his cap.

Then, someone brushed against me to my right. I was shocked to see Josef. He didn't look my way, smile or say hello, but only looked ahead. This was a fine predicament. Due to the long hours I spent each day in Josef's company, I couldn't help but notice what an excellent young man he was.

We had a lot in common. He enjoyed a simple life, and we both liked children. In truth, I'd never known another man like Josef. He spent so much time with the girls, and actually got down and played with them. Rare indeed. He had a fine testimony, and like Papa, he wanted to own land in America and till the ground. I liked that.

Staring ahead, I tried to concentrate on Elder Drummond's speech, but before I heard a full sentence, I felt Lars's movement on my left.

Lars was shorter and stockier but exceedingly handsome and fun. We had things in common, too, such as his appreciation for the night sky, and he also had a strong testimony. He liked to take charge of each situation, perhaps a little too forcefully, where Josef was quieter and more reserved.

Lars constantly remarked on my beauty. It made me uncomfortable as I didn't believe myself a beauty, and I knew that good looks should not be given true consideration in choosing a spouse.

I inhaled deeply and tried once again to focus on our morning worship. I needed the spiritual boost. At the sound of my sigh, both men glanced my way, seemingly ready to fulfill my every need. I stared straight ahead.

Josef had never given any indication that he wanted more than friendship. I'd given him the perfect opportunity the other night to kiss me. And he hadn't.

"Up." Ana tugged at my apron.

As I reached down to pick up my little sister, Josef bent down. "Allow me." Our hands touched, and once again I felt an invisible current pass between us. Goosebumps rose on my arm, and I glanced over to see if Josef felt the same. He wore long sleeves, though his lips curved into a smile. What did that mean? I straightened and turned my attention to Elder Clark— when had he started talking?

Josef touched my hand again. Mama would ask too many questions if I left the meeting now—it's what I reasoned as I savored Josef's fingers lingering timidly over mine. I am a wicked, wicked girl, I told myself.

When Lars put his arm casually around my shoulder, I glanced nervously at Josef. He let my hand loose and looked away. Lars smiled reassuringly, somewhat triumphantly. Did Lars know that Josef had held my hand? Not knowing what else to do, I smiled, although I felt frustrated and confused.

As soon as the meeting ended, I scooped Ana from Josef's arms, startling him. I took Mary's hand and rushed away. I was in a fine predicament, indeed. Was I delusional? Was I suffering from cabin fever? These were the only reasons I could muster for thinking Josef would kiss me two nights ago. I had no explanation for his holding my hand just now. What had Elder Clark spoken on? Had Josef thought I needed comforting? If so, I felt far from comforted.

"Where are we going?" Mary demanded.

"I've got to get our book of scripture. Then we're going to get Orla and Engla." I dragged the complaining girls with me to Vestergaards' berth. With them in tow and on the way back outside, we made a long, rushing procession.

"You girls sit here and play nicely while I read."

"We want you to play with us," Mary complained.

"I can't." Frowning at the still standing girls, I made myself cozy and opened the book. "Sit. Play."

Reluctantly the girls sat on deck. Engla put a handkerchief on her head. Orla grabbed it and folded it into two babies in a cradle. Although I pretended not to notice, Ana bent down and looked under a woman's skirt as she walked past. Mary giggled and peeked, too. I grabbed Ana and sat her aright, and then gave the girls a short scolding. Regardless, they made no real effort to play on their own.

"I'm bored." Orla said.

I continued my reading.

All too soon, I noticed Josef's approach from the corner of my eye. He was probably returning from his shift below. My heart fluttered anxiously as he neared, and I knew that I had not read nor repented nearly long enough. I'd been trying to be good by ignoring the girls' pleas to have me join their play and had read ten pages counting the two from last night.

I chewed my bottom lip, concentrating all the harder on my reading, and pretended I didn't see him approach.

"Good morning, girls."

They all rushed to his side in greeting—the traitors.

"Miss Catherine and I have some private matters to discuss. Mary and Orla, could you watch over the younger girls for a moment?"

They both agreed, but I couldn't allow it. "Nej. They cannot be alone." Josef didn't know our danger.

"Your mama is sewing with some other sisters not far off. We'll take them there." With a determined expression, he grabbed Ana up and held her in the crook of his right arm. He took my elbow with his other. "Follow along, girls." Josef nodded to the other three, with me trying to voice a protest as he hurriedly walked to Mama.

A fine predicament. Now Mama would be asking questions, and I swear I had no answers.

Chapter 22

We were aft of the ship in as private a place as possible. I glanced around, regarding the nearby Saints. Though I was sure we were out of earshot, some peered at us from the corner of their eyes. I was not the only one who had a hard time in living the Mormon Creed. Surely I would be the subject of their fine afternoon chat.

Josef loosened his hold on me. "Catherine, tell me what you felt this morning during our services." He studied me, and pulled a loose strand of hair from my face. His green eyes were brilliant this morn. I felt drawn to him, wanting him to hold me once more, but I held still.

"It was a nice worship." Not having heard a word during services, I chewed my lip hoping he wouldn't ask for details.

Upon my reply he rubbed his forehead. His eyes were closed and he looked as if he was thinking of something painful.

I knew what it was—me—caring for him when Lars had announced his intentions. What had gotten into me? Wishing to ease his pain, I stepped toward him and put my hand on his shoulder.

"You needn't worry over me any longer," I whispered. If my desires caused him grief, I wouldn't have them. We were friends, after all. Why had I ruined things by trying to make it more?

He took my hand and held it. A thrill went through me—

an unfortunate response since I'd just vowed to let him be. We were standing close. Too close. I studied every particle of Josef's face as I noticed him studying mine. At the same time, something kept pestering my mind.

Being here, close to Josef, felt so right, and yet seemed so similar to that unfortunate moment not too many days ago. He had put me in my place that night, letting me know by his actions that we were no more than friends.

"There's something that I need to tell you." He took my other hand in his, and held them both. The hairs on my neck prickled. Surely he wouldn't turn me away like he'd done before. Although there were people nearby, I saw only Josef.

"Oh, there you are!"

Startled, I jumped. Josef nearly pushed me over in his effort to distance himself. I was humiliated. Again. I turned to greet Lars's smiling face, and realized that reading God's Word hadn't thwarted my evil ways near enough. I needed to pray harder. I didn't want to hurt Lars. He cared for me in a way that Josef did not.

"Your mama said I could find you here." He scowled at Josef, and then beamed at me. "The girls are aching to go for a walk and I promised to escort you." He linked elbows with me. "Shall we?"

I turned back to address Josef, but he averted his eyes. I stepped away, ashamed. "I'm sorry, truly." I curtsied.

Josef merely wanted to find a nice way to let me down. Although he hadn't quite gotten around to it, I'd count his effort as good and save myself the humiliation of having him spell it out.

"A penny for your thoughts," Lars said.

The sound of his voice startled me. "Pardon?"

"So serious. My bumbling brother didn't upset you, did he?"

"No pennies, I'm only thinking—sorry."

"Don't be sorry." He rushed in front of me, walking backwards and taking my hands. "Only let me be a part of your thoughts—your dreams."

Remembering Josef's hands in mine, I pulled free of Lars and turned away.

My sisters ran forward. "Catie, Catie, let's go for a walk," they called in greeting. I knelt, and scooped them into my embrace. Today I was grateful for this small ship. The scant opportunity for private conversation was an occasional benefit.

"Let me show you something." Lars knelt and showed them a magic trick.

"Do it again," they squealed.

Lars looked up at me and winked. He seemed as capable of entertaining four young girls as Josef. He showed them more tricks, and needless to say, the girls were sad when we returned from our walk. Lars bowed and left us with Mama.

I was glad for the break. Men were exhausting.

"Mama, can I ask a question?" I blurted it out before thinking. What would I ask? Or rather, how could I ask her what to do? I chewed my bottom lip in frustration while trying to decide how to leave unnoticed. I'd changed my mind about the conversation.

"What is it, Princess?" Mama looked up from her embroidery when I didn't reply right away. "Ja?"

"It's nothing, Mama. I'm merely feeling tired." Tired and going crazy from want of privacy. What I wouldn't give for a green field to wander in, to be alone, to think uninterrupted, or to smell wild flowers. The luxury.

Tending Orla and Engla had helped me focus on someone other than John. I'd recovered, or mostly recovered. But now my problems lay with Josef and Lars. They were both good choices. Lars would make a fine husband, so why did I long for Josef when he kept pushing me away?

If I spurned Lars, would anyone marry me, or would I end up alone like Mary had predicted? I did care for Lars, and it was pure foolishness to reject the hand of a worthy suitor. Papa would not approve. But if I did marry him when I didn't love him—it seemed dishonest. It felt like a betrayal to John to marry someone I didn't fully love, when I'd rejected him for that very reason.

With a gleam of pure inspiration, Mama said, "You've been such a good help lately. Why don't you take some time just to be Catherine again for a while?"

"Oh, Mama, thank you. I do need some time alone."

I hurried away, wondering how to make the best use of private minutes alone. I needed time away from Josef and Lars. Oh, and away from nosy sailors. A couple of them stared down at me from above.

Because of its thick, dank air, we seldom stayed below during daylight hours. I would be safe there. We still used guards to protect our belongings, and best of all, no one would think to look for me below.

I glanced about to make sure no one saw me then I sauntered to the hatch and raced down the stairs. Again, watching for the guards and making sure no one saw me, I sneaked to my berth and climbed onto the paper-thin mattress. Heaven.

Sitting up and pressing myself into the corner, I wrapped the blanket over my legs and intended to read the Holy Scriptures. The book lay open in front of me. I closed my eyes instead, and my mind wandered to our farm back home. I loved our fields of alfalfa and their pretty purple blossoms. I pictured myself there, running and twirling with Berta like we enjoyed doing just before harvest.

Someone stood in the distance. He waved, and I waved back. My heart quickened as he drew near—he had auburn hair. Josef. We embraced, and he kissed me. I melted into his arms, wishing to stay there forever. My cheeks warmed with pleasure.

"I have loved you since Denmark. Will you marry me?"

I heard him speak the longed for words, but curiously, his lips didn't move. However, I responded immediately, "I will."

Josef frowned and stepped aside. Lars came forward then, and put a ring on my finger.

Startled, I gasped aloud, and then snapping back into reality, I grabbed the Holy Scriptures.

After having read chapter after chapter of scripture, I felt even more confused and frustrated than ever. Perhaps they didn't contain guidance for someone such as me.

I climbed the stairs to the dining hall, ate, wished I knew what to do, returned to our berth with Mama and Papa, brushed Mary's hair and braided it, all while worrying how to behave if I bumped into Lars or Josef at the social.

"Mama, let me stay here with the girls. You and Papa should go to the social alone." Mama glanced up from brushing her hair and considered me with suspicion, so I continued, "Please, let me do this for you."

"I think it's a wonderful idea." Papa squeezed forward, grabbed Mama around the waist and hugged her tight.

"Now, Papa. Behave yourself." Mama smiled as she swatted at him.

"I am behaving." Papa twirled Mama and himself together. Then he leaned in and kissed her.

Mary and Ana giggled. Embarrassed, I turned my gaze away. But because of my parents' tomfoolery, I got to stay and didn't have to deal with the two Hansen brothers.

"Tell us a story, Catie." Ana jumped onto my lap.

"Okay." I pulled the blankets up and tucked the girls in, settling into our berth beside them. "Which one?"

"The mermaid, the mermaid," Ana and Mary chanted.

I recounted the stories of "The Little Mermaid," "The Ugly Duckling," and "Little Tiny" before the girls were finally both asleep. With my arms tucked under my head, I stared at the ceiling, feeling contented, and listened to the ship's sounds.

Music floated through the cracks in the wood, lending wing to my comfortable mood. I thought of Lars and Josef wondering where I was. Being away from them for the afternoon and evening had done me some good, although I had a feeling I shouldn't slack on my prayers regarding them.

"You're looking mighty cozy tonight." Bishop Iversen stood beside me, smiling sardonically.

"It is you." I sat up. "It's been you all along. The hunger aboard ship is at your hand." I kept my voice low and pretended to be brave.

"Not me." He leaned against a support beam. "I'm known as the 'Good Bishop.' Anything else is your word against mine." He pushed off of the beam and leaned forward. "I just came to reiterate my previous warning." One of his eyebrows rose. "Mind the Mormon Creed, or your days may well be numbered."

"I've done nothing wrong. You wouldn't dare harm me," I hissed, not feeling the least bit sure.

"It's not me you need worry about, miss. I don't care much for violence, never have. Just heed my warning. Remember the Creed."

"What do you mean?" I asked. I hadn't done anything wrong. Yet it was too late—he had disappeared.

I backed up against my sisters and peered into the darkness. My plans of spending the night in thoughtful contemplation were ruined. I found myself unable to do more than shake under the covers. Not the kind of shivers that come from the cold—no, these originated deep inside my soul.

But I could find solace in reading the Holy Scriptures.

We kept the lantern lights down low in the evenings to spare the oil. The second and third decks below were a shadowy haze with barely light enough to ensure safety in moving about. But I needed inspiration. Although the girls beside me were sleeping, I reached for the lantern near our berth and twisted the knob that allowed the light to shine a little brighter.

Turning through Papa's book of scripture, I opened to Alma chapter five. Desperate for knowledge and comfort, I began. In this chapter, the prophet Alma admonished the people to repent. As I read, "... whosoever bringeth forth evil works, the same becometh a child of the devil...." my mind turned to the man who called himself bishop. "... And whosoever doeth this must receive his wages of him...."

That's fine. The bishop needed punishment. But what could I do? If my parents wouldn't listen, if John wouldn't believe me when he'd been there, how could I get anyone else to believe? The Lord needed to show me the right thing to do. I read on. "... I have fasted and prayed many days that I might know these things...."

After reading this passage again and again, I put the book in a little cubby and began pondering my situation. What could I do—what should I do? I didn't know for certain the bishop had stolen the money from the Saints. Nonetheless, he was in cahoots with the sailors. They wouldn't threaten me without reason.

But ponder as I might, I couldn't come up with any safe solution to my dilemma. For now, I could do only one thing: fast and pray as the Holy Scriptures had admonished. Mary and Ana were bundled too closely for me to get out of bed and kneel, so I folded my arms and closed my eyes.

Chapter 23

"Sister Vestergaard has delivered her baby!" "It's a girl! It's a girl!" The exciting news reverberated all through the ship. It was good news to be sure.

"Your mama had her baby." I squeezed Orla and Engla into a hug. "Let's go see!" Excited for something happy to brighten this ever-monotonous voyage, I took hold of the girls and we rushed to the Vestergaards' berth to see their new little sister.

Sister Thompsen was there, wiping Sister Vestergaard's brow. Brother Vestergaard paced, his hat wrenched between his hands, a look of pure agony on his face.

I skidded to a stop. This was not the joyous occasion that I'd imagined.

Sister Thompsen looked up. "If she hadn't been in such poor health during her pregnancy," she murmured.

Brother Vestergaard saw Orla and Engla, and sat at the foot of the bunk, motioning for his girls.

Engla crawled onto her papa's lap. He kissed her forehead. "Meet your baby sister." He reached down and stroked the baby's face. "Your mama worked so hard to bring her here."

I knelt down to help Mary and Ana get a better look. The baby was cradled between Sister Vestergaard and the bed.

Little Lila as they named her, had such a tiny body, smaller than any baby I'd ever seen before. A sob caught in my throat. I touched her tiny fingers—I'd seen earthworms bigger around—

and marveled at how perfectly they were formed. Yet Lila was weak, her little arms limp. She didn't seem to have enough energy to cry.

Orla kissed the baby's cheek. "I love you," she whispered.

Engla crawled off her Papa's lap and repeated Orla's expression of love.

"Can I hold her?" Orla asked.

"Nej, child." Brother Vestergaard pulled her into his embrace. "Let's give her a chance to recover from being born." His voice seemed to catch, and he held Orla tight. "Papa loves you."

The baby's health was not good, yet Sister Vestergaard appeared worse, having used all of her strength in delivery. She lay limp and pale. Brother Vestergaard proved a devoted husband and never left her side. He took a damp rag and wiped the perspiration from his wife's face.

"Sleep, my love, and wake rested on the morrow." He brushed his wife's hair and kissed her cheek.

Unable to bear such a sight, I grabbed Orla and Engla, and rushed with the four girls to the companionway. They struggled to keep up with me as I bounded up the stairs, but I didn't stop until we had arrived on deck.

"You'll be good here, ja?" I settled the girls down where they wouldn't be in anyone's way.

"Mama!" I ran to her. "Did you see the baby?"

Mama nodded. "It is so sad. The baby will not survive and it's doubtful that Sister Vestergaard will either."

"Is there nothing we can do?"

"We can always pray, but I've never seen a mother or child in such poor health who survived."

"Oh." I started to turn away, my vision already blurring.

"Princess, it's especially important that you keep the girls away from their berth." Mama squeezed my shoulders. "Entertain them and keep an eye on them until eve. Ja?"

Unable to speak, I nodded and took my place beside the girls. We played until later that day, when in subdued silence, Mama came.

"Catherine, it is time for the girls to go back to their parents."

"Mama?" I wanted to ask if the baby had not survived, but my voice caught and I could not bring myself to ask in front of the girls.

Mama took Orla's hand and led the way. I didn't want to follow, but Mama expected me to bring Engla. When we arrived below, the girls rushed into their papa's arms. He clung to them, sobbing.

Sister Vestergaard, still so weak, clung to her recently departed infant.

"I'm so sorry," sobbed Brother Vestergaard. "You wanted to hold your little sister. I should have let you, and now it is too late."

Orla looked over at her mother and the infant. "Can I hold her now?" she whispered.

"Ja, ja." Brother Vestergaard guided Orla and Engla to their mother. "Hold your little sister, Lila, and tell her goodbye."

They snuggled into their mother and kissed her on the forehead. Engla patted her mama's cheek lovingly. Sister

Vestergaard carefully laid the swaddled baby into Orla's waiting arms.

"Where is Lila going?" asked Orla.

"She's going to heaven to live with God," murmured Brother Vestergaard.

I did not want to witness this scene but Mama held fast to my hand.

"Mama, Lila's color is wrong." Orla peered at the infant, and touched her face.

"Nonsense, her color is perfect," assured Sister Vestergaard in a broken whisper.

I could see the infant and I agreed with Orla. The baby's color was all wrong.

"Why doesn't she open her eyes?" Orla sounded confused.

"Orla, Engla, you must listen to Papa." He took the infant, and placed her with his wife.

I didn't want to stay—I couldn't. If I did, I would soon die myself.

"Catherine." Mama expected me to stay with her and help, but I couldn't.

I stepped back, looking to her for permission to be excused, and saw Orla and Engla crawling onto their papa's lap. Mama's lips pursed in disappointment, but she nodded and I tore myself away.

In an effort to be polite, I took slow steps at first but I gasped for air, feeling as though my heart was being ripped open. Soon my steps turned quick. I sprinted through the maze of narrow aisles on the second deck below. The steps took me to fresh air. I bolted up them and ran onto the deck.

Pushing through the others, I searched for solitude, and finally stopped at the place aft of the ship where Josef had taken me to talk. I crumpled to the ground and gasped great gulps of air while releasing my sorrow.

"Why?" I moaned. "Why did she have to die?"

It wasn't fair for the baby to be taken away. The Vestergaards were good people. I didn't understand why such a horrible thing had happened. Yet, Mama had lost some babies. I was younger then, like Orla, and hadn't fully understood. Mama hadn't been sick like Sister Vestergaard, but her babies were taken nonetheless. How did she cope? How could Mama stay there and help when she knew the sorrow of losing an infant?

Someone stood beside me, but I continued grieving. Eventually that person knelt down and put an arm around me. It was comforting, but I didn't open my eyes to discover his or her identity.

How long I lay on deck tormented by the unfairness of life, I did not know. However, I could not quit my crying. My tears and anguish persisted until I had no strength to continue.

Then, with little encouragement and after taking one long, gasping breath, I settled into his lap. Snuggled against his chest, I felt quite at ease while these male arms, possibly Papa's, wrapped themselves around me. My bonnet constricted, so I untied it.

I rested.

It had been a long while since I'd felt so unburdened, and I soon became conscious of him stroking my hair. Not ready to open my eyes, I enjoyed the sensation. As a small child, Papa stroked my hair while telling me bedtime stories. Yet, in my subconscious I felt this person, my comforter, was not Papa.

He bent over and kissed my forehead. At last I forced my eyes open, curious to see the face of compassion.

"How long have I been here?" I asked, the heat of embarrassment warming my face.

"Not long." Josef brushed a wisp of hair from my cheek.

My blush deepened, and I worked my way off his lap. The sun appeared considerably lower in the sky. Josef had stayed with me for well over an hour. If I stayed longer, I'd probably try to make more of his kindness than he intended, and I could not endure the pain of his thrusting me from his arms once again.

Chapter 24

"Mama, why do these bad things keep happening to me?" I took two stitches of embroidery and looked up waiting for her answer.

"Princess, these things have not happened to you." Mama frowned. "Lila's death is for the Vestergaards to mourn, not you." I started to protest, but she continued. "It is sad, ja, and we can feel sympathy for them, but this is not your tragedy."

"But John—"

"Nej, he was not yours to mourn either." Mama's eyebrows lifted. "You know it is true." She finished stitching a beautiful daisy and knotted it off. "We all cared for Brother Rasmussen. He was a good man, ja, but you have grieved enough over a man you did not love."

"But I did," I insisted.

"Catherine, what are you to do?" Mama put her sewing down. "Will you throw yourself into a tizzy each time someone you know passes on? What about the gospel? What about these people going home to their God in Heaven?"

I knew about all of these things, but I did not feel comforted. "Mama, I prayed for John. Why didn't my prayers work? Why can't I keep the people I care for safe through my prayers? Isn't my faith strong enough?"

"Of course you have faith." Mama's countenance softened. "And it's served you well so far." She put her hands on my shoulders and held my gaze. "Your faith gave you the strength to end your relationship with Isaac. Your faith gave you the strength to leave Denmark and join our voyage to America. I know you didn't want to."

I ducked my head, embarrassed that Mama knew the truth, but she squeezed me into a hug.

"Our faith helps us through trials, Princess. It doesn't prevent them."

Mama believed in me. This gave me great relief. If she said I had faith, then I did. I smiled in appreciation.

"It's a hard thing to grow into womanhood and have to live so many hard life lessons," she said. "John was a good man, but you know he is happy with his wife now, so why do you still mourn him? And, as sorry as we are that the Vestergaards lost their baby, we know that at least the little dear isn't suffering, and that she will be reunited with her parents one day.

"You are young and should not let yourself get bogged down each time something bad happens. You need to move on now, be happy. There is plenty of life left for you to live. Open your heart and let love find you."

I didn't know if love would find me. I'd prayed for it but didn't know if I could ever have true love for myself. Nor did I believe that I deserved true love. Even if I did, I didn't desire coming between brothers, and I didn't desire to cause either of them pain. Nor did Mama understand that finding love was probably not the worst of my problems. I nodded and walked away deep in thought.

My wise Mama never complained about anything. I would try to be more like her—which meant no more moping.

Talking with Mama gave me an idea. I shouldn't sit around and wait for my fate. I needed to do something about Mr. Iversen and those dangerous sailors. It wouldn't be sensible to worry Mama, but I could possibly discuss the matter with Elder Clark at the social. He always presided. I could take him aside for a chat without drawing any suspicion to my motives—especially since the crew never socialized with us. The bishop, if he came, would be visiting with a group of women as always.

"Miss Catherine." Lars tipped his cap and bowed with a flourish.

Unsure of whether to be happy or sad at his appearance, I merely curtsied in greeting.

"A ship off port side!" a sailor shouted.

"Let's go see it." Lars slipped his hand into mine and led the way. Many of the other Saints had also gathered around to see it. When Lars pushed our way to the front and I saw the vessel, I knew why.

My eyes widened in amazement. "I've never seen anything so large."

"I read a book on modern ships of the world," responded Lars. "Before us is the most outlandish invention of modern times. It's called the *Great Eastern.*"

"The *Great Eastern?*"

"Ja, ja, it's the largest luxury liner in the world. It's also known as Brunel's folly."

"What do you mean?"

"The ship was the brain-child of a man by the name of Brunel." Lars secured his arm around me as he talked. "It combines all of the newest technology and can run on steam with paddle wheels. It's also driven by sixteen-hundred-horse-power engines and as you can see, it also has sails. However, weighing in at over 22 tons, it's much too large to be practical." Lars leaned closer and murmured. "The poor girl has had one disaster after another."

I couldn't help but be intrigued and impressed by his knowledge on the subject.

"The ship is so large, it's rumored they accidentally sealed one of the workers inside its double hull—alive." He stopped for effect and nodded his head. "People have actually heard him clanging and trying to get out."

"How could something like that happen?" It sounded horrifying.

"No one knows." Lars shook his head sadly. "Only the ship's been doomed since its construction. One of the times when they tried to set sail, a large explosion in the boiler room killed five workers. When Mr. Brunel heard the news, it upset him so much that he had a sudden heart attack and died."

"That's horrible!" I shuddered at the tale.

"Mr. Brunel died a broken man and his financial backers cursed the day they got involved with him." Lars stood behind me and rubbed my arms.

"The ship doesn't look cursed." It did, however, look big enough for someone to get lost inside its walls. Although we were some distance away, I imagined that I could see passengers lounging on deck, drinking and laughing. They probably had lots of room, and I wondered if perhaps the Danish island, Langeland, could fit within the vessel, but that was absurd.

"The ship's backers are probably trying to regain some of their losses by catering to the wealthy. Maybe they're going to Denmark," he mused.

I waved to the passengers. Could they see me?

Others also cheered at the sight of the mighty ship, waving and shouting in a futile effort to gain the attention of those aboard. Yet I felt sorrow for the extravagances that had gone into the building of such a monstrosity as the *Great Eastern* and felt that, indeed, the name Brunel's Folly was a fitting title.

"Come with me." Lars led me through the crowd of Saints to the other side of the ship. When we stopped, he brought my hands to his lips and kissed them.

Embarrassed that he would do such a thing in the light of

day, I looked around to see if anyone watched. At the same time, I wondered if he was the one I should open my heart to.

"I missed you last night." He started kissing my fingers one by one. Unnerved by this, I pulled my hands away and put them behind my back.

"Mama asked me to stay with Mary and Ana again." It was a lie, of sorts. I had asked once again to be left in solitude.

"I'll need to have a talk with your mother." Lars stepped forward, causing me to step backward until I discovered myself backed against the bridge of the ship. "Mmm, I've got you right where I want you." He growled playfully and kissed my cheek.

It seemed wrong for him to kiss me in public like that, and I felt at that moment as though he didn't respect me. Could a person use another for their own pleasure and still claim to respect them? And yet, if a person loved another, couldn't they kiss that person even in the daylight?

We were in a relatively secluded area. I remembered Mama's words again, Open your heart to love.

"I'm having the hardest time keeping my promise to wait until we reach America to propose," he murmured into my ear.

I wanted to heed Mama's word and open my heart to love. Still, I couldn't be sorry myself. I needed as long as possible to sort out my feelings. He leaned forward and nuzzled into my neck.

"Mama needs my help today." I scooted sideways and away from his attentions. "I must return to her." I stepped away.

"Must you leave?" He pulled me back and gave me a boyish pout.

"Ja, ja. Orla and Engla are spending the day with their parents." Mary and Ana tended to get a little bothersome when bored.

Lars walked me back without further complaint. When we reached Mama, he bowed politely. "I hope to see you at the social this night." He looked at Mama while he spoke.

Her lips pressed together, and she nodded once.

The girls and I gathered other playmates and played a twirling game. However, Mary bumped into an older woman. She asked me to kindly control my sister. We held hands and weaved our way through the maze of other passengers. We were still giggling over the woman's scowl when we accidentally bumped into Josef.

"Oh. I am sorry." I stepped back, but the other children bumped into me before they stopped, and I lost my balance.

Josef wrapped his arms around me. All my senses came alive for one brief moment.

"Good afternoon." He grinned as he put me straight and held me away from his body.

"Ja, ja." My heartbeat quickened, and I ran away with the girls in hand, angry with my traitorous heart.

Chapter 25

"Brothers and Sisters, it is with deep sadness I inform you of the death of our dear and beloved Sister Grette Vestergaard." Elder Drummond clutched his hat in front of his person. It was he who had first brought them the gospel message. "Her services will be tomorrow. For the present, Brother Vestergaard has asked that we continue on with our social, and so to honor his wishes, we will. However, let us spend a moment in silent prayer and contemplation before we begin the night's pleasantries."

After the benediction, the Saints started down the stairs. We waited while Papa visited with Elder Drummond. What would Orla and Engla do now? They must be grief stricken. Although I didn't know Sister Vestergaard well, I did know her children and was devastated for them. How could they go on without a Mama?

Without my permission, one tear and then another fell. I hated this watery life. Mama hurried over and comforted me in her arms. Before long I noticed Papa as well, and rushed into the security of his embrace.

After a moment, I remembered my promise and took a deep breath. I refused to be whiney or morose any longer. Pulling away from Mama and Papa, I wiped away my tears. "I'll be fine." I clasped their hands in reassurance, but I felt vulnerable.

"Catie, come dance with us." Mary tugged at my skirt.

"In a moment," I said. However, I could not make my feet move.

What if Lars disregarded me on this night? What if Josef continued pushing me away? I glanced at Mr. Iversen waiting his turn to descend the steps. "Miss Erichsen." He tipped his hat.

I refused to acknowledge him. He had threatened me several times in my berth while I tended Mary and Ana. How could he threaten me and then dote over the Saints in his care as he did?

"Catie, come now." Mary tugged my skirt. Ana clung to my leg.

"Ja, ja." The music began, but I didn't feel like dancing.

So far, I hadn't been able to convince myself to love Lars any better than I'd been able to convince myself with John. Having him behave as my beau when I didn't share his feelings was torture. If only I loved Lars the way he wished me to.

I should be fearful of going unassisted to my berth, yet that was precisely my desire. Solitude.

I tapped Mama on the shoulder. "I would like to tell stories to the girls in our berth instead of dance." I looked pleadingly at Mama.

"But we want to dance," complained Mary.

"Brother Vestergaard has asked that we continue in joy." Mama's eyebrows rose.

"Please." I gave her a look of desperation.

"Nej, Princess. You have spent far too long grieving for others. It's time you learn to live for yourself."

"Hooray!" Mary and Ana bounced up and down.

I took my sisters' hands and the three of us went to the social, dancing on the sidelines, and watching the others.

I stole a glimpse of Josef, wishing it was he with whom I danced. I caught him watching me and didn't know what to make of it. Yet no sooner did I look than he glanced away, making me question if I'd seen correctly. I should not have run off when he comforted me after Lila's death. I should have thanked him for his help.

After the girls and I danced for a while, I remembered my resolve to seek out Elder Clark and discuss with him the sailors and Mr. Iversen. Who pretended to be a bishop? Why would he do such a thing? I scanned the room but didn't see Elder Clark anywhere. He could be comforting Brother Vestergaard.

Mr. Iversen was talking to a small group of women. They seemed to be having a merry time. I had noticed that about the man. He worked expertly at covering his iniquitous heart with lots of happy chat and offerings of help.

I made sure Mama and Papa were in sight. "I need to go on an errand," I told the girls. "The two of you stay here and be good until my return." I slipped away amid their protests while pretending I didn't see Lars approaching from the other direction.

Hurrying down the corridor toward the Vestergaards' berth, I hoped I'd been correct in assuming Elder Clark would be there. It wasn't proper for me to interrupt such an occasion, but I needed to talk to him without drawing attention to myself.

I needn't have worried because as I drew closer to the Vestergaards, I saw Elder Clark approach and hastened to greet him.

"Elder Clark."

"Yes?" He stopped and waited for me to continue. Suddenly I felt nervous. I wanted to talk to him—I needed to talk to him—my mouth opened and closed while I tried figuring out how to begin.

Before I had a chance to utter a word, a hand grabbed hold of my arm. I gasped, surprised, and turned to see who had handled me. To my horror, Mr. Iversen stood beside me. He gave a brief glance of warning. My heart jumped into my throat, and I gulped.

"Elder Clark." He tipped his head in courtesy. "Don't worry yourself over this girl's complaints. I've been counseling with her myself."

"I'm sure I don't understand, Bishop." Elder Clark reached out and shook his hand.

Then, still holding my arm with his left hand, he moved closer to Elder Clark and murmured, "She's misguided at best and terribly distraught over the loss of Brother Rasmussen, the infant, and now our dear Sister Vestergaard. Whatever she might have said could only be a fabrication due to grief."

"Yes?"

I started to struggle, and opened my mouth to protest. Mr. Iversen cut me off with his lies.

"Yes. And her sisters, they're a constant worry. They've almost fallen overboard twice. It's difficult keeping curious girls such as those in check."

His mention of my sisters made my knees go weak. Mr. Iversen's vise-like grip kept me standing.

"Elder Clark, I assure you that all is well here." He smiled patronizingly at me and then making a show of letting go, he patted my shoulder and linked arms with me before I could stop him. "I know you are expected at the social, and we wouldn't want to keep the good Saints waiting." Mr. Iversen bowed. "I'll go ahead and escort this poor lass to her parents." He then hurried me away.

"Now, dear." His smile changed to a sneer. He nodded his control of the situation by glancing at my arm. "Let's not bother Elder Clark with your problems any longer. Why don't we go to a private corner and I'll pray with you."

I looked desperately, helplessly for a familiar face and was disheartened to discover no one. It seemed that everyone, out of respect for Brother Vestergaard, had gone to visit and dance. In a moment of misguided inspiration, I stomped on his foot and pulled myself free, but Mr. Iversen regained control and shook me unmercifully.

"Stop, you're hurting me." I tried wrestling away again, but he held tight.

"Listen here," he growled, "I see the Mormon Creed means nothing to you, so I'll have to teach you another. It's called 'family first.' I'd hate for one of your little sisters to accidentally fall into the ocean."

"You wouldn't!" I shivered and hoped my eyes didn't betray my alarm. "If you hurt my sisters, I'll—"

"You'll what?" he challenged. "Do you think for a moment that anyone on board will trust the rantings of a poor girl, delirious with grief, over my word? Ha! I think not."

With me in hand, he stormed up the steps and out into the cool night air.

"Please!" I begged, "Please let me go!"

There were a few people on deck; some knew him and nodded a greeting. He pretended to console me. And in truth I was hysterical. They probably felt I could use a good talking to.

We were near the ship's edge—too near—with my body pinned against the bulwark. He had pushed me backward until I leaned precariously over the side. Upon glancing down to the frigid water below, I closed my eyes and uttered a silent prayer for my safety. I shuddered at the thought of receiving my own, premature, burial at sea.

"I'll tell you what's going to happen," he growled. "I don't want to hurt you, but test me again and I will. It's only at my doing you've remained safe from Pierre and Louie this long." He glared at me. With a shrug of his shoulders he continued. "I'm going to show my good faith by letting you go, and to prove to you that it's not my desire to bring harm to anyone. In return, you'll tell no one your suspicions. You don't really know anything for certain, do you?"

I shook my head, terrified.

"I thought not." The corner of his lip curled up into a sneer. "Now, if I see you talking to Elder Clark or if you talk to anyone about this matter ..." He shook his head, his eyes sorrowful. "I've been planning this for a long time now. Much too long. I'll be parting company with the Saints as soon as we get to America. You can wait that long before turning in Pierre and Louie, can't you? I'm going to start up my own business. This is the only way."

Seeming to snap back into his evil mood, he shook me. "Now, I suggest you go back to your berth," he snapped. "Spend some quiet time, soul searching." He let me free then. Without looking back, I rushed away thanking my Lord with every step.

Chapter 26

My heart pounded. My breath heaved from me, and I held to my wooden berth as though it kept me safe. But I wasn't safe. Not alone, not ever. I straightened my hair and dress so as not to cause alarm and stumbled back into the social to get my sisters. Mama would be upset that I left them.

Josef was there, as usual, playing for everyone's enjoyment. I kept my gaze toward the floor, unable to look at him for fear I may break down and cry.

Lars, once again, had not spent much time without a dance partner. He appeared to be enjoying himself with Ester. She saw me enter the room and winked at me. Perhaps it was all for the best.

Mama expected me to be upset because of Sister Vestergaard's passing. She regarded me accordingly, and in truth, I must have looked frightful. My heart still hadn't settled to its normal rhythm.

"That Lars Hansen has asked about you, as have several other worthy suitors," said Mama. "The social is nearly over, however, and the girls are tired. You may as well take them to bed."

This I was glad to do.

Amid my worries that night, I fell into a fitful sleep with the image of Mr. Iversen pushing me overboard and the echo of his menacing laugh.

I gasped awake. It was still dark with night. Quiet whimpering, the creaking of the ship, the animals' lowing all joined together like an out of tune chorus. Each new noise startled me until a notion entered my mind. I had been awakened for a reason—the bishop would not continue to let me be. Now was the time to act.

My heart pounded, and I hesitated, praying for the strength to achieve my goal. I slipped from bed, dressed, wrapped my woolen shawl around my shoulders, and crept away. The footsteps of sailors could be heard above. I knew to be quiet so as not to alert them, or anyone, to my activity. A baby cried in the night. Worried parents shushed. Sneaking past unnoticed, I made my way to the bow of the ship and toward Elder Clark's berth.

An unfamiliar sound startled me and I glanced into the blackness. Shivers of apprehension prickled my neck. I couldn't tell if someone was following me, but I could not turn back. I hurried a little faster, determined not to return to my berth until I'd talked to Elder Clark. The creaking continued as well. Was it me? Was Bishop Iversen lurking nearby? I could not tell. All I knew was each time I stopped, so did the sound.

I hugged close to the side of the ship, moving cautiously as I hastened through narrow passageways, and hoped I wasn't seen. I stopped and listened again. The sound stopped. Was there a noise separate from the creaking of the ship? I took another step forward, my heart pounding. In echo, the sound persisted.

I peered in a berth. This was not Elder Clark's sleeping quarters. Frantic, I peered in the next, and the next. He was in none of them. I thought I knew his whereabouts, yet I had no idea. Did he sleep below with the Saints or somewhere near the captain's quarters? I closed my eyes, rubbed my temples and tried clearing my mind of fear so I could think.

The thought came. I should go above and test the sound. If it followed, it was of human origin. I crept up the stairs and out into the moonless night.

I looked up. A sailor on the rigging stared my way. Why had I come out here? This was not safe. I didn't know what to do and began to panic. Once again I had put myself in a foolish situation. If I started back down the stairs I might come upon Mr. Iversen. If I stayed above, those evil sailors might find me—alone.

A silent prayer soared heavenward from my heart. I needed safety and to know what to do. Then, franticly feeling my way around, I tried to decide the right course of action. The noise still accompanied me. This was not the innocent rocking of the ship. Someone was following.

Some crates were nearby. I slid between them and waited. The creaking noises came closer and stopped right in front of my hiding spot.

I gasped. "It's you! Why are you following me?" Pulling myself out of hiding, I stood before the person who confused and irritated me with each breath he took.

"I might ask you the same question." Josef lifted his eyebrows. "Why are you sneaking about in the middle of the night?" His hands went into his pockets. "It's not safe for a woman alone. That's why we've set our own guards out."

"What I'm doing is none of your business." The faint sound of a baby crying reminded me of the need to whisper.

"You should leave now." I waved him away with my hand. "Go back to bed."

"Go ahead." He stood firm and swept his arm dramatically for me to take the lead. "I'll not leave you wandering around in the middle of the night by yourself. It's dangerous! What would your parents say if I allowed harm to come to you?"

"Oh, honestly." I folded my arms across my chest. There

was no getting around this situation.

Upon hearing another creak, the possible footsteps of another, yet less harmless immigrant, I grabbed Josef's arm. "Be quiet—someone's coming."

He followed, and we crawled into a crevice between the crates. The creaking sound stopped. I wanted to peek but didn't dare.

If someone came, we could still be seen. I scooted back until I was leaning against the furthermost crate. Then I tugged at Josef, who moved silently toward me. As he did, the image of Mr. Iversen came to view. He looked to the right and to the left, and then he peered into the crates, straining to see.

I froze with terror, not even daring to breathe for fear of being discovered.

Mr. Iversen turned and stood in front of our only exit. "It's a fine night for mischief," he said.

"There'll be no mischief aboard this ship. Your Saints are too suspicious. Guards are everywhere." I recognized this voice. It was one of the sailors who had accosted me.

"Yes, it's a pity you won't get more—deserving men like yourself."

"We're here to discuss the girl—the feisty young wench we found lookin' through our belongings." This sounded like the other blackguard.

"You needn't worry yourselves about her," Mr. Iversen said. "I've seen to the girl myself. She'll not talk."

I felt Josef's accusing stare. Surely he knew they were talking about me. If so, he must wonder what madness befell me. I was ashamed and cast my eyes downward, thankful for the darkness.

"My sources tell me the lass has already tried speaking with your leader, Mr. Clark. I'll not be risking the brig or my life because of your cowardice in removing the threat."

"I've harassed her sufficiently." Mr. Iversen placed his arm on the sailor's shoulder. "The girl is scared out of her wits. She'll not be talking. I give my word."

"We won't be trusting the word of a lily-livered bloke like you."

"It's for your benefit that I don't harm her," Mr. Iversen replied vehemently. "Should something happen, I fear that her parents would cause a great upheaval. Captain would be forced to search the ship. If I go down, I'm pulling you with me."

"We don't go for threats around these parts," the man growled.

"And I would never stoop to using them on my fine cohorts. This is merely a gentleman's agreement. It's worked for us so far. Let's not be getting hasty, there's such a short time left before this is all over."

"Indeed. You'll be getting your wish with the young wench, for now. But if we get word of anything more, both you and the girl might be a-findin' yourselves tryin' to swim ashore." The sailors turned and walked away. Bishop Iversen straightened his vest, looking nervously about. Then he hurried in the opposite direction.

"What is the meaning of their conversation—and why are you hiding here?" Josef implored.

"I'm in trouble and don't know what to do." I choked out the whispered words. With my face in my hands, I took deep breaths to calm my racing heart. What would I do?

"Let me help." Josef put his hand on my shoulder.

"I can't." I shook my head without looking up. "I can't let anyone help me." The combination of fear and the chilly pre-dawn air caused me to shake uncontrollably.

Josef fussed with my shawl, snuggling it tight around me.

"I tried telling Elder Clark. Mr. Iversen caught me and almost threw me overboard. He's threatened me if I speak. If you get involved, he'll do the same with you." I felt helpless. I looked at him, but in his eyes I saw strength.

Had the Lord sent Josef to help me? With that thought in mind, I continued. "This burden is too great for me to carry by myself." Closing my eyes, I shook my head, and rested against his shoulder. "I just don't know what to do. No path seems to be the one to keep me and my family safe from harm."

"Let me share your burden. I'm here and I'm willing. Allow me to help." Josef put his hands on my shoulders. "Catie, you must trust me."

I savored the way my sisters' nickname for me sounded on his tongue. After a moment's hesitation, I shared with Josef my predicament—of being discovered in the crew's quarters—overhearing Mr. Iversen as he talked to Pierre and Louie—discovering that Mr. Iversen was not even a bishop.

"He's taken their money, I know he has. And I don't believe he's a true bishop." I looked upon Josef and trusted him with my life. I needed him to believe me. Josef remained still, but I continued. "Tonight, I woke from my sleep. Thinking the Lord had awakened me to go undetected on this dark night, I arose to find Elder Clark, but I got lost." I heaved a shuddering breath. "He probably won't believe me. Mr. Iversen said he wouldn't. He said no one would."

"I believe you." Josef stroked my cheek with his thumb and brought his forehead to meet mine.

A loud creak stopped our whispering and I wondered if Mr. Iversen or one of the sailors was still on the lookout. We waited, breathless, listening, yet no one materialized.

"It's too dangerous for you to attempt a meeting with Elder Clark," Josef whispered. "I will go."

"Nej, I cannot put your life in danger." I would die if harm came to Josef, my protector—my love—but I knew he didn't think of me that way.

"Catie—"

"Nej." I put my fingers to his mouth. "I will pray about it and give my answer on the morrow."

He nodded solemnly and started to back out of the crevice. My fingers still tingled from the feel of his lips when I reached forward and touched his arm. "I'm afraid."

"I would not have harm come to you." He clasped my hands in his. "It is better to resolve this quickly. I'll expect to hear from you as soon as possible. Don't worry. I'll not let anything happen to you or your family." He climbed out of the crevice and lent me a hand, pulling me up. "Let me take you to your family before one of them awakens and discovers you missing."

Josef took my hand in his, and we walked quietly along the shadows and back to my berth.

"Thank you." I leaned in and gave him an awkward hug. "We will talk tomorrow, ja?"

"Ja, but I have duties tomorrow and will be busy after morning worship. I'll meet up with you in the afternoon."

"Don't speak to anyone about this unless I tell you. Promise?"

"I swear it. I'll wait for your word before talking to Elder Clark. No one will be suspicious since I talk to Elder Clark regularly and play with your sisters almost every day."

"Your kindness tonight has meant the world to me."

Josef started walking away then turned back, seeming to convince himself of something. He took my hand, kissed it, and bowed. "Till morning," he said.

I watched, dumbfounded, as he slipped away.

Chapter 27

My parents and I stepped on deck with Mary and Ana, and joined ourselves with the other Saints awaiting morning worship. I inhaled the crisp, salty air, feeling invigorated.

Elder Clark stepped onto a crate. "Good Morning, Brothers and Sisters," he said. "It's time to begin."

Lars pushed through the crowd to my right. "Good morning," he murmured, smiling.

No sooner had I returned his greeting than Josef pressed beside me on my left, pulling Ana from my grasp as he did so. "Josef!" she cheered, and patted his cheeks.

The woman in front of me turned with a glare. This felt a little too familiar, too similar to our previous worship service. I squirmed.

Before I could even think of what to do it seemed, Ester appeared from the throng of Saints and slipped to Lars' right. "Good morning," she said.

"Good morning," I greeted, my chest feeling tight.

Sister Andersdatter stood on a crate to lead us in song. Ester was a good fit for Lars, I decided. A better fit than I was. "*Gird up your loins; fresh courage take. Our God will never us forsake.*" My heart swelled in testimony as I joined the song. This was a hymn we'd learned after our conversion and greatly loved.

Even with the confusion of young men on either side of me,

my eyes grew misty as we began the last verse, "*And should we die before our journey's through.*" I blinked, embarrassed by my tears.

"Oh, Lars, that verse always touches my heart," exclaimed Ester. "I love it, though I pray we live to the end of our journey."

"Amen," I whispered.

Josef nudged me. "Have you prayed for a solution?"

Did he think I wished to discuss our agreement of the previous night here, with listening ears on every side? Although I cared deeply for Josef, sometimes he was exasperating. I turned my attention to the front.

"... There will be a special memorial for Sister Vestergaard early this afternoon," said Elder Clark. "We invite all those who had special acquaintance with her to attend."

Orla and Engla were with their papa. I would bring Mary and Ana, and we would go together to comfort them, and accompany them to the memorial.

Josef tapped my shoulder. "Do you have anything to tell me?" He asked right in front of Lars. Of course Lars overheard and became curious.

"What would she have to tell you, brother?"

I shared with Josef my angriest look, disappointed that he would be so careless with my life. Last night before sleeping, I'd prayed about the matter and hadn't received any direction whatsoever. This was probably why—Josef could not keep things secret.

At that moment I couldn't swear what I had ever seen in him.

Having nothing polite to say, I turned and walked away. I found my sisters not too far off, and took them in hand, marching nearly to the ship's stern before sitting them down to play.

"Catie, I don't want to be here," Mary complained.

"Me too." Ana crossed her arms and frowned.

"Well, it's a sorry notion because I told Mama I'd keep you busy for the morning." I flounced down onto the deck, leaned back, and allowed the sun to shine on my face, praying once more the west wind would hurry us safely and quickly to America.

"What are we going to do?" Mary stood over me with her hands on her hips. "You didn't bring us anything to play with."

"Hey, girls." Lars waltzed forward. "Can I keep you company?"

He received a quick glare from me before I returned my attention to my sisters.

"Why are you here?" Mary was a perfect miniature replica of Mama when she was angry. I fought to keep my expression neutral.

"Mary," I tried to scold. "Don't speak rudely to Lars. You know he is Josef's brother." If he thought this an insult, let it be so. He shouldn't have left Ester so soon.

"Where is Josef? I want to play with him." Mary stomped her foot on the wooden deck.

"Mind your manners," I scolded in earnest, "or I'll take you right to Mama. You know where you'll go from there." But if she continued, I'd have a good reason to leave.

"I'll be good." She gazed up with a look of pure angelic innocence, nearly making me laugh.

"Fine," I grumbled, forcing a stern look upon my face.

"Fine," she mimicked.

"What do you girls usually do?" Lars asked, sitting on deck beside me.

"We usually play with—" Mary bit her tongue upon seeing my irritation. "dolls," came her quiet and more appropriate response.

Lars had never given my little sisters more attention than politeness demanded. His motives for spending time helping to amuse them on this day seemed suspicious. It kept me wondering. Had Josef discussed my situation with him?

Mary and Ana jumped into Lars's lap.

"Oomph!" He winced, but then put his arms around them. "What shall we do?"

"Tell us a story!"

"Once upon a time," he began.

I couldn't concentrate but spent my time wondering about the two brothers. Had Josef betrayed my trust? The thought upset me. It hurt my feelings. I didn't need Josef's interference nor did I need his brother's. Their loose tongues could very well get me killed.

Lars stayed right by my side as though someone had sewn his breeches to my skirt. It seemed he made a point to be sweet to the girls—overly sweet. But he helped me to keep them entertained until Mama came to take over their care.

"Why don't you two go enjoy some of this fresh air?" Mama smiled and picked up Ana.

I kept my displeasure in check. Lars hadn't done anything wrong—and, should he propose, I could not reject him as I had John. Spurning two worthy men would keep another from asking, and secure my lot in life as a lonely maid. The thought of being Lars's wife, however, did not soothe my nerves. I needed to think of something.

Lars linked elbows with me and whisked me away with a grin as big as Jutland. He was a good man who loved the Lord. As we walked, his hair flitted in the breeze like Grandfather Erichsen's had done. The thought lifted my spirits.

"Oh, Catherine." Lars pulled me into an unexpected embrace and twirled me off my feet. "It's a beautiful day to be alive, don't you think?"

He had my heart racing to be sure.

"I can't wait to get to America. Can you imagine it? It's so large! How will we ever find our way to Zion except by the Lord's hand?" Lars swept his hands across the width of the horizon and I felt his excitement.

While we gazed into the sea, Lars turned me to face him and began leaning forward. I saw with horror that he intended to kiss me on the lips! If he kissed me here, now, Papa would insist we marry right away. I leaned back, placing my hands in front of my face just as his lips brushed across my palm.

"What kind of woman do you think I am?" I flushed with irritation and stepped back.

"Catherine," he pleaded, sounding contrite. "Please forgive me. I got carried away." He touched my arm wishing me to face him, but I wouldn't forgive so easily. "Your beauty overwhelms me at times, and I'm afraid I lost my manners."

We weren't raised to give much stock in beauty so his words didn't flatter me as he probably desired them to. I faced him, wondering. Was I more to him than a pretty face?

"It's much too fine a day to spend it being cross." He pulled off his cap and held it between his hands. "Please give me a chance to redeem myself. Let's go for a stroll. I won't even hold your hand if you don't wish me to—just let me spend more time with you."

Though he seemed sincere, I hesitated, wishing he'd throw his attentions on Ester. He tilted his head and peered at me with doleful eyes. At last I extended my arm, having not entirely forgiven him.

He took the longest route back to where we'd left Mary and Ana, and by the time they were in sight, I'd forgiven Lars his bold actions. After all, he had stated his intentions to marry me.

Lars didn't understand. I was more private. I preferred a kiss in private as well. He didn't know I was stricken with worry that he would kiss me, that he would marry me. Would

Josef even care? I pushed the painful notion away. When we approached Mama, she and Papa were sitting and talking by themselves.

"Where's Mary and Ana?" I asked.

"Bishop Iversen took them."

My muscles constricted. "Where?" I cried, lunging toward Mama and Papa. How could I ever forgive myself if they were hurt while I wasn't watching?

"Do not be upset," Papa said. "Because you don't care for him is no reason others shouldn't. We took the opportunity to visit with the good bishop last night at the social. He was very pleasant."

Hadn't Mr. Iversen just threatened me last eve?

"You don't understand." I wiped my brow, fighting to appear calm. "I need to get the girls. Where did he take them?" Would he throw them overboard? Would I be able to save them?

"I don't know their exact location," Papa said. "He took them after the memorial service." Papa patted the ship "Why don't you and your young man sit with us and visit?"

"We shall discuss later why you weren't at the memorial," Mama said.

"I must find the girls first," I said, knowing I should have been there.

"Weren't you planning to spend time in the Holy Scriptures and in prayer?" Mama eyed me.

"I will. Please let me find Mary and Ana," I plead. Why did she waste precious time with questions? I fidgeted, waiting for directions, wishing to save my sisters from that evil beast.

"Catherine, you are overexcited." Lars stood behind me, rubbing my shoulders, thinking he would calm me. His condescension had the opposite effect.

Mama and Papa exchanged glances, smiling, as they focused on me and Lars.

"Oh," I gave an exasperated sigh, "I cannot talk now. I need to find the girls." I rushed past Mama and took the companionway stairs two at a time. Lars followed close behind. I ran through every small corridor but didn't find them. With panic rising in my chest, I realized I should have stayed on deck. I almost couldn't breathe. Had this mistake cost my sisters' lives? I headed for the stairs again.

"Catherine, this is ridiculous—you are making yourself sick." Lars took my arm and pulled me to a stop. "End this nonsense now. I insist. You behave as though your sisters are in trouble when they are merely playing with the bishop."

"He's not a bishop, and no one asked you to follow along," I fumed. "If it offends you to accompany me while I'm looking for my sisters, by all means, don't!" I tore myself away from his grasp and leapt up the stairs and into the sunlight. Once outside, I disappeared in the crowd of Saints.

"Have you seen my little sisters?" I asked a woman.

"*Jag vill inte tala danska.*" She shrugged her shoulders and looked apologetic. "*Beklagar.*"

I tried again with a nearby gentleman. "Have you seen two little girls, and Bishop Iversen?"

"*Jeg har ikke tale danske.*" He patted my head.

I wished I could speak other languages—I wished they could understand me. I hurried away, frustrated, and didn't try again.

I stopped to scan the crowd. My sisters were nowhere in sight. I continued making my way through, bumping and pushing as I went. My stomach was sick. Acid rose in my throat.

A small group was clustered near the bow of the ship. My skin chilled, and I ducked through the crowd toward them. Elder Clark was there with his arm around Brother Vestergaard like a mother hen with a baby chick. They were teary eyed, and others nearby were consoling them as well.

"What has happened?" I asked.

"The memorial services for Sister Vestergaard." Sister Thompsen frowned. "Your parents were here. Elder Clark buried her privately yesterday."

I should have been there, not strolling with Lars. My shoulders slumped. I should have helped comfort Orla and Engla.

"I'm so sorry, dear." She put her arm around me. "I know you've been upset by the loss of our dear Brother—"

"Nej," I interrupted. "I meant to be here, but my sisters are missing. Have you seen them?" I couldn't share with her that I'd been lollygagging about with Lars.

"They're with Bishop Iversen, just over there." She pointed down the gangway opposite from where I'd come, "He's such a wonderful man to—"

I rushed away before she finished. Wonderful? If she only knew. I swallowed the bile in my throat and grimaced. When I spotted them, I ran the short distance.

"There you are," I sobbed. Kneeling down, I held them to me.

"Now, Catherine, dear." Mr. Iversen reached out to touch my elbow.

I jerked away.

"Don't worry over your sisters like this. They're in good hands." He leaned down and kissed Mary and Ana on the forehead. "We've become the best of friends, haven't we, girls?"

"Ja, ja," Ana took the Bishop's hand and held it. He bent down to her and she climbed into his arms.

I grabbed Ana around the waist, and pulled at her. Mr. Iversen held her with a firm grip. "Someone help me!" I screamed. "This man is trying to harm me and my sisters!" I pounded on his arms with my fists. "Let her go!"

Bishop Iversen didn't slacken his hold on Ana, instead

he placed his hand on my shoulder. "Now, Catherine," he murmured, "Just because we've had a disagreement, there's no need for going sour. You're much too sweet for that." Then for the nearby Saints' benefit, he talked louder. "Take your sorrows to the Lord, dear girl. He will help you overcome your pain." Mr. Iversen patted my head as though I were an infant and let Ana down to stand by Mary.

Everyone on the bow of the ship stared at me. The Bishop appeared triumphant. "Don't worry, dear Saints, the good Lord says it's a fool who takes offence, and I am no fool." He laughed cordially. "Apparently our dear Sister Erichsen is still overly distraught from losing the recently departed Brother Rasmussen and now her good friend, Sister Vestergaard. It has caused her to be a bit delusional, I fear, for I received permission from her parents to escort these delightful girls on a stroll."

Trembling with fear and exasperation, I grabbed Mary and Ana's hands and made my way through the crowd.

"But Catie, Bishop Iversen said he'd play games with us today." Mary tried putting her feet down to stop but I pulled until she had no choice but to follow.

"I like him, he's nice," said Ana.

I stopped and kneeled to Mary's height. They didn't understand the situation. "You girls must never go anywhere with him again. Do you understand?"

"I'm going to tell Mama." Mary put her hands on her hips and glared. "I bet she'll let us play with him."

Fear roiled inside of me and my heart skipped a beat. How could I make the girls obey without upsetting them?

"Nej. You need to listen to me. Do not go near that man again." I chewed a nail as I tried thinking of a plan.

"He was going to teach us a new game," Mary complained.

They saw a new friend in Mr. Iversen and a new repertoire

of things to do. I needed to find them a diversion and do all in my power to take their mind off of that wicked liar.

"I'll tell you what," I said a little more calmly. "I'll go get Christer and Grete. We'll play dolls—pretend we're on the train—or anything you'd like."

Chapter 28

"What are you making?" Lars hovered over Mary.

"Cornflowers," she replied.

I had no notion that helping the girls with their embroidery would be a problem. Mama and Papa were in sight, as they would be for the rest of our voyage. I watched after their safety and they watched after mine, though they did not know of our danger.

The problem came with Lars—he had decided once again to be my personal shadow. I hadn't completely forgiven him his near kiss, nor had I forgiven his telling me to calm down, for no one knew better than I my reasons of not being calm. I was disappointed in him. For someone always professing his love, Lars should have more faith in me.

"Orla, do it like this." I took her needle and showed her the proper stitching.

No sooner had I resigned myself to his presence when I developed another problem—Josef. I pretended I didn't see him walking near. What was going on with those two?

Seldom had I seen the two of them together the whole voyage. And, all of a sudden, they were hovering over me like great pelicans waiting to snatch up a fish.

"Catherine, I knew I could trust my brother to keep you safe in my absence." Josef bowed with a flourish and then stood beside me.

His strange manner puzzled me, but his comment helped me understand the situation more clearly. Josef had indeed confided in Lars and asked him to be my protector.

"Brother." Lars nodded with a scowl.

"Lars." Josef sounded accusatory. The girls rushed to Josef, clinging to his breeches and shouting his name. "I'll take over from here." Josef smirked. "Your presence is no longer needed."

I glanced back and forth between the two, trying to understand their sour moods.

"Did you see the great ship?" I asked Josef, hoping to diffuse the tension.

"Yes, but who cares about such nonsense when there are beauties such as yourself aboard this ship?" Josef replied airily.

I had never seen Josef act so peculiar. Had he accidentally gotten hold of the crew's liquor? I leaned toward him ever so slightly, hoping to be inconspicuous, and sniffed his person. He smelled fine enough—there was no stench of alcohol anyway.

"Are you all right?" I asked. Perhaps he'd hit his head on something while scraping the floors.

He became downcast and my heart softened toward him.

"As always, Josef, your manner is too abrupt." Lars scoffed. "When in the presence of ladies, one must use style. Good manners would be a welcome change for you, brother." Lars's expression indicated he teased, but their uneasy undercurrent intensified.

"Well, what is good manners to one is merely the meaningless flapping of jaws to another," snapped Josef. "It's all irrelevant at this time, however. The young lady and I have business to discuss." Josef placed his elbow out as a sign for me to take hold and accompany him, which, ever so reluctantly, I did.

"I think not!" Lars challenged. "Catherine and I were having a most pleasant conversation until the wind became sour in your direction." Lars took hold of my other arm in an effort to tug me away, but Josef did not let go.

Their personal tug of war startled me. I hadn't realized before that these very different young men had at least one thing in common—their sense of competition. Yet it needed to stop before it escalated into something even worse—me losing an arm.

I stomped my foot, and, startled, they let me loose. I had half a notion to stomp on their feet. Sternly, I looked from Lars to Josef wondering what to do.

"Catie," Josef murmured. Because of the emotion in his eyes, I could not help but step toward him. Perhaps he wanted to apologize for sharing my problems with Lars.

The little girls wanted to follow us, but I knew Josef would like to communicate in private. Mama and Papa were near enough to watch over them, so I lifted my shoulders sheepishly. "Excuse me. Ja?"

It seemed that a shadow of anger passed across Lars's face before he masked it and agreed. It happened so quickly I couldn't be sure. Perhaps it was merely my guilty conscience since I'd been visiting with him first. However, I took Josef's proffered elbow while promising myself I wouldn't be long. After all, how long could it take to tell Josef exactly how I felt about his betrayal?

We walked in veritable silence. I glanced up and saw his jaw clenching. Was he angry about something? Indeed. I was the one who should be angry.

"Do you know the first time I noticed you?" He stopped aft of the ship and rested his arm along the taffrail.

This set me off my guard, and I reflected on my memory of first noticing him and Lars coming off the ferry. Upon coming to my senses, I gave him a more solemn look. This was the man, after all, who made light of my fears by telling Lars of my situation. And Lars held a special regard for Mr. Iversen.

"It was on the ferry from Fyn." Josef looked into the sea. "You tossed your bonnet into the air."

I scowled at the remembered embarrassment. Why would he make fun of me in this manner?

"Some thought the gesture scandalous, but, I don't know." He looked around as though distracted.

I surmised that he was keeping an eye out for his brother. The two had become less than cordial to one another. Boredom could be the cause. It had become quite difficult for Elder Clark and our other leaders to keep the peace.

"... but soon after, he informed me of your betrothal to the older gentleman, Brother Rasmussen."

Did he think to censure me as Lars had? My forehead wrinkled in thought, trying to understand. Was this his explanation for only wanting me as a friend? I needed to say something to put his mind at ease.

"Josef—"

He put up a hand to silence me. "After Brother Rasmussen's passing," Josef continued, "Lars bragged that he had claimed you as his own."

"Claimed me? You make me sound like a prized horse." Why was he doing this?

"Nej. Catie." Josef put his hands in his vest pockets. "Lars only recently confided his plans of waiting to propose in America. This leaves me with only a small window of opportunity." He took a deep breath.

"Opportunity?" Had I missed something?

"Did I remember to mention your beauty?"

I winced back at the unwelcome remark and turned to leave.

With shaking hands, he took mine, and knelt on the deck. "I beg you to forgive my forwardness, but will you consent to be my wife?"

What? I'd longed for a proposal—prayed for one—but to

hear the desired words spoken thus cut me to my core. I stared at him in stunned silence for an eternity.

Josef stood and reached over, kindly closing my mouth. It helped me to come out of my shock. I stepped away from him, thoroughly stung.

Once again I had fallen for a man who did not love me as he should.

I turned to a woman not too far off. "Did you hear this, Sister Pedersen?" Appalled, I faced Josef. "You ask to marry me, not out of love, but to keep your brother from asking first?"

"Catie." Josef reached for me. "Let me start over."

I backed away from his touch and straightened. "Start over? I've given you chance upon chance! And, not only that, you've betrayed my confidence." My balled fists rested on my hips. "I hope I can feel confident that neither you nor Lars will ever call on me again!" I veritably spat the words and rushed away, pushing myself through a throng of strangers. My heart was broken, my vision blurred, and barely noticing as I approached Lars and the girls. I wanted nothing more than to collapse and shed myself of this grief.

"I've been missing you." Lars stood in greeting.

I didn't doubt he missed me, seeing as he wasn't used to tending little girls. I wiped my face dry with my sleeves and scowled at his grinning face. "I'll tell you as I told Josef." My voice cracked. "I'll not be treated as some game between quarrelling brothers. I am not to be trifled with nor bargained for, and I insist you and your brother leave me alone this instant!"

"Catherine." Lars reached out to me, but I twisted away and avoided his touch.

"Go!" I pointed my finger west. At that moment I wished him to follow in this direction till he fell overboard.

"What has my fool brother done?" Lars took off with the heat of a charging bull—and I had no doubt who his horns would gouge.

As soon as he left, I crumpled onto the deck, hiding my face and trying to get my emotions in check.

"Catherine?" Mama asked as she walked near. "Are you all right? What was that about?"

"I've had enough with those two!" My voice was too loud. People were watching. I needed to calm down. After taking several slow breaths, I lowered my voice. "They're both proposal crazy and I fear they have no goal in mind except to be the first brother betrothed to someone they term beautiful."

Emotion choked my words, and I drew in another steadying breath. "They treat me as though I'm some trinket to be purchased with the right amount of flattery."

"I see." Mama frowned. Extending her hand, she helped me up and we walked toward Papa and the girls. "They've both proposed to you?"

"Ja." I nodded for emphasis. "Lars proposed after we first boarded the ship. He was being fresh and I told him so." My jaw set with indignation. "Although he has promised not to repeat the expression until we land, he has continued to remind me of it and he pursues me with the grace of a starved hog with a bin full of corn."

"My heavens, that sounds dreadful." I saw the corners of Mama's mouth turn up ever so slightly, but she would not make light of my anger. "And the other boy?"

"Josef?" I gulped, and closed my eyes. A tear squeezed through, so I wiped it away and blinked. "He's another problem altogether."

My shoulders drooped. "He has spent so much time with the girls while I tend them. I have developed feelings for him. Yet, to my complete and utter disappointment, he has given no indication that he returned the sentiment."

Mama put her arm around my shoulder.

"We're just friends! And then at this moment, he proposes." I rested my elbow on the arm clutching my stomach, my knuckles against my cheek, and blew out my hurt in a loud breath of air.

"Josef proposed to you on this day?" Mama's half smile was gone and I saw that she began to understand.

"Ja! The presumptuous imbecile said he wanted to ask me before his brother did—not because he loved me."

Mama pulled me into her embrace. Because of her compassion, my emotions released from me like a grand river of regret and frustration.

"Catie, why are you upset?" All four girls gathered around my skirts and hugged me tight. I lost my balance and nearly toppled over. However, their love and concern helped lightened my mood.

"I shan't be upset any longer if you will be good girls and lend me all of your affection for the day." I wiped my eyes and turned my attentions to them.

Mama joined in the fun and we merged into one large, giggling heap. Their silliness was a healing balm to my love-weary soul and helped cheer me for a time.

Chapter 29

"I'd much rather we stay here as a family." I patted the mattress. My lips tightened and I pressed my arms against my stomach.

Mama and Papa believed that only the most extreme circumstances should keep us from attending any and every church function—including evening socials. I believed we were in an extreme circumstance for I had no desire to face Lars or Josef ever again and feared staying in our berth alone.

"Catherine, I'll not have you hiding behind the blankets every time you have a disagreement with a young man. The girls need the exercise, and I will not spend the evening hiding in our berth like a family of church mice."

With her jaw set just so, I knew Mama would not give up even if she had to drag me there herself. I felt inclined to insist she do just that and stood my ground.

"Catherine dear, come along and listen to your mama. After that debacle on deck with the Hansen brothers you need to make an appearance. We'll keep an eye on the young men and not allow them to make themselves unwelcome." Papa put his arm around me.

I leaned in to his embrace. When at last he took a step toward the social, I went with him while still nestled in the security of his arm.

Upon our arrival, I scanned the room and was contented

that the Hansen brothers, in respect of my wishes, had kept themselves away. Josef wasn't even playing the harmonica. I danced one dance with the girls, and saw my friend Ester standing alone. I went to visit with her.

"Have you seen Lars?" she asked.

"I hope never to see him again," I grumbled.

"What is it you do? How do you have everyone chasing after you so?"

"You exaggerate," I said, trying to make light of her comment. After all, there were nearly a hundred single men aboard ship. I only had problems with two.

"If you have no interest in him, will you help me gain Lars's attention?" She took my hands in hers. "Please?"

I opened my mouth to reply. I would gladly help.

It was then Lars Hansen ambushed me. "Don't be cross, Catherine. Dance with me, please." Lars extended his hand.

"I cannot dance with you." I would not. "However, my friend, Ester, would like to dance."

"That would be nice, ja." She smiled and curtsied.

He glanced at her and bowed. "Another time?"

I searched frantically for Papa, but his back was turned so I started toward him.

"Catherine." Lars stepped in front of me and would not let me pass. "This is a silly misunderstanding. Let me explain." He reached for my elbow, but I pulled away.

"Can't you see that the lady does not desire your company?" Josef stepped forward, shoved Lars aside, and held my arm.

I jerked away from Josef as well. "Do neither of you understand?" I shot them an icy glare hoping to hide my hurt. "I no longer desire to keep company with either of you."

"Catherine, give us another chance." Lars and Josef hurried to either side of me, both determined to win their point, both taking hold of me, pleading.

"Give you another chance to what—pull me from limb to limb?" I looked pointedly at their hands. This was not love, it was competition. I'd been foolish to ever think otherwise.

"Boys, there is no need for this." Papa rested his hands on their shoulders. "My daughter is a good girl, and this behavior is very distressing."

"Thank you, Papa." I pulled loose from their grasp and rushed to the companionway.

He would give them a talking to, but I did not desire to stay longer. Being anywhere near the Hansen brothers was a bad idea. Anguish powered my legs until I discovered myself out on deck, alone. A shiver of warning wormed up my spine. I should not be there.

The stars were out. I slowed my pace and walked to the bulwark. Nervous to be alone, I glanced around, making sure Mr. Iversen, or his cohorts, weren't about. The area was vacant. I forced myself to calm down and enjoy the splendor. The moon hadn't appeared in the sky and nothing interfered with the scene of millions of stars shimmering from heaven. Again, the feeling that I was vastly insignificant overwhelmed me—I was nothing but a speck in the universe. How could God know me?

"Catie."

I clenched my jaw and steeled my heart against the hurt there before turning. Josef stood not too far off, yet I couldn't speak his name. Viewing the stars had unruffled me some, but upon seeing him, my lip quivered. I could not bear the idea of my being a mere competition between brothers. It was cruel.

"Catie, it's too dangerous for you to be out here. Come in with me."

Had he not come, I'd have gone back inside. I didn't need Josef to inform me of the danger. Yet I paid no attention to the desperation in his voice, for I could not go to him. To do so would be to rip my heart into a million shreds and cast the pieces out to sea. How I wished I had never met Lars or Josef! How I wished I had never walked aboard this ship!

"Leave me alone." I did the only thing I could—I ran away from him. Although upset, I still felt a certain amount of self-preservation. So, as I ran, I looked for somewhere to hide until I could bear to return to my family.

Before I found a hiding place I fell onto the deck. Too weary, too distressed to pick myself up and run farther aft of the ship, I scooted to the side of the bridge and buried my face in my hands. I'd made a big mess of things.

I hadn't thought of Isaac in a long time, but he entered my thoughts as I sat there. I didn't feel anything toward him—no heartbreak—no anger. It surprised me. My life and surroundings had changed so much since I'd seen him last. His memory felt like a dream.

I compared Isaac with John—the man I cared for and should have loved. If everyone was like John, the world would be a better place. He had a strong testimony, a sense of adventure, and polite manners. Manners were something the Hansen brothers could both take lessons in. A sob escaped my throat as I thought of them.

Had Lars never cared? And Josef? He had pointed me out to Lars when we were still in Denmark. Had Lars taken the opportunity to step in where his brother was too shy? The thought hit like lead in my stomach.

Even after this quarrel, Papa may insist I marry Lars, if he asked. Though Lars was a good man with a strong sense of faith, it seemed to me that we both wanted different kinds of lives. Lars wanted fame and fortune. He was obsessed with social appearances.

None of these things mattered to me. Couldn't he understand that? Yet, if a good person with a strong testimony of the Savior desired to marry me, should our different aspirations matter?

Thoughts of Lars led to unwanted thoughts of Josef. As much as I believed our goals were similar—family, living a simple life free from society's expectations, and farming—I couldn't allow myself to care for a man if he only wanted to steal me away from his brother. I would never have thought to do something so horrible to Berta.

I needed to give serious reconsideration to Josef and the kind of person I'd thought he was. I wiped at my cheeks and started to get up. I needed to get below to safety.

"My, my."

I gasped and looked up

"Just when we was thinking of going fishing, the whale come and jumped into our net."

My blood chilled at the sound of the sailors known as Pierre and Louie. I stood slowly, as if by doing so they wouldn't notice.

Chapter 30

"Leave me alone!" I inched along the sterncastle, hoping to make it to the hatch and down the stairs.

Louie huffed. "Now, missy, let's spell out the reasons we can't." He bent down to my eye level and extended his pointer finger. "For one, yer just too nosey." He held out another finger. "For two, ya can't keep quiet." He put up a third finger. "For three, we warned ya not to go rattin' us out." They both took a step forward. "And we heard ya very clearly as ya were screamin' yer betrayal. T'was our good fortune no one believed ya."

The two men, now on either side of me, grabbed my arms and began walking away with me.

"Stop! Help!" Overcome with panic, I kicked and screamed and tried my best to stop them from taking me anywhere. They were taller and lifted me till my feet didn't touch the deck while carrying me closer to the ship's edge.

I shuddered at the thought of becoming whale bait and struggled all the more. They would not throw me overboard. But how could I stop them? With a wisp of an idea, I forced my body to go limp. It barely hindered their progress as they tugged me forward.

"Don't she seem a might heavy for her slight frame?" Louie stopped. "I think she's been holding out on us."

"What're you saying?" Pierre scowled.

"I'm saying that when we was searching for their coins, we was lookin' in the wrong place." He leaned down and lifted the hem of my dress.

"Nej!" I kicked and twisted. "Someone help me!" I screamed. They could not have my parents' money.

"Ya know we can't let the little brat live after this." Pierre stood behind me, holding me with his arms locked in mine while Louie ripped off my underskirt. I kicked him in the head and he fell backward, my petticoat dropped from his hands.

"Yer a feisty little wench," Pierre snapped. Then, a spark of evil shone in his eyes. I dreaded his expression. I'd seen it once before when John was there to save me. "What say ye Louie? I like my women with a little spunk. How about we have a bit of fun afore we get rid of her?"

"Aye," said Louie, and scrambled back to aide Pierre.

"Leave me alone you vile, repulsive dogs!" Someone would hear. Someone had to. "Help!" My throat was getting sore from screaming, but I screamed again. "Help!"

Pierre leaned forward, his eyes full of lust. I turned away as well as I could, yet his slobbered kiss landed on my cheek. This could not be happening. Not here, one stairway from seven-hundred Scandinavian Saints. Not now, only weeks from shore. Not ever.

Pierre took my face in his hands and planted the kiss on my lips. "Now that ain't so bad." He showed his brown teeth in an evil grin.

I spit his kiss back into his face.

He slapped me and prepared to hit me again.

"Someone'll probably come looking for her quick-like." Louie pushed Pierre's fist down. "Don't be getting too carried away."

I kicked out, and my foot connected with Pierre. This gave me a short-lived satisfaction. Pierre groaned and doubled over.

Trying to make use of his distraction, I squirmed and wrestled, but Louie held me firm.

"You're hurting my arm. Let me go!" I kicked at Louie as well. He masterfully avoided contact with my foot. This made me angry and I kicked all the harder.

Pierre stood and made his way to where Louie and I wrestled. He took hold of my arm. "Ain't no woman treats Pierre LaBrue like that." He reached out and slapped me. The force of it snapped my head backwards.

Searing pain shot through my head, and my knees went limp. Pierre shoved Louie away and tried forcing his lips upon mine again. Turning my head back and forth, I avoided his lecherous attack and fought him off with the best of my ability.

"She ain't worth our necks, Pierre. Let it go." Louie grabbed me and started dragging me—for I resisted with all the strength I could muster—and he stormed to the bulwark.

Pierre came forward and drew his arm back to punch Louie, but Louie hit him first and Pierre stumbled backwards. Louie proceeded with me to the edge.

My life would soon be over, yet I clung to the ship for all I was worth. While Louie wrestled me and tried prying my arms and legs loose, I tried pushing down my panic as I repositioned my hands each time he set one free.

Little flashes of my reasons for living came to mind, giving me strength. Mama. Papa. My little sisters. Berta. The man I loved. I could not leave them in this manner.

I pleaded for mercy over and over again to no avail. As I begged for my life, my petitions turned to my Creator.

"O, Lord!" I sobbed the words from the depth of my soul knowing my only salvation was through my Lord and my Savior. Surely I could not save myself. I was powerless in the hands of these monsters. "Please spare my life!"

"Ain't no one here's gonna save ya," Louie growled while prying at my fingers.

"Not so quick." Pierre threw himself on top of Louie and began wrestling me up and onto the bulwark. "I ain't had shore leave in months."

Louie let loose of me to punch Pierre. I climbed over the

side of the ship and onto the deck. They began brawling and seemed to forget me.

I took one step and then another. While keeping a watch on them, I started to run, but bumped into something solid.

"Now, what do we have here?" Mr. Iversen snatched hold of me.

Pierre and Louie stopped their fighting and rushed toward me again.

"Thought she'd get away, did she?" The two sailors joined forces in pulling me from Mr. Iversen's grip, and proceeded once again toward the bulwark.

"Help me, bishop!" I cried. Did the title mean nothing to him? "Help me!" I thrashed about, hoping Mr. Iversen would do the right thing. "Please let me go."

"Now, lads, I know she's been a bit of trouble, but let's not be hasty." Mr. Iversen rushed forward and stood between me and the sea. "Murder holds a much harsher punishment than thievery."

"If you ain't got the stomach for it, ya best be getting outta the way," snarled Pierre.

Mr. Iversen hesitated and my heart took courage. Perhaps he would fight them off after all. In that hope I was disappointed. Mr. Iversen skulked away and never laid a hand on either man.

I could barely resist, so tired was I. My only defense lay with my Father in Heaven. But would he hear me? Would he help me? "Lord, carest thou not that I perish?" I breathed these words of scripture along with my own plea. "Please, save me from these wicked men."

"Listen to the little wench—praying like someone can hear 'er." Pierre laughed and shoved me onto the bulwark. I felt myself slipping over the ship's side and toward the sea, and lunged for safety, barely securing my grip.

Dangling precariously over the edge, I glanced at the turbulent waters below knowing I had no chance of survival should they succeed in loosening my grip. The current would most likely pull me under and send me quickly to the bottom of the sea.

"Please, Lord, I'll do whatever you ask." The words escaped my lips in a shaky whisper. I'll marry Lars if you want me to. "Just don't let me die tonight." I continued my fight, unsure of which answer I would receive. Then, with strength I never knew, I swung myself up, and clung to the bulwark.

Louie snarled and pried my legs loose. Pierre was beside him, helping. I tried swinging one leg up and lifting myself back to the safe side of the ship, but my strength faltered. The monsters pried at my fingers. I could not fight them much longer.

"Thank goodness you've arrived." Mr. Iversen sounded anxious.

Who was he talking to—Pierre—Louie—or someone else?

"Ya stubborn little wench! Let go!" Pierre doubled his hand into a fist. I moved my hand just as he slammed it onto the ship's side. He cursed, spouting words I'd never heard before.

"Help me!" My fingers slipped. I reached out and gained a meager hold on the ship.

"I tried persuading the scallywags to let her loose—but what could I do? They wouldn't listen to reason," whined Mr. Iversen.

Had I not known the truth, I'd have believed he wished to help me. My fingers began slipping. "Help me!" I shouted, my voice hoarse. "Help me, please!" I clung to the bulwark in a final effort to save myself before falling to my death.

The captain peered overboard. He looked as sinister as ever. I didn't know if I should trust him, but when Pierre and Louie stood aside and the captain offered his hand, I took it.

"That's a good lass. Be careful now—that's the ticket," he encouraged as he helped me back aboard ship.

"Thank you! Thank you." I shook from the strain of my fight and struggled to stand.

"Now yer welcome," responded the captain. He didn't realize I was thanking my Father in Heaven.

"You helped save my life," I murmured.

"Catherine!"

It sounded like Mama and Papa. I turned. They rushed to me and took me in their arms, nearly suffocating me with their embrace and their kisses.

"Tie these men up and then take them to the hold," ordered Captain Boyd.

From the safety of my parents' arms, I watched the commotion unfurl before me as streams of people came onto the deck. Had someone heard my cries after all? Why were these people here now?

Then I saw Josef. He seemed to be ushering everyone onto the deck. "They're near the bulwark," he shouted. "This way!" People gathered around and watched the sailors struggle for their freedom while being dragged away, just as I had struggled for my life only moments before.

"Mr. Iversen. He's with us." They cursed, and spat. "Sailor's honor, he's in on it."

"Now, see here." Elder Clark came forward to address the captain and his prisoners. "There's no need to tarnish the name of our dear bishop."

"You're thieves and liars!" Several bystanders shouted. "The bishop is innocent."

"He's no more innocent than we are. He came to us." Pierre struggled against his ropes. "Stealing your loot was his idea!"

Mr. Iversen was right. No one believed the sailors. Would they believe me? I hesitated. Those who had come onto the deck looked on the verge of mutiny. Josef tried to get them to settle down, but no one would listen. They seemed incensed by the accusations against the bishop.

He looked around, careful not to move at first. Then, taking advantage of the upheaval, Mr. Iversen took one slow step to the right and then another. Gradually, and unnoticed by anyone except me, he worked his way to the edge of the crowd. He hoped, I think, to disappear until charges against him were forgotten.

"Ask the girl," shouted Louie before being forced below.

At that moment, the crowd hushed and all eyes turned to me. They waited for my answer, expecting me to confirm Mr. Iversen's innocence.

If I charged him of his crime, would they set him free anyway? If so, he would then be at liberty to inflict any punishment upon me or my family his demented soul could fathom. My outburst of the other morning had gone unnoticed.

I looked to my trusting and anxious parents, the shock of the truth dawning on their faces. They expected me to tell, yet I'd spent the better part of our voyage keeping his secret to myself. My silence, though, had nearly cost me my life. I glanced at Josef who gave a nod of encouragement.

"Mr. Iversen is no bishop," I finally said. Nikolaus, his mother, and the others under his care deserved restitution, and I knew my family and I would never be safe so long as he walked free. "It was he who stole the Saints' missing money. He was also in collusion with Pierre and Louie."

When I said these words, a great calm descended upon me. I had done the right thing.

"Keep him under guard until I have time to investigate the matter," commanded Captain Boyd.

"This cannot be!" "She is a dreamer." "The girl cannot know this." "She is too upset to know the truth!" There were many things shouted about me, and many tried denying Mr. Iversen's involvement by saying he was too good a man.

I knew better.

Two of the captain's officers stepped forward and grabbed Mr. Iversen by his arms.

"Don't listen to the girl. She's nothing but trouble." Mr.

Iversen turned red in the face "She's delusional. I've been counseling with her since Brother Rasmussen passed away."

The officers dragged him toward the hatch. The scene looked almost comical.

Almost.

Mr. Iversen kicked his captors and with a forceful twist pulled himself loose. "You owe me girl." He charged at me with all the energy of an angry bull. "I kept you safe from Pierre and Louie—and this is the way you repay me?" With his hand outstretched, he lunged forward to grab me.

I gasped and pressed myself tighter into Papa's arms. Papa instantaneously moved me out of the way.

Mr. Iversen stumbled, and something dropped from his overcoat. A pool of creamy-white muslin rested on the deck in front of him. My petticoat. "That's mine!"

The captain stooped and picked it up, looking at it curiously. "Take him to the brig," he commanded.

To my relief, and in spite of the Saints' protests and those of Mr. Iversen, the officers scrambled forward. Shoving Mr. Iversen to the deck, they tied his hands behind his back before standing him up.

"This is not what it seems," Mr. Iversen shouted as they marched him away.

My knees trembled. Moisture filled my eyes.

"There, there, Princess." Papa gave me another hug. We walked through the throng of staring Saints, down the steps, and to our berth. Mama climbed in the bunk beside me and hummed while stroking my hair until I fell into a fitful sleep.

Chapter 31

"Papa, please don't make me do it."

"It is right and good." His eyebrows rose. "And I insist."

I'd spent all morning talking to the captain, telling him everything I knew about the thievery, and of the threats made against me. The two sailors' belongings were investigated. Papa now had his watch, and the other stolen heirlooms were returned.

Captain Boyd, accompanied by Elder Clark, had checked Mr. Iversen's trunk and found the embezzled money. The captain entrusted it into Elder Clark's safe keeping until he could determine how best to return it to those from whom it had been taken.

Every moment I spent in Mama's sight, she coddled and smothered me with tearful kisses. My limbs ached, and my first wish was to spend the rest of the voyage in my berth, recovering.

Though I didn't have the strength or the desire to listen to the praises of some, nor to take in the accusatory glances and whispers of others, I knew from past experiences that solitude was not the path to healing. I must face my life head on.

Except Papa wanted me to speak with Josef. I had no desire to face him or ever speak to him again. How could I? Yet, there he sat faithfully tending my sisters.

"He saved your life," Papa insisted. "When you went on

deck last night, he came to me. It was Josef also who gathered Elder Clark and the captain." Papa glanced down, appearing uncomfortable for what he would say. "Lars insisted on alerting the bishop, or, rather, Mr. Iversen."

This news didn't surprise me. Lars had great faith in Mr. Iversen and held him in high regard. It must be devastating for him to discover his error in judgment.

"The lads got into quite an altercation over the issue. In the end it didn't matter because Mr. Iversen saw the ruckus and left to investigate. I've never seen a lad move so fast as did Josef on Mr. Iversen's absence." Papa took my shoulders and turned me around so that I faced Josef and the girls. "I think the poor boy is smitten with my oldest daughter."

"Nej, Papa." A tear formed and I brushed it away. Papa had it backwards, but Josef did deserve my gratitude for his actions last night. His quick thinking had saved my life.

"Mary?" I knelt beside her. "Do you mind taking charge while I talk with Josef for a moment?"

"Ja, ja. It is well and good." Mary leaned over and hugged me.

"Josef?" Biting on my lip, I glanced at him, but he had already risen and moved beside me. He motioned for me to lead the way.

We walked in silence half the length of the ship. The air between us had never felt so troubled, and I realized nothing was being resolved with my silence.

"I wanted to thank you." I paused and looked up into his green eyes. "You saved my life last night." My heart fluttered, and I tried in vain to silence it as he brushed his fingers across my face to tuck an errant strand of hair behind my ear.

"Nej, it is not necessary. I did nothing." He looked down, clearly embarrassed with my praise.

Unable to think of another thing to say while he stood so

near, I turned, thinking to help Mama or play with the girls.

"Catie." Josef reached out as if to stop me, his hand brushing against mine.

"Ja?" I left my arm dangling at an awkward angle hoping he would take my hand and never release it—willing with all my heart for Josef to declare his love for me—a love that had nothing to do with sibling jealousies.

His hand felt like a whisper so light was his touch and then it was gone, leaving me empty in its wake.

"It is nothing." Josef repeated, his eyes looked soulful, sad, as he walked away.

In my heart I yearned for him and couldn't bear for us to be parted. My feet took me to him, running without my telling them to do so.

"Josef." Not thinking, I reached out and took his hand in mine. He glanced anxiously at me and then my hand. Embarrassed with my bold behavior I released him. "I, I only wanted to thank you again," I murmured against the wild beating of my heart.

He nodded and continued on his way, his head lowered.

I had nothing left to do other than return to Mama. My heart hurt—all twisted in knots somehow—and I remained silent the remainder of the afternoon.

I sat alone in the shade of the sterncastle, watching Ester and the other girls from a distance and wishing I was more like them.

She must have sensed my watching; she waved, and then she stood and came over.

"Catherine, how can I ever thank you?"

"Not to worry. All is well and good," I said.

"All this time, you were in danger." She shook her head, her hand to her heart. "If I'd known." She knelt down while touching the pendant on her neck. "I have this because of you, but I would never have wanted you to die for it. I'm so glad you're safe."

I nodded, too troubled to speak.

"Would you join us?" She indicated the others as they sewed.

"Nej. Thank you, though."

She have me a quick hug, and left while wiping her eyes.

Mama sat beside me. "You are so quiet. Is everything good?"

"Ja." I continued watching Ester.

"Can you talk to me about it?"

"I have been thinking of my little friend, Nikolaus, and all those under Mr. Iversen's care. Is there nothing we can do for them?"

"We cannot make more food on the ship than there is," Mama said.

"I know." I rubbed my cheek. "It's just, have you seen those sea biscuits? They have to flick the weevils off before they can even eat them."

"Ja." Mama shuddered. "It is a terrible thing."

"And they are so hard. They have to soak them in tea or coffee to soften them enough to even eat."

"It shows us the widespread influence of one wicked man." Mama motioned to Ana, who toddled onto her lap.

"Among those who were fooled by him, there are many whose faith has faltered."

"Nikolaus?" I asked.

"I'm afraid so, dear. Many of the adults as well"

"I should have helped more. I've been so neglectful." I hung my head.

"There is nothing you could do differently." Mama touched her hand to my shoulder. "It is of their choosing whether to be offended or not." She tucked a lock of Ana's hair behind her ear. "And what of the Hansen brothers?

"Oh, Mama, I do not know. Lars is a good man. Very handsome." The corner of my lips turned up with my confession.

"And very ambitious. He would make a good husband." For someone.

"It all sounds very wonderful," said Mama. "So, tell me about Josef."

My legs ached so I resituated myself by wrapping my sore arms around them and resting my chin on my knees.

Mama watched me, waiting for me to continue.

"Josef is so gentle and kind, and we both enjoy the same things. I have grown to appreciate him." I hesitated, timid of saying more.

"You are my daughter," encouraged Mama. "I'll not judge the things you say."

"I merely wonder what life would be like if he cared for me the same way," that I care for him, I continued silently. I glanced at Mama, afraid of her disapproval.

"It is unwise to trifle with men's hearts." Mama took my face in her hands. "You can't have them both."

Nodding, I remained silent. I didn't want them both.

"Have you taken it to the Lord?" Mama asked.

I didn't admit that my relationship or rather lack of relationship with Josef had consumed most of my daily prayers for what seemed an eternity. So far, true love seemed just out of my grasp. Perhaps instead of praying for Josef's heart, I should pray for my heart to open toward Lars.

My stomach churned. Would I be compelled to marry a man who had nearly cost me my life? It was grossly unfair. Though if that's what the Lord wanted. I gulped. I had given Him my vow.

Papa came near with Mary in hand. When Mary saw us, she pulled away from him and rushed forward.

"We're hungry!" Mary jumped into Mama's lap. "It's time for supper."

"Let's eat," Ana said. She pulled at my hand. I scooped her

into my arms and we went below.

We ate our simple meal and were thankful for it, although I'd never felt completely full since the whale had eaten all of our potatoes. After supper, Papa pulled Mama and me aside, his eyes twinkling with some type of happy mischief.

"I think I've cleared this matter up between the Hansen brothers." Papa winked.

I did not wish Papa to arrange things for me. My heart sank, and I groaned.

"I've talked to them both. They're very nice lads, and they both express an interest in courting you, so I've done the logical thing." Papa squeezed Mama's hand. She nodded for him to continue.

I was horrified and dared not hear more.

"I am allowing them both to court you three days each," Papa said. "After that, you will make your decision and choose one brother." Papa put his thumbs in his vest pockets and rocked back and forth on his heels. He looked very pleased with his arrangement.

"But Papa," I protested.

"Nej, I've seen how you care for both men." Papa frowned. "It's not proper."

"But, Papa." What must they think of me? Three days each to decide. How could I face them again? Did Papa think I was the Princess of Denmark to receive such consideration?

"Catherine Erichsen, don't give me that look. You already know both men, and it's not fair to keep them waiting longer. Lars is the oldest and asked to be first. You'll meet him tonight at the social."

"It's almost time for the social now." I rushed down the companionway to our berth and grabbed the brush. How could Papa do this to me? Frantically I grabbed at my bonnet and unbraided my hair. Had I been so obvious that everyone could see my feelings? It's no wonder Papa took such a bold move—I must be the object of lots of fine gossip.

Mama and Papa waited patiently near our berth, encouraging me to hurry.

"Can't we do this tomorrow?" I looked at Papa, pleading. "I do not feel social this night." I rubbed my hand across my forehead. "I would just like to sleep."

"Daughter." Papa gave me a stern look. "I have given my word."

I nodded my understanding and held his arm for support. Surrounded by family, perhaps it would be good. I could do this.

As we entered the large room, Lars came forward and took my hand. "I'm so relieved you came," he said.

The music had already begun, but Josef was absent from the group. We didn't dance right away, instead we meandered around the room. I suspected he wanted to get far enough away that Mama and Papa couldn't hear our conversation.

"I am ashamed by my behavior yesterday." Lars stopped and took my hand, kissing it softly. "Can you please forgive my rash behavior?" His brows lifted.

I had planned on forgiving him and agreeing to marry him should he ask. However, my near bout with death had put me in an unforgiving mood, and I wasn't near ready to socialize. Why Mama and Papa kept forcing me out when I wanted nothing more than to stay in and study the Holy Scriptures I did not know.

Things might have been different in the morn. I might have been happier, ready to face Lars and feel for him the way he wanted me to. Perhaps by morn I would have forgiven him, for on this night I felt that he begged forgiveness far too often, and possibly his behavior was rash more often than not—at least when it concerned me.

"I see," he said of my silence, his voice barely above a whisper. "Is this the end? You don't wish to see me anymore?"

"Lars, why do you ignore the other girls when I am around?" I looked into his blue eyes and realized they no longer affected me. "Why do you court me?"

"I—I—" Lars stammered. "The other girls aren't as beautiful."

"What happens when I get old and fat?" I raised my eyebrows.

"You would never." He looked horrified.

"What happens if a rooster attacks me, and leaves a scar across my face?" I put a hand on my hip. "This happened to a friend of mine."

He remained silent.

"Don't you see? You would be much happier courting someone with your same ambitions." I rubbed my temples where they had begun to ache. "Please escort me to my berth."

He held his arm out for me to take it, his lips forming a thin line of disapproval as we walked toward the companionway. He then brightened with an idea and paused.

"You like walking at night," Lars said, his voice light with hope. "Instead of dancing, we could take an evening stroll on deck and get to know one another better."

"Nej, honestly." Couldn't he understand I was spent? "I'm tired. I just need some sleep." I turned my lips up at the corners in a weak attempt for him to believe me. "I'm sure I'll feel better in the morn."

We descended the stairs in silence. Because of this, I felt better about Lars. He did trust me. He did respect my judgment. I would see him on the morrow as he desired. When we neared my berth, however, I wanted him to turn and leave, expected him to, but he didn't.

"Catherine, your father gave me only three days to persuade you of my deep devotion. Let's not waste a minute of it by quarreling." He took my hand and kissed it. With strong arms he drew me into an embrace.

His touch repulsed me. This gave me strength to continue. "Lars, do not feel bad." I pushed him away. "I cannot do this any longer." My heart had made its choice—and Lars didn't reside there. To lead him on even one minute longer was wrong.

"What do you mean?" He released me but kept my hand in his.

"You have not lost me, but you've gained an opportunity to find someone better suited for you. My friend, Ester, for example. She holds your same values and similar dreams. It is Ester you should love." I shook my head. "We are not alike. I cannot make a good companion for you."

"But I gazed at the stars with you—Josef said you liked the outdoors. I've even spent hours entertaining your little sisters in an effort to please you." He tilted his head, his brows furrowing. "Just forgive me, and I'll make everything all right." He lifted my chin and peered into my eyes. "You care for me, I can see it."

"Nej, I do care for you. Eventually I will forgive you, but everything will not be all right. You cannot make it so." I pulled my hand from his. "You never trusted me, even when my life depended on it." I could no longer believe the Lord had sent Lars in answer to my prayers.

"Let's not do this tonight." He caressed my bottom lip with his finger. "You are tired, I can see that now."

He sounded earnest. Had I made the wrong decision? Perhaps my feelings would change in the light of day.

"You wouldn't honestly choose Josef over me." Lars frowned. "I've got an education, ambition—all the things Josef doesn't have. He wants to own land and be a farmer." Lars pulled me close to him and whispered, "You're better than that. Don't do something you'll regret by morn."

I knew I would not feel different tomorrow or any other day.

If I remained unwed the remainder of my life I could never bind myself to Lars—to do so would be to bind Josef as my brother-in-law.

It would be too painful.

Chapter 32

"Mama, Papa," I whispered. Mary and Ana were tucked in bed and sleeping. "I cannot sleep. I wish to take a walk around deck." It was safe now.

"Nej. It is not proper for a young lady to be unaccompanied at this hour." Mama pursed her lips.

Uneasy with the accusation, I glanced at Papa hoping he would change her mind.

He shook his head. "Nej. Your mother is correct. I cannot have you walking about alone at this hour."

"But Papa—"

"Nej." He regarded me sternly. "Sneaking around when you shouldn't have is what got you in trouble to begin with. I'd say you've spent far too much time on this voyage doing things you shouldn't ought. However," he continued, with a mysterious twinkle in his eye, "if you'd like to walk with your papa, I can escort you."

"But you are tired." I didn't wish to say I'd rather be alone.

"Nonsense." Papa rubbed the sleep from his face and slipped into his wooden shoes. I sneaked out of bed so as not to disturb the little girls, and wrapped my Faroese wool blanket around my shoulders.

"Thank you, Papa," I whispered as we climbed the steps.

"I understand you are no longer considering Lars." Papa held his hands behind his back as we walked.

I glanced sideways at him wondering how much I should reveal, or how much he knew. "He is not the one for me, Papa. And you are correct, it would be unjust to make him wait."

"Do you believe Josef is the one for you?"

Papa, I know, took great pains in keeping his expressions neutral, trying his hardest to appear disinterested. I knew better.

My heart raced in my chest at the mention of Josef's name but I couldn't fool myself. "He might be the one for me Papa, but I fear I am not the one for him." Unexpected tears welled in my eyes. How could I make Josef love me when he thought of me only as a friend?

"Ah, daughter, I think you are mistaken there."

"Nej, Papa." How I wished I were. I shook my head trying to push back a wave of despair.

This had not been a good voyage for me and I hoped never to set foot on a ship again. Perhaps I'd find someone to love me that I could also love on the way to Zion. The Lord will provide. I remembered Papa's words, the Lord will provide.

"How then do you explain Josef's sleepless night?" I followed Papa's raised arm and saw Josef leaning against the bulwark and staring into the sky. At my step, the floor creaked and Josef turned to see us. His look, at first surprised, appeared hopeful or anxious, I could not tell which but wished for hopeful.

"I'll leave you two to talk things over. Perhaps he can convince you of his feelings?" Papa said this to Josef. I closed my eyes, humiliated. If Josef had feelings for me, wouldn't he have said so before now? However, I noticed Josef's eyes shinning. Could it be possible I was wrong, and Josef did care for me, or was he merely pleased with my discomfort?

"I ..." Speechless, I turned to Papa for direction, but Papa had already gone below. Uncertain of what to do, I looked back to Josef. Oh, my, should I hurry and follow Papa, or should I stay?

"I understand you and my brother are no longer courting." He took a step nearer to me. My heart thumped in response.

"This is true." Lost in his eyes, I stepped forward.

"Why?" His head tilted, and his eyebrows creased in puzzlement.

I marveled that he didn't know. How could he not know how I felt? What should I tell him? I tried desperately to think of a safe response. There were several reasons, and after pondering I went with the safest one. "He didn't have faith in me."

A crooked smile crept on his face. "I did," he whispered, stepping forward again. He was so close. Did he hear the loud beating of my heart? I glanced downward, trying to rein in my emotions. His hand touched mine, sending a thrill through me. "Will you see me tomorrow as your father arranged, or do you wish me to stay away as well?"

I wished to see him every day for the rest of my life, and nodded. "I would very much like to see you tomorrow." A blush warmed my face.

With both my hands in his, Josef gazed into my eyes. "Before I take you back to your family, I have one more question."

"Go on," I encouraged. "You can ask me anything."

His eyes searched mine, for what, I did not know. I wished him to trust me with his thoughts.

"May I kiss you?" His words, barely audible, caused butterflies in my stomach to dance excitedly the "*Bondepigen.*" I gulped, and nodded almost imperceptibly, afraid to breathe for fear the moment would pass and I'd find myself with Mary and Ana, only dreaming.

However, Josef moved closer and touched my face, timid at first. He leaned forward until his lips met mine. Softly they caressed my soul, transforming me. No longer was I stranded on this despicable ship, but I floated into another world—a place green and alive with meadows, butterflies—and the man I loved by my side.

Too quickly for me, he pulled away. Still in my imaginary paradise, I nearly lost my balance. He held me, keeping me aright.

"It's late," he whispered, his forehead touching mine. "I must get you back."

Now the butterflies had all flown into my chest. I dared not utter a word but nodded only. He took my hand—a sensation so sweet I almost sighed with contentment—and he led me back to my family.

"Tomorrow?" He brushed my cheek with his fingers.

"Ja, ja, tomorrow," I whispered. And then he was gone.

After I climbed into bed, trembling from excitement with the memory of his lips on mine, Papa said, "Nice lad. You chose well."

Smiling in the darkness, and feeling absolutely safe for the first time in a long while, I soon drifted off to sleep.

"Brother Erichsen, sir?"

My eyes flew open at the sound of Josef's voice. What was he doing here? It was still dark out and I knew I'd just closed my eyes.

"Ja?" Papa's scratchy voice answered.

"I've come for your daughter?"

"Oh, right." Papa cleared his throat. "Give us a minute, son."

"Shall I wait on deck, sir?"

"Ja, ja, she'll be right up."

I listened to their conversation, and to the sound of Josef's retreating footsteps with brief trepidation. Would today be different, or would Josef still care for me as tenderly as he had last night? I placed my hand over my heart with a sigh—Josef didn't place his feelings lightly. If last night wasn't a dream, Josef did care for me the way I wanted him to.

Shaking, not from fear or the chilly morning air, but for another reason altogether, I left our bunk. I covered my sisters so they wouldn't awaken, dressed, ran a quick brush through my hair, braided it, and donned my bonnet.

"Enjoy the morning," whispered Papa. "We'll expect to see you at morning worship."

"Ja, Papa," I whispered in return and then dashed away, trying not to make any noise, but eager to meet my Josef.

He surprised me at the top of the stairs by pulling me into

his arms before I'd even seen him.

"I'm glad your papa didn't send me away. I worried he would." Josef glanced at me with a timid smile.

"It is surprising," I mused.

The deck was almost deserted and provided as close to a private walk through the meadow as we could currently hope for—a gift in itself. "I've never been on deck at daybreak. Feel the breeze." I stood with my arms outstretched, taking in the cool sea air in a large sigh.

"Come. I have something to show you." He took my hand and led the way. At last, a non-dangerous adventure! What would we do?

Occasionally as we walked, I glanced toward him only to catch him glancing at me as well. A field of tulips couldn't contain the joy in my soul. What more could there be on a morn like this? As though in answer to my question, he paused and took my face in his hands.

Still cautious but more confident than last night, he drew me near, causing my heart to beat wildly just as the night before. His kiss was tender, pleading, coaxing me to give him my heart. I already had. When we parted, I felt lightheaded from the sweetness of it.

Looking into my eyes, he pulled me into an embrace. Then, with our arms still securely around one another, we walked again toward the stern of the ship. It wasn't a stroll through the meadow, but it still felt like heaven as we walked on the hard wooden deck and smelled the moist salty sea air.

Near the sterncastle where we'd hidden before, Josef already had a blanket spread out on top of the crates with a few slices of dried apple.

I choked back emotion at his thoughtfulness.

"I couldn't wait to see you again and to share with you my favorite time of day." He helped me onto the crate and offered me a slice of apple. "Mother sent them with me. I saved them for a special moment." He joined me then, with one hand resting on the blanket and the other hand on my shoulder. "Behold

God's miracle."

My brows furrowed in question. I didn't see anything.

"Be patient." Josef held my hand in his, and the two of us sat in awed wonder as the deep pink of the sunrise reflected in the ocean. I had never seen anything like this before.

In comfortable silence we sat for a time, watching as the sun grew larger and started to peek out from the distant horizon. The vibrant pinks turned to orange. Then, a shock of gold filled sky and sea, dancing playfully among the waves. The surrounding sky changed from indigo, to misty purple, and then to a striking blue.

"It's so beautiful," I whispered.

"Catherine Erichsen?"

Curious as to why he used my full name, I glanced over. I much preferred his calling me Catie. His gaze held mine and I was unwilling to turn away. "Josef?" was my whispered reply.

"I have loved you since Sjaelland, and I've had to watch and wait in the shadows through John Rasmussen and then my brother." He shook his head slightly and squeezed his lips together momentarily before speaking. "But I can't wait any longer. I need you, I love you, and I want you in my life. Forever." His eyes pleading, he took my hand and kissed it. "Catherine Erichsen, will you consent to be my wife?"

If only I'd known. Why hadn't he shared his feelings so thoroughly with his first proposal? At his words, my heart confirmed what I had suspected—I had always longed for this gentle man and could not bear to be parted from him any longer.

"I will." I wrapped my arms around his neck and he slid me onto his lap. "I love you, too."

The kiss he gave me then started as before, sweet, tender. But he did not let me go, nor did I wish him to. My hands moved along his back, taking in the feel of him as our kiss deepened and we shared our hopes and dreams of an eternal future through the passion of our kiss.

"Shall we go ask Papa's permission?" I asked, though I felt I knew Papa's answer.

Josef grinned. "I already have. And if it meets your approval, I'd like to marry when we first set foot on American soil."

I blinked back my surprise. It was soon, to be sure, but it couldn't happen fast enough for me.

We stayed there near the sterncastle for a while longer, enjoying one another's company and enjoying the first moments of our newly declared love before joining Mama, Papa, and the Saints for morning worship.

My heart rejoiced in the Lord, and I realized—He knew me. My troubles and fears were not unknown to that God who created all life, as He had proven so many times along the way. And, I realized, I was now eager to arrive at America—to be an American and to start a new life with my Josef.

The next morning, Josef sat nearby while I instructed Mary and Orla in their embroidery, and I thought he had never looked so handsome, nor had he ever looked so at ease.

I closed my eyes and let my mind wander to a picture of Josef in a field of gold, a scythe in his hand, tired from a long day's work but with a song in his heart. I stood in the doorway of our home, watching him approach.

"Your husband is starving." He placed the scythe against the fence and came into the yard. "What is for supper?"

Two little blond heads peeked around my skirt and then raced forward yelling, "Papa! Papa!"

He grabbed them both in his arms, twirling them and laughing.

I felt the soft stroke of Josef's hand on my cheek, and when I opened my eyes he was only a few inches from me, his eyes sparkling. "Will I have a wife who sleeps in the daylight?"

My face warmed with embarrassment, but before I could respond, Mary did.

"Catie was awake," she said. "Just dreaming. She does it all the time, ja."

I wanted to protest, but how could I? Instead, I looked down, not daring to meet his gaze. He lifted my chin and looked into my eyes. "As long as she dreams of me," he said.

"Always of you," I whispered, feeling my blush deepen.

It was then we heard the long-awaited cry, "Land ahoy!"

The girls and I threw our handiwork aside, and we rushed to see our first glimpse of our new land. America.

The days were slow in their passing as we waited first to dock, and then for our ship to be declared disease free before disembarking at Castle Garden, New York, in America. But I enjoyed each moment with Josef and loved him better with each day.

As I walked hand in hand with Josef, I still felt nervous about this new country. Yet, when we made our way onto American soil, my feet actually tingled when they met the earth.

"I will be an American now," I whispered, realizing I would love this land or any land where Josef and I were together.

Lars strode past us with Ester clinging to his arm. He tipped his cap and smiled. I knew then that Lars hadn't wasted any time in mourning over me, and I was glad. Silently, I wished the two of them well.

"You will soon be Mrs. Josef Hansen." Josef stood beside me, his voice soft. "Are you glad? Did you make the right choice?" He was earnest, his eyes pleading and yet full of love.

I reached up and stroked his cheek. "My heart made the choice long before you ever asked me, Josef Hansen, and I only love you more today."

He caught me by surprise with his warm lips in an eager and passionate response. When he released me, I blushed as the Saints around us cheered. We walked forward then to Elder Clark who waited to perform the simple ceremony that would bind us on earth as man and wife.

Book Club Questions

Part of this story took place in Denmark. Did the author succeed in giving a general feel for the area?

Catherine is brokenhearted to leave her sister, Berta. Do you have a close bond with one of your siblings?

The Erichsens are a tight-knit family. Were your family circumstances similar? What might Catherine's parents have done differently when she tried confiding in them?

Have you lived in a place where you felt especially strong ties? Where?

As the immigrants travel, Catherine sees and experiences new things. How might you feel in a similar situation?

Since Catherine's curiosity often got her in trouble, do you agree with her assessment that learning about new things is good?

How might Catherine have behaved differently in her relationship with John? Would you be able to marry someone you didn't love?

Who would you have preferred to marry - Lars Hansen or his brother Josef?

Do you have Danish ancestry? Did you learn anything new about Denmark? Is it a place you might like to visit?

Did you find the ending of the story satisfying? Why, or why not?

Author's Notes

This novel is meant to pay homage to the many Danes and other Scandinavians who faithfully left the only home they ever knew while struggling through poverty and other hardships in order to follow the words of a living prophet. It is my hope that I portrayed Denmark and its people in a way that is pleasing to them, and that I also gave readers a small glimpse into the Danes' charming kingdom and their valiant lives.

I used the Danish spellings for the islands of Funen, Zealand, and Jutland, as well as for the Danish cities, including that of Copenhagen.

While this is a novel and all the characters are fictional, many of the elements of the novel are based on true events. This voyage portrays the second voyage of the John J. Boyd and the Saints' route of travel from Copenhagen.

The icebergs, the whale incident, the dolphins, sighting the Great Eastern, and even the thieves were all mentioned by my great-grandmother and other immigrants who traveled aboard the John J. Boyd.

According to the Mormon Immigration Index, there were only a few deaths aboard this voyage, including a middle-aged man, a mother, and her baby. It is believed that this is largely due to the rigorous schedule the immigrants kept of scraping the floors clean with a holystone. The first burial at sea caused much distress and fainting among the Saints. Because of this, the other burials were performed privately.

The Mormon Creed—to mind your business and let others do the same—was mentioned in several life stories of passengers aboard the John J. Boyd.

Knowledge of Shakespeare's Hamlet and Elsinore Castle were obtained by a personal visit to Helsingør. A statue of Holger the Dane resides in the dungeons of the Castle.

Knowledge of Faroese wool was obtained through a personal visit to the Viking Ship Museum, in Roskilde, Denmark. Also in Roskilde is the Domkirke, where royals have been buried for centuries.

The tradition of burying Viking Chieftains inland with their ship was told to the author by a Danish couple near Ringe, Denmark.

Hans Christian Andersen—Information on his life and stories was obtained through a personal visit to the Hans Christian Andersen Museum in Odense, Denmark.

"A penny for your thoughts," was first recorded in 1546 by London-born John Heywood.

Atlantic white-sided dolphins—information on the dolphins most likely to be in this area can be found at: http://marinebio.org/species.asp?id=347

Humpback whale—the whale most likely to have caused the upset: http://www.callifemagazine.com/Page_3.php, http://en.wikipedia.org/wiki/Humpback_whale

Hymns of the Church of Jesus Christ of Latter-day Saints. Salt Lake City: The Church of Jesus Christ of Latter-day Saints, 1985. #30 "Come, Come Ye Saints." #31 "Oh God, Our Help in Ages Past." #100 "Nearer, My God, to Thee."

The hymn, Come, Come Ye Saints was originally known as, All Is Well. http://www.mormonchannel.org/history-of-hymns/16.

The Book of Mormon. Salt Lake City: The Church of Jesus Christ of Latter-day Saints, 1989. (see http://www.byui.edu/english/mlaguide/works_cited.htm under Religious Works) Alma, chapter 5

Information on the Great Eastern was found at: http://www.atlantic-cable.com/Cableships/GreatEastern/ and http://en.wikipedia.org/wiki/SS_Great_Eastern

Lawnmower: http://www.oldlawnmowerclub.co.uk/mow-info/mowhist.htm

Bicycles—In Denmark, the author visited Eskov Slot which has a bicycle museum on its grounds, and obtained some information on bicycles of this era.

To ensure the authenticity of the Danish names used, the author went to: www.names-meanings.net/names/male-danish, and www.rootsweb.ancestry.com/~dnk-cen/.../1000surnames.html

Denmark did not cede control of its German duchies, and lose nearly a third of its total area and population, until after a final war with Germany in 1864. This information is found at: http://www.denmark.dk/NR/rdonlyres/E0AE-5FAD-227C-4C99-8999-59E160377338/0/History.pdf

Clothing of the era, and information on Danish Folk dances was found at: http://vofl3450.homeunix.net/DanishFolk/Costumes/FC-Lund/home.html

Nautical terms: http://phrontistery.info/nautical.html Information on immigrant sailing conditions can be found by visiting the LDS Church History Museum in SLC, Utah.

Information on the John J. Boyd was found at: http://www.dastrup.org/history/images/f/fb/THE_VOYAGE_OF_THE_JOHN_J_BOYD.pdf

The Storebaelt Bridge wasn't approved until 1986 and none of the 1863 immigrants would have seen any part of it. The pillars seen by Catherine are fictional. http://www.storebaelt.dk/english/bridge

For Danish folk dances, go to: ttp://lavigne.dk/oldfolk-dance/

A vague reference to Kai Nielsen's sculpture "The Water Mother" is made while Catherine and her family are on the train. However, the traveling Saints would not have seen this on their journey.
http://www.welcome-to-my-København.com/glyptotek.html

Other references include:
Countries of the World—Denmark, By Patricia J. Murphy
Denmark—Enchantment of the World, by R. Conrad Stein
Of Danish Ways, by Ingeborg S. MacHaffie, and Margaret A. Nielsen

About the author

Tina Peterson Scott was born and raised in Mesa, Arizona. For much of her childhood she could be found nestled against a branch high in their pecan tree and reading a book. Her favorites were fantasy, and mystery, and it delighted Tina when her mother read to her from Grimm's Fairytales and the stories of Hans Christian Andersen.

Tina and her husband have seven children and a growing number of grandchildren. Other than large family get-togethers involving lots of food and fun, she enjoys writing, watercolor painting, long walks, ice cream, and traveling to Europe—especially to her father's ancestral home of Denmark.

Tina writes freelance for a few select publications, has won awards for her writing, and loves best to write about ordinary people in extra-ordinary circumstances.

Connect with Tina on social media:
http://www.facebook.com/TinasWritingAdventure/
http://www.pinterest.com/tinascott161214/
www.linkedin.com/in/tinapetersonscott
Twitter: @authortinascott

Other Titles by Tina Scott:
Surviving Denmark on a Bag of Peach Rings
My Sweet Danish Rose
Menopausal fairy Mischief